FAKING *for* NOW

REBECCA JENSHAK

Bloom books

Cover design by Nicole Lecht/Sourcebooks
Cover art by Elizabeth Turner Stokes

Published by Bloom Books, an imprint of Sourcebooks
1935 Brookdale RD, Naperville, IL 60563-2773
(630) 961-3900
sourcebooks.com

Cataloging-in-Publication data is on file with the Library of Congress.

Printed and bound in the United States of America.
VP 10 9 8 7 6 5 4 3 2 1

ALSO BY REBECCA JENSHAK

Frost Lake High

Stealing for Keeps

Playing with Forever

CHAPTER ONE

Rowan

"It's a beautiful day to play some soccer, boys." Our captain, Vaughn, is all smiles as he tosses out blue scrimmage jerseys.

"It's like a thousand degrees out here," Eli mutters as he adjusts a hat on his head like he's attempting to shield himself from the sun, high in the sky, hitting him. "Can't we just take our shirts off instead of adding layers?"

"Nobody wants to see your six-pack." His twin, Eddie, rolls his eyes.

"It's not that hot," Austin corrects him. "When we visited my grandparents in Arizona last week, it was 118 degrees."

"That's not right." Eli shakes his head and then grimaces as he pulls the jersey down over his T-shirt.

The chatter from my teammates is a welcome change from the past few weeks. I love summer vacation as much as the next person, but with everyone doing family shit, traveling out of town, or working summer jobs, I barely saw some of these guys. And I guess I missed them.

Vaughn, for instance, spent his summer in Ireland. The twins spent all of June at their lake house; Hunter worked at the golf course, cleaning clubs and washing carts; and Blake had to babysit his three younger siblings.

And me, well, I mostly sat around waiting for people to be available to hang out. It sounds more desperate than it was. Nearly every day someone was up for kicking the ball around or grabbing lunch, and there were parties nearly every night. But it's good to have everyone back together.

Soccer practice doesn't start until next week, but today we're doing our annual scrimmage against the girls' team. It's mostly fun. No spectators aside from the coaches, who are here in an unofficial capacity to give us access to the field. Tryouts for the freshmen and new students are done, and our team is set. Now we get to see how we play together.

Vaughn's dad, Coach Collins, sits on the bleachers. Dark sunglasses shield his eyes. He looks almost bored, but I bet he'll be watching carefully to see what we look like after months off and with a new group of guys. We lost a few starters to graduation and added two freshmen and a sophomore transfer. The overall mood today is light and fun, but after losing last season so close to the state title, there is an air of excitement and anticipation too.

Senior year. This is it.

I take my jersey, pull it on over my T-shirt, and head onto the field to warm up. The girls are on the far side, doing the same.

Vaughn falls into step beside me as I start a light jog toward the goal line. He's only been back from Ireland a week, and he's spent most of that time with his girlfriend, Lacey.

"You ready for this?" he asks with the sort of grandiose enthusiasm that only Vaughn could pull off over a scrimmage game. I've never known anyone who loves soccer as much as he does. I guess it's what happens when you're born into soccer royalty. His dad, Coach Collins, was one of the best to ever play the game. He has records and trophies highlighting a career I can't even fathom.

I never aspired to be that type of player. I love the game and enjoy playing it more than just about anything else, but it's always been just a game to me. I appreciate the difference and what that means for my future. I won't be selling out arenas filled with screaming soccer fans, not like Coach C did and not like Vaughn most definitely will.

"Yeah, of course," I say, letting some of his excitement bleed into my own. Maybe I'm not meant for great things, but I can't think of a better way to spend a sunny afternoon than out here on the soccer field.

His lips pull into a half smile. "Did you touch a soccer ball this summer?"

I shove at his shoulder playfully, but he bulked up over the past two months and barely budges until I put a little weight behind it. "Hell yeah, I did. Every morning, I woke up and the first thing I did was get in three hours of drills and conditioning."

The other side of his mouth lifts and he gives me an expression that calls bullshit even before he says, "Yeah, I'll bet."

I most definitely didn't train for three hours. Or any hours, really.

"Don't worry about me, Cap. I spent my summer relaxing and recharging."

"You mean slacking and partying?"

"Isn't that what I said?"

He lets out a deep chuckle.

Austin falls in on my other side. He's smiling so big you'd think we were about to play a title game. He comes the closest of anyone else I know to matching Vaughn's love of soccer. It's hard to believe these two are my best friends in the world. They're all drive and determination, and I'm more of a take-things-as-they-come sort of guy. I like to think I balance out their ambition.

"How do we do this?" Austin asks as he surveys the field.

I forget that he wasn't here for the previous scrimmages. His family moved to Frost Lake just before school started last year. It feels like he's been part of the team, and my friend, for much longer.

"Twenty-minute halves, no goalkeepers, no offsides, no slides, and no three-point touching," Vaughn rattles off our scrimmage rules. "If you score, you sub out for a minimum of two minutes."

"For real?" Austin asks, clearly not liking that rule.

"It's supposed to be fun," I say. "We want to make sure everyone plays as much as possible, and it keeps Vaughn from destroying them."

Which he could, easily. Probably without any of our help.

"And no referees," Vaughn adds. "We call our own fouls. The coaches will jump in to make any final calls if needed, but it's lax."

"Awesome. I'm ready to do this." Austin's steps have an extra bounce.

"Don't go too hard. We don't want to beat them so badly they're all pissed about it," Eddie says, having overheard us as he and Hunter join our warm-up jog.

"Yeah, no kidding. Two years ago, we kept them to one goal and the after-party was a major bummer." Hunter shakes his head, and his eyes widen as if he's remembering it.

"You're still pissed that Penny turned you down that night." Eddie's shoulders shake as he laughs at his friend.

All I remember from that night is playing truth or dare with Amanda. My gaze drifts down to where said ex-girlfriend is standing, one leg pulled up behind her in a hamstring stretch.

Ex-girlfriend might be too definitive a label for what we were. We talked, we hung out, we hooked up. She's cool and we had fun. I thought maybe we could date for real, be a couple and all that like Vaughn and Lacey or Austin and Claire, but then Amanda found someone else.

I haven't seen her since the beginning of summer when I ran into her at one of Boone's parties. Rumor has it that she's single again, and I was certain we'd start things back up and I'd have another shot, but then she left town with her family for vacation and never texted when she got back. I wonder why. Maybe we're done for good this time? The idea has a pit forming in my stomach. I'm not sure why that is either.

As we get closer, she glances up. When she spots me among the group of guys, a slow smile spreads across her face. She lets her leg drop out of the stretch and starts toward me.

"Are you two talking again?" Austin asks me.

"Nah," I say at the same time Eddie says, "Not yet."

They keep mouthing off about the likelihood of me and Amanda resuming our...whatever we are, but I stop listening and jog away from them.

Amanda meets me halfway between our collective groups.

"Hey." Her voice carries a hint of hesitation as we stop a foot apart from each other. Her blond hair is pulled back in a ponytail and her skin is a golden tan from the summer sun. She looks good.

As soon as I hit her with a smile, her shoulders relax, almost like she wasn't sure where we stood with each other either.

"Hey, beautiful." The endearment slips out. There's an ease between us. Perhaps it's because of our history, or maybe it's just part of the connection we share. I've never dissected it that carefully, to be honest. We just click.

I wrap my arms around her shoulders for a quick hug. Her body is stiff at first, then slowly melts into me.

"Hey, Blakenship. How was the rest of your summer?" she asks when we break apart.

"Good. Yours?"

"Mine was good too."

"Great."

We stare, bob our heads in unison. Forget what I said, the usual ease between us is cloaked in an unfamiliar awkwardness.

"Hot out today," I say finally to break the tension and then inwardly groan.

"Yeah." Her responding chuckle is strained.

Dear god, this is painful. It's like listening to my parents make small talk about the weather with business acquaintances. Fake, forced, and uncomfortable.

"Are we good?" I ask, hoping to squash whatever weirdness is going on.

"Yeah." She shakes off more of her discomfort. "Of course. I wasn't sure. After everything that happened with me and..."

Her voice trails off and I find myself wondering how she'd end that sentence. Instead, she smiles and says, "We're good. I missed you."

"Yeah, same."

"Are you going to the twins' house tonight?"

It's tradition for us to have a small get-together with the girls after the scrimmage. I've never missed it. To be fair, I rarely miss any party.

"Yeah. I'll be there."

"Great," she says. Neither of us moves, but a little of that awkwardness creeps back in. I hate it. No matter what happened in the past, I don't ever want there to be tension between us.

In the absence of anything else to say, I find myself scanning the rest of the girls' team. I've come to be friendly with most of them as an extension of Amanda and spending time with her, and because the boys' and girls' teams often share space and sometimes even travel to games together.

"How's the team looking this year?" I ask.

She snaps to attention, reminding me a little of Vaughn. She's not as die-hard as him in her routine, but she takes her position as captain and leading the team just as seriously. "Actually, pretty well. I think we have a chance at districts. Maybe regionals."

The girls' team hasn't been that successful in the three previous years I've been in high school. I always feel a little bad with us winning so much and getting attention from the school and community and them...not.

"Really?" Try as I might, I fail to conceal my surprise.

"Yeah. One of the freshmen is showing real promise in the net and Sophie grew two inches over the summer, and somehow it's really balanced out all her clumsy tendencies. Watch out for her on defense today. She's quick."

"Nice." I find her friend Sophie on the field doing high knees and note she does look taller and somehow more graceful.

"What about you guys? Any notable additions?"

Before I can answer, I'm distracted by a flash of red hair. One of the other girls is dribbling a ball down the field at a speed that seems more suited for a game than a warm-up. Her curly red hair is pulled up in a ponytail that blows wildly down her back and behind her as she goes. She kicks the ball and then stops. When she lifts her head, I get a better look at her.

Fair skin, big eyes, round face. She has on a thin black headband, a lot like the one I wear, to keep her hair out of her face.

It's then I remember Amanda is waiting for my answer.

"I'm not sure yet," I say, distracted as I watch the redhead retrieve the ball from the back of the net. "Who's that?"

She turns, following my line of sight. I pull my gaze away from her teammate in time to see Amanda frown. "Ugh. No one."

Someone blows a whistle, and both teams glance up while moving to their respective sides.

"I better go," Amanda says as she steps backward. The first real smile I've seen out of her dances across her lips. A mixture of playful and determined. "Good luck. Try not to sulk when we beat you."

A small huff of surprise leaves my lips, and that earlier ease I'd been hoping for returns. "You wish, Jones."

It turns out we didn't need to worry about taking it easy on the girls. With a minute to go in the first half, we're tied. And it is not because we aren't trying.

I lift the hem of my shirt to wipe the sweat out of my eyes. It might not be the scorching Arizona heat, but for Michigan, it's pretty damn hot out here. The redhead I was watching during warm-ups is next to me. The girls are in a zone defense and she's playing midfield in the number ten spot.

She's continued to play with that edge and intensity, almost like she has something to prove. If she's a freshman, then I get that. A lot of the new guys come in looking to make an impact right away. The rest of us have played together, some of us as far back as elementary school.

There's something else about her play style though. It's scrappy and all out, nearly to her detriment. It's borderline sloppy, but somehow she continues to control it.

Hunter passes me the ball and the girl shifts, putting herself between me and the goal. My legs are tired and the months of not playing have me sucking in air through tight lungs, but something about her determination has me pushing everything else away and focusing. I want to help my team, but I also want to see what she's capable of.

I dribble, taking my time, focusing on my footwork, scanning the field to see where my teammates are, and moving us closer to the goal.

She's right there with me, every step. Her gaze is laser-focused on the ball. She's handsy, too, tracking me with a forearm almost like she's attempting to push me backward.

If this were a real game, I'd be pissed and probably push back. Instead, I do a Cruyff turn and get a half step around her. She latches on to my arm, surprising me and even pulling a laugh.

"Not giving up that easy, huh?" I ask, slowing down again to let her catch up. I'm purposely baiting her, but also giving the guys a little breather.

Austin's found a nice position on the right wing and calls for the ball. He and Vaughn are the only ones who are going at full speed. Well, them, and whoever the hell this chick is. Actually, the entire girls' team seems much more conditioned than we do. Something Coach C has no doubt noted as well. I see a lot of running in our future.

"You're not bad for a freshie," I say because, well, I guess I really just want to see how angry I can make her. If I'm right and she has a short fuse, then I know exactly how to push her buttons.

She says nothing but releases her hold on me as she places herself in front of me again.

If she is a freshman, that means when I was in sixth grade she would have been a…third grader. I've always made it a point to know people. I never had that stick-to-your-own-grade mentality when it came to making friends, but three years is a big enough difference that I guess our paths never crossed. Pity. I think I might like her…or at least I like trying to rile her up. I get the feeling when she does blow a fuse, there'll be fireworks.

While I'm trying to summon enough energy to get past her, she lunges forward and tries to swipe the ball. She misses, but in the process lands an elbow in my gut. Intentional? Probably, but her eyes still widen with surprise as I let out an "ooof."

"All right," I say, strained. "Stop fucking around. Got it."

With everything I have, I dribble, step over, and then hit the gas. I blow by her and send a hard pass to Austin, who finds the back of the net before the defense has time to shift.

I glance to my side in time to see the redhead's mouth pull into a tight line of disappointment. Huh. I think I expected her reaction to be…angrier. Instead, she looks like she might cry. Well, damn. The victory I was feeling seconds ago trickles off to something more like guilt. I really hope she doesn't cry.

The buzzer sounds and there's a collective sigh of relief from both teams for the break.

I jog off toward our bench with the rest of the guys.

"I think I ruptured my spleen," Blake mutters, holding onto his right side and gasping for air as he takes a seat.

"Wrong spot, genius." Hunter opts to sit on the ground, falling onto his back in the grass and flinging one arm over his eyes.

Eli is panting and squirting water from a plastic bottle over his head. He's peeled off the practice jersey and his T-shirt to cool down or, more likely, to show off the abs Eddie taunted him about.

I'm gassed too but also thoroughly impressed. "To be fair, Cap, I don't think we're any worse than usual."

We always show up rusty at the beginning of the season. Well, everyone but Vaughn and now Austin. It's a week or two of long practices and Coach Collins breathing down our necks before we pull it together and start playing like a championship team. The only difference between this year and the previous three is that the girls showed up ready to play.

One girl in particular. I find the redhead easily. She's off on her own again. I have no idea who she is, but she's responsible for one of their goals. There probably would have been more, but it's like she's playing a game separate from the rest of the team. They're barely acknowledging her, let alone passing to her, but she's so scrappy out there she hasn't needed it.

She's quick and smart.

"Who the hell is that chick? Freshman all-star?" Parker,

one of our new freshmen asks with a glint of hope in his dark-brown eyes.

"Nah, she doesn't look timid enough," Eli says. "Also, when did Sophie get so good? And did she get hotter too?"

"Maybe if you stopped checking out Sophie, you could manage to hold onto the ball," Eddie quips at his twin.

Hunter's laugh carries up from where he lies. "Maybe you should go show her your six-pack."

"Can we all focus here?" Vaughn asks. I can tell he's trying to walk a careful line between friend and captain. He knows today is supposed to be fun and casual, but he also wants to strangle the lot of us for sucking so badly.

We fall silent, appropriately chastised and tired as fuck. After a few beats of panting and heavy sighs, Vaughn waves a hand toward the field. "They aren't the problem. We are."

There are some grumbles of disagreement before Hunter's question centers back in my thoughts. "Seriously, though. Who is that chick?"

I'm glad he asked the question again because I can't stop thinking it.

She's already back on the field by herself, practicing shots. The rest of the girls are still taking a break. Her cheeks are stained red from heat and exertion, nearly matching her hair. She has on the same white practice jersey as the rest of the girls, but instead of the blue shorts the others wear, hers are purple. Just one more way she seems to stand out.

"You don't recognize her?" Vaughn asks, a hint of a smile tugging up one corner of his mouth.

I look back at her, narrowing my gaze and searching my brain for any recognition. The hairs on my arm lift. Actually, now that he mentioned it, she does look familiar. But I'm certain if I'd met her, I'd remember. The hair, for one, makes her stand out. Not just the color but the curls. I dig it.

But looks aside, there's something in the way she holds herself. From the tilt of her chin to the way she moves down the field.

Before I'm able to piece it together—though to be honest, it's unlikely I would have on my own—Vaughn says, "That's Summer Lindsey."

"Who?" Eli and Eddie ask at the same time. They do that often, but it never ceases to make me grin. Twins are cool.

I run her name over and over again in my head. Summer Lindsey. Summer. Lindsey. Holy shit. Summer *Lindsey*.

My attention snaps back to Vaughn, and my expression must give away my thoughts because he nods, smiling bigger. "That's Silas Lindsey's sister."

There's a chorus of comments and questions from the guys.

"No way."

"His sister is hot."

"I hate that guy. I'm so glad he graduated."

"Who?" This from one of the freshmen.

"He played for Oakley," Vaughn says.

"Total asshole," Eddie adds.

"I still think about that time Rowan broke his foot sophomore year." Hunter's eyes dance with amusement.

"It was an accident." I clarify so the new guys don't get the wrong idea. I'm not a fan of the guy, but that was a freak thing where we collided, and he went down. Not that I hadn't thought about punching him a dozen times before.

"I always wondered why that guy hated us so much," Austin says, looking at me like he's pieced together something he'd been thinking for an entire year.

Finally, Hunter asks the question on the tip of my tongue. "What the hell is Silas Lindsey's sister doing here?"

By *here*, he means Frost Lake High instead of Oakley. The purple shorts now make a lot more sense—they're Oakley's colors.

Vaughn shakes his head. "I'm not sure. She's pretty good though."

Pretty good is an understatement for anyone but Vaughn.

"Well, now I understand why they aren't passing her the ball," Austin says with a hint of compassion in his tone. When he first came to the team, some of the guys did the same to him. And he wasn't from a rival team.

Seriously, what the hell is she doing here? I can't imagine she came willingly. Her brother must be shitting himself.

As I continue watching her during the break and then back on the field, I see the family resemblance more and more. The way she moves with a soccer ball, for one. Part of the reason we all hated Silas so much was because he was quick, racing down the field with the ball and an ease that defied the speed. He was a damn good soccer player and tough to defend. She is too.

She has a little of his temper, as well. While he was more verbal, talking shit any chance he got and trying to get under our skin, I've taken enough elbows from her today to get a feel for her personality on the field.

Outside of their game play, they also have the same big eyes and round face. I don't remember what color Silas's eyes were, but hers are hazel. His hair, from what I remember, was a dark brown with maybe a hint of red. I guess I didn't stare at him as much as I'm staring at her.

I don't have as much time as I'd like to catalog all their similarities and differences because we—the guys' team—manage to pull it together and start playing like we all know we can. We score back-to-back early in the second half and then the girls struggle to respond.

We end the game 5–2.

Coach Collins comes over from the bleachers to remind us we start practice next week and suggests maybe we spend the weekend preparing. The smile he flashes before he walks off basically promises a week of conditioning hell.

Eli strips out of his jersey and shirt, laying both over one shoulder. "I'm going to jump in the lake. See you boys later."

One by one, the guys start to trickle off. I spot Amanda still lingering nearby. Summer too. Austin steps in front of me. "What time are you heading to Eddie and Eli's house?"

"Not sure. You need a ride?"

"Nah. Claire's picking me up. I'll see you there."

"Later." I jut my chin at him as he takes off.

I walk toward Amanda without a plan, but it's Summer I run into first. She turns, duffel bag on one shoulder, and nearly collides into me.

She barely looks up as she mutters, "Sorry."

"Hey, you're Silas's sister, right?" I ask.

Her steps falter and those hazel eyes flick to mine. She doesn't reply, but I can't tell if it's because I'm wrong or for some other reason.

"I'm Rowan." I hold out a hand. "You were good out there today. What year are you?"

"I know who you are." She adjusts her bag, wrapping her fingers around the strap tighter before stepping around me.

"Well, that wasn't very friendly," I mutter to myself while wondering what the hell that was about.

"Hey." Amanda appears before me. Her smile is welcome

after the chilly reception I got from her teammate. "See you tonight?"

"Yeah."

"Great. Let's hang out. I've missed you."

"Yeah. Same."

She backs away, then turns and jogs back to join Sophie and Penny.

I grab my bag and head for my truck. The night is looking up.

When I pull up to my house, there's a brand-new shiny red truck in the driveway. It's so new it doesn't even have a plate yet, just dealer tags. I bet it has less than a dozen miles on it. Top of the line too. Best trim line and all the bells and whistles. It can only mean one thing. My parents are home.

I head inside with a mixture of excitement and anticipation and a hint of unease. My parents are hard to keep track of. They travel a lot and change plans so frequently I've stopped trying to remember where they are and when they'll be back. Though the last thing doesn't matter much because of the frequent-change-of-plans thing.

"There he is!" My dad's deep, warm voice greets me as I walk into the kitchen. He's dressed in a crisp, white short-sleeved shirt and tan pants—the picture of resort casual.

"You're back early," I say, dropping my bag on the floor.

He opens his arms and I walk into his embrace. He pats me on the back several times, then pulls back and smiles at me.

"Your mother was tired of the beach." He grins. "Where've you been?" He looks me over. "Soccer practice?"

"We had a scrimmage against the girls' team. Practice starts next week. School the week after that."

"Right," he says like he's kept track.

I love my parents. When they're around, they're loving and warm. My dad started as a car salesman and built an empire. Four dealerships across the county. He bought the land and built them from the ground up. He made partnerships with local banks and repair shops. He's smart and friendly. People love working for him and with him. And my mom is impressive too. She was in sales, then eventually joined forces with him. He always says she's the real magic behind his success.

From there, they made other investments in real estate and business. I've lost track. I have a lot of childhood memories of running around the car lots, sitting in their offices, and watching them work. They sacrificed a lot of time for their success.

Once the businesses were running well, they were able to take a step back, and that's when they started traveling. They've earned it, and I'm happy for them. But the point is they were never the type to volunteer at school or keep the school calendar bookmarked.

"Where's Mom?" I ask as I open the fridge and grab a handful of strawberries.

"She had a hair appointment."

I nod. "Did you have a good time in…"

"Miami."

"Right." I toss one of the berries into my mouth.

Dad grins. "We'll tell you all about it tonight at dinner."

"Dinner?"

"Yes, at the club."

"I have plans with the guys."

He gives me a look like he can't imagine why I'd rather hang with them than go to dinner with my parents. Which I guess is fair since I haven't seen Mom and Dad in weeks.

"Kristy Leigh is coming, the VP of admissions at FLU."

Frost Lake University is my parents' alma mater. It's a good school to which my family has donated significantly.

"Why?"

"What do you mean, *why*?" Dad chuckles. "You're a senior this year and, as far as I know, still haven't committed to a college."

This isn't the first time my parents have said something about me attending FLU. It's been pretty much assumed for me as long as I can remember.

I swallow down the lump forming in my throat. I know he won't be happy, but I suppose it's time to be honest. "I don't know if I want to go to FLU."

"Don't be silly. It's a fantastic school, and you'll be close enough to do internships at the dealership over the summers." He smiles like it's the greatest idea he's ever had. Another thing that's always been assumed: I'd work at the dealership.

I don't have the heart to tell him that not only am I uncertain about FLU, but I have zero interest in working at the dealership. Instead, I nod. It's one dinner.

CHAPTER TWO

Summer

"There must be something you can do." I follow behind my mother as she carries a laundry basket down the hallway in our house.

"We've been through this, honey." She steps into the bathroom and sets the basket on the floor. "You know if there were any way to keep you at Oakley with your friends senior year, I would have already done it."

The compassionate expression on her face makes a sliver of guilt wrap around the anger consuming me. I already knew that was true. She's always had my back. Always.

But…

"Isn't there someone we can appeal to? Maybe if we just asked the schools for some sort of leniency? The Frost Lake girls don't want me there any more than I want to be there."

When she finishes with the towels, Mom grabs the laundry basket and rests it on one hip. With her free hand, she reaches out and cups my cheek. Her thumb slides along my face. It's comforting in a way I don't want right now. It feels like giving up.

"I'm sorry."

"It isn't your fault," I mutter. Aside from picking out this house twenty years ago, she didn't do anything. Stupid school boundary laws. We've always been right on the line. Our block and everything to the east was in the Oakley school district and everything west part of Frost Lake.

Until now. They redrew the district maps and the line moved, placing us in Frost Lake. There is only one other house that was impacted. Across the street, a little boy is starting school this year, so at least he isn't being moved after spending the past twelve years at Oakley.

"My friends are all there, Kevin, my team." My voice is a whine, frustration bleeding into every word. "This is so unfair."

My mother's hand falls away and her look of sympathy morphs into something more like steely determination. She isn't a big fan of wallowing. Her life hasn't been easy. She once told me she didn't have time to sit around and feel sorry for herself when things were tough. Which I guess is true. She works two jobs to provide for our family, takes care of Dad when he's having a rough spell, plus maintains the house, the yard, and everything else Silas and I need.

Knowing that makes me appreciate her so much, even now in my frustration, but it doesn't solve my problem.

"Those Frost Lake girls hate me," I say, following her out of the bathroom.

This time she turns into my room and sets the basket on my bed. I take a seat next to it and grab my soccer ball off my pillow. The worn leather is a comfort under my palms.

"They don't even know you," she says after emptying the contents of her laundry basket into tidy stacks beside me.

"Yeah, well, they don't want to know me. I'm the enemy."

Her eyes, the same hazel color as my own, spark with amusement, silently calling me on my dramatics. But she didn't see the way those girls looked at me today. I *am* the enemy to them.

A knot forms in the pit of my stomach as acceptance, or at least acknowledgment, washes over me. I'm switching schools senior year. Everything that I was excited about for my final year at Oakley is now gone. No first day of school with Charlotte and Jill. No going to dances and football games with Kevin. And no run at state with the team I've known and played with all through school.

There's nothing to do about this shitty turn of events and no one to save me. Like it or not, this is what's happening.

I hate it.

"You can only do what you can do. Keep your chin up and work hard, like you've always done." It's advice she's given me countless times over the year. No-nonsense, tough, slay your own dragons—that's the Lindsey family motto.

I nod my agreement and feel my stomach muscles relax the tiniest bit. Her words soothe me more than the truth of them. I know it won't be that easy, but I have twenty-four hours before I have to face the girls on the soccer team again. Practices start tomorrow and then school in two weeks. The scrimmage was a prequel to what it'll be like (awful), but at least for the rest of today, I can pretend nothing has changed.

"Now." Mom straightens with the empty basket on her hip. "It's your turn to unload the dishwasher."

My face scrunches up.

"Don't give me that," she says as she heads for the door. "And shower too. This room smells like a locker room."

“Hi! I’m sorry I’m late.” I tie the black apron around my waist as I step behind the concession stand at the Frost Lake Country Club. I’ve worked here for the past two years. During the school year only a few times a week, less during soccer season, but it’s basically my home away from home during the summer. It helps that my best friend, Charlotte, works here with me.

“It’s okay.” Charlotte hands a kid a red Popsicle with a smile and then turns to me. “I had a hunch you might be running behind today.”

“Why’s that?”

“First day with the Frost Lake girls,” she says with an expression that adds *duh*. “Were they awful? Did you spend all afternoon plotting revenge and lost track of time, or did they hold you hostage so they could haze you?”

I snort a laugh. Leave it to Charlotte to pull me out of the funk I’ve been in all day. “Neither. Mom had me doing chores. I barely had time for plotting and scheming.”

“That Momma Lindsey is a genius. Keeping you distracted so you don’t get into any trouble.”

I grunt my begrudging agreement. Although I think it was more necessity than anything else. Dad’s had a tough week.

“You didn’t answer my first question. Were they awful?”

“Pretty much.”

I can still picture my new teammates’ faces as I walked out onto the field. Their look was a mixture of shock and outrage. I think they thought I was there to mess with them. Like it was some elaborate prank that I dreamed up with my friends at Oakley. I wish.

Coach Bradley knew I was coming. My old coach

contacted her on my behalf to explain the situation, but it was clear she hadn't shared it with the team until I walked onto the field.

"I'm sorry." Charlotte steps over to me and wraps me in a tight hug. She's four inches shorter than me and tiny, but she squeezes me like a big, burly man. All annoyance, as well as the air in my lungs, leaves in a *whoosh*. We've been inseparable since second grade. Her hugs are her superpower and I've never needed one more than now.

"It'll be okay," I say with more belief than I truly feel. "Right?"

"Right." Her voice sounds more convinced than mine.

Our boss appears at the front of the concession before Charlotte can reassure me further. Brent gives us a forced, tight smile. He's worked here as long as I have. He graduated from Oakley two years ago, but he acts like he's way older and more mature than us. Then again, I once saw him doing a keg stand at a party, so I'm not fooled on the mature part.

"Jackie needs one of you in the restaurant tonight," he says.

Charlotte and I share a disappointed frown. The best part of this job is working together.

"I can do it," Charlotte offers, but I know she's only trying to do me a favor. She hates working in the restaurant. We both do.

"No, I've got it." I take a deep breath that lifts my shoulders and let it out slowly. I'm already having a shit day, no reason to ruin hers too.

"Are you sure?" she asks.

"Whoever is going, decide quickly. They're slammed tonight." He looks down at his cell phone as he waits for us to make a decision.

"It'll keep my mind from plotting and scheming," I tell Charlotte. "Plus the tips will be nice."

Brent looks up long enough to confirm we've reached a decision and then nods. "I'll let Jackie know."

Charlotte groans as soon as he's gone. "I was looking forward to catching up tonight."

"I promise to fill you in soon."

"You're still coming over Sunday night to help me and Jill pick out first-day outfits, right?"

It's a punch to the gut after the day I've had to add another item to my list of things I won't do with my friends this year. Oakley starts a week before Frost Lake, so while they're preparing to go back and do all the things we talked about for the past three years, I have to sit by and watch. "Of course."

"Good." Relief smooths out her features, and she smiles.

Inside the restaurant, I have a moment of regret when I step into the kitchen. Instantly, the frantic movements of everyone working has my pulse rate increasing, and I don't feel at all prepared for this level of chaos tonight. I grab a notebook and pen. The club refuses to buy tablets so we can input orders at the table and instead has one very old and unreliable computer just outside the kitchen.

"Hi." Jackie smiles when she spots me. "Thank you. Thank you."

Her gratitude makes it hard to hold on to my annoyance that I won't get to chat with Charlotte all night.

"No problem. Where do you want me?" I force myself to think of the tips. I can buy new cleats and add to my college fund.

"Section two. Tables five and six are almost finished, seven has drinks but hasn't ordered, and eight was just seated."

"Does eight have waters yet?"

"No. Group of four."

"Got it." I move to grab glasses and fill them with water. As I walk across the restaurant, I scan my tables to find them as Jackie described.

I go to eight first. Four people are seated at the corner table. A stylish woman with dark-blond hair sits next to a man, presumably her husband by the way she smiles at him, with thick, dark hair, peppered with gray. They're both dressed in what Charlotte calls *country club casual*, him in a starched white polo and her in a modest pink dress with pearls.

Across the table is another woman, maybe a tad younger than the couple but dressed similarly in slacks and a silk top. She has her back to me so I don't get a good look at her. To her left, a younger guy sits sort of off to the side, almost like he's trying to escape them. His hair is the same shade as the woman sitting across from him. The ends curl at the nape of his neck. His skin is tan and the polo shirt he's wearing feels less snobby. Maybe because it's wrinkled. Or maybe it's the way his arm muscles distract me from the clothing all together.

Few kids our age eat in the restaurant, most preferring to sit outside by the pool with friends or avoid this place entirely. In all honesty, the restaurant is 99 percent couples and groups in the fifty-plus age bracket. And 100 percent rich or rich-adjacent. You know, people who work with or for wealthy people. I can always pick them out. Rich people have an ease about them that most people can't fake in this environment. Myself included. Luckily, no one expects me to. Smile, be friendly and polite, and most importantly, be invisible.

Smiling, I approach the table on the right.

"Good evening." I hold the tray up and place the waters down. First in front of the man, then his significant other, followed by the other woman, and finally the younger guy.

Once I've successfully delivered the waters without spilling, I tuck the tray under my arm and let my gaze roam the table.

The man has kind blue eyes that put me at ease. There's something a little unnerving about some of the people at the country club. It's like they can see that I'm not one of them.

The man's partner is as pretty and put together as she appeared from afar. The other woman has a more business-like feel to her. An accountant or lawyer maybe, something that requires her to always look important. It's the power suit she's wearing almost like armor that gives her away.

"Can I get you something to drink besides water?" I ask. When my stare lands on the younger guy, my eyes widen. He's looking back at me with something like amusement in his expression. It's the same way he stared at me on the field today.

Rowan Blakenship. He's a senior on Frost Lake's boys' soccer team. A midfielder, like me. Except nothing like me. His style of play is different from mine, something I already knew from watching him play against my brother but found out for myself today. I wasn't expecting to see him. Not earlier today (though I should have been) and definitely not now.

He's the picture of cool indifference as he watches me grapple to rein in my surprise. I'm flustered, and I *loathe* being flustered.

I straighten and pull the tray at my side in front of me

like a shield. Only I'm too close to the table and I knock over a water glass.

A polite but strangled sound leaves the man in front of me. The man, who I'm now sure is Rowan's father, is soaked. I just dumped his entire *full* water glass directly on his nice black pants. I reach for a stack of napkins on the table and shove them toward him.

"I'm so sorry," I say in a rushed jumble of words.

"Oh my goodness!" The woman—Rowan's mother, most likely—gasps. She does her best to help mop up some of the water with the napkins, but when she sees it's hopeless, her gaze lifts to me like she expects me to fix it. And I guess I should, but I'm frozen.

"I'm really sorry," I say again, wishing the words could take back my clumsiness, or maybe the floor would just swallow me up.

Tense silence falls over the table.

"It's okay." Rowan's father's jaw is tight, and his expression is filled with polite irritation. I know he's as annoyed as his wife, but he's better at hiding it.

"Maybe we could use a few more napkins," the other woman says with a smile that's pitying.

Right. More napkins. I'm thankful for something to do and flee quickly. But not before I mistakenly glimpse Rowan. He's smiling like he's watching the greatest comedy routine of his life.

I'm glad he finds this entertaining. Meanwhile I'm probably going to get fired for this. My stomach clenches. I can't lose this job. They're great about working around my schedule, and Charlotte is here. Now that I'm going to Frost Lake, it's likely the only place I'll see her once school starts.

Hot, angry tears blur my vision as I walk back into the

kitchen. I can't believe I was so stupid. I don't have long to bask in self-loathing.

"What the hell happened?" Brent asks as he comes to stand in front of me.

I open my mouth to defend myself, but a glance back at the table has me hating myself all over again.

"It was an accident," I say in case that wasn't obvious. I don't make a habit out of spilling drinks on people.

He blows out a breath, looking tense enough that I almost feel bad for him instead of myself. "This is bad," he says. "That's Lee Blakenship."

My blank stare prods him to say, "Of Blakenship Ford and Blakenship Bank."

I don't know anything about the Blakenships except that Rowan is a jerk who my brother hated his entire high school career. But it seems that who they are and what they own is of great importance because when I glance back toward the table, Jackie is there next to Mr. Blakenship. I don't need to hear her to know she's apologizing profusely.

Shame heats my cheeks. Of all the people to dump water on, it had to be Rowan Blakenship's dad. I care less that he's someone important and more that Rowan was the one to witness my failure. The guy gets under my skin. It's no wonder Silas hated him.

I grab a stack of napkins, enough to soak up three times the amount of water I spilled, and start back to the table.

Brent steps in front of me. "Where do you think you're going?"

"I'm taking these to the table." I can't bring myself to say their name.

"Oh no. You've done enough. Let Jackie smooth things over."

"Really? I can't even show my face?"

He offers what is probably a sympathetic expression, but it only makes me feel worse.

"What about my other tables?"

His mouth opens and twists before he speaks like he's choosing his words carefully. "Just…don't move for a few minutes."

"Fine." I hand him the napkins, and after a brief pause, where he seems to be making sure I'm going to stay put, Brent leaves me in the back and beelines for the table.

I watch from the safety of the kitchen. The way that everyone is acting, you'd think I doused Mr. Blakenship in blood and tar and then feathered him.

I'm still hiding in the back, eyes glued to the commotion at table eight, when movement catches my eyes. I hadn't seen him stand up or start this way, but Rowan is heading right for me. I stiffen and seriously contemplate sprinting in the opposite direction. Since I'm in trouble enough as it is without adding another faux pas, I stand my ground.

"That was wild, huh?" His smile is sheepish as he shoves both hands into his jean pockets. He's casual, bordering on messy, but there's an air about him that I'll never have. Just like his father. I could dump water on him too, and he'd fit in better than I would regardless. Or maybe that's just my own insecurity talking.

He quirks a brow as if waiting for my reply, but I have no idea how to respond to him, and the gravity of the situation has also made it hard for my brain to focus on anything but my job.

He takes another step forward and ducks his head slightly to catch my line of sight, which is how I realize that I'd been staring at the floor between us. I blink and am mortified when a tear falls from my eye. I swipe it away quickly and stare hard at Rowan.

"Do you need something? The kitchen is off-limits to customers." I pull my shoulders back and blink a few more times until I'm certain I won't start crying for real in front of him. How humiliating would that be?

"Look, it's no big deal. Stuff like this—"

"No big deal?" I cut in.

His brows pull together and he looks at me with genuine confusion. Of course he wouldn't understand.

"I'm probably going to get fired, and you think it's no big deal?" I scoff. "Maybe for you, but I need this job. Okay?"

"Fired?" He glances back at the table. To his credit, it seems as if the thought never occurred to him. When his stare returns to me, there's more sympathy there, but it's still laced in confusion. "For spilling a little water?"

Brent returns. His face is a mask of polite professionalism—no sign of the keg-stand guy here. "We've got it from here. You can return to the concession with Charlotte."

"But I—" I stop and look at Rowan, which has Brent also acknowledging him. He gives Rowan a stiff nod.

Rowan lets out a small disbelieving laugh. "Look, it's not a big deal. Accidents happen, right? There's no need for all the dramatics."

"We appreciate your understanding," Brent says, then looks at me, brows lifted in a silent signal to get the hell out of here.

Which is exactly what I do.

CHAPTER THREE

Rowan

Summer unties the apron around her waist and sets it on the counter before turning on her heel and leaving the kitchen.

I give the dude who just chastised her a what-the-fucking-hell look and then follow after her. She practically runs, exiting out a side door into the warm night air. Her steps slow and she raises both hands to the top of her head as she turns in a half circle. She looks like she's either going to burst into tears or punch a wall.

"Are you okay?" It's a stupid question. Of course she isn't okay. I watched her fight her emotions on the field today but right now she's not pretending.

"Fine," she says, voice wavering and teeth gritted.

"Seriously, don't sweat it. My dad is fine." I wave back toward the restaurant. So my dad got a little water spilled on his lap. He doesn't even like those pants. He was griping about them fitting snug the entire ride over to the club. He had told me with a wink that it was a problem that he was sure had nothing to do with him getting a little soft around the middle.

"Yeah, well that accident probably cost me my job."

"Then it's a stupid fucking job."

She laughs, short and bitter-sounding, as she turns away from me. I should go back inside and leave her to spiral on her own, but I can't seem to make my feet move.

Her red hair is pulled up in a ponytail like earlier today but without the headband. She's in the standard khaki-colored pants and white shirt that everyone else here wears, but she looks a lot better in it than anyone else. I doubt she'd like me to notice she's hot right now, but she is. Silas Lindsey's little sister is a stunner. Who would have thought?

"I need this job even if it is stupid."

A woman comes out the door behind us, the same one who had been at the table earlier apologizing and comping our meal.

"Summer," she says, a hint of condescension in her tone.

Summer's mouth pulls into a forced if not totally believable smile. Her eyes plead with me to go.

I clear my throat and then look at Summer as I say, "Thanks for your help. I'll see you around."

Back at the table it's like nothing has happened—except Dad's water glass is pushed as far away from him as possible.

"There he is," my mom says as I take my seat. "We thought you'd skipped out the side door and taken off." She looks good. Happy. She always is when they get back from a long trip, which makes it hard to resent her for it.

"The thought did cross my mind," I joke, and they all laugh.

If there's tension at the table, it's only coming from me. This is weird. Weird but nice. I can't remember the last time I had dinner with my parents. They're gone more than they're home. Traveling for work or pleasure. They work hard. They play hard too. I get that from them—the last part that is.

Kristy twists slightly in her chair as she says, "Rowan, I don't think your parents told me what you plan to study at FLU."

She's a *friend* of my parents in the loosest sense of the word. Not that she isn't lovely and not that my parents don't like her, but their relationship is based on mutual benefit. As in my parents donate a lot of money to the university, and she'd like them to continue doing so. I've met her before at parties and events, probably other dinners like this. She's head of admissions at FLU, a fact I had forgotten until today. But it makes the reason for this dinner all the more obvious.

I give Kristy a small smile. "I haven't decided."

"Nonsense. He'll study business management or maybe finance. Either one will set him up nicely for managing the dealerships after college." My dad's grin is so proud and confident as he looks at me.

My stomach swirls with unease as I nod at Kristy. "That's what I meant. Something business-related, but I haven't pinpointed my focus."

It's hard to hold her gaze or meet my parents' eyes. All my life, my parents have talked about my future like it was set in stone: finish high school, attend FLU, and work for the family business. I knew it was their plan for me, but it always felt so far away. And their attention is so fleeting that I wasn't sure they'd even remember I'm graduating this year. This dinner tells me that they not only remember, but they also haven't given up the dream.

There's a slight look of apprehension on Kristy's face that tells me she understands at least some of the dynamics here, but she forges ahead anyway.

"FLU has a great business program."

"Yeah, I've heard great things about the Blakenship Business School," I tell her, wondering if anyone else thinks it'll be weird for me to enroll in a major my family funded. No one but me, I guess.

My parents laugh and I take another drink of water, wishing it were something stronger.

The conversation moves to other university news—recent updates and professor happenings I don't care about. It isn't that I'm opposed to FLU, or any college, really. It's just that I've never been able to look ahead and see my life like my friends seem to. They have interests and goals, ambition. I've never loved anything enough to imagine planning a life around it. Certainly not business or finance.

While they're talking, I look out the restaurant windows to the pool area. Summer walks by carrying a stack of towels, disappearing from my line of vision as I stare after her. Looks like she didn't get fired, so that's a plus for the evening.

My phone vibrates in my pocket. I pull it out under the table.

Amanda: Where are you?

Me: Running late. Dinner with fam. Be there soon.

I stare at the screen for a beat, waiting for her reply.

"That sounds great. I'm sure Rowan would love to help out with that," my dad says. It takes me a second to piece together the sentence while I'm preoccupied, but when I do and look up, all eyes are on me expectantly.

"I'd love to help with what?" The uneasy sinking feeling in my gut tells me I will definitely not love it, but I'm probably going to be forced into it anyway.

Kristy faces me again. "FLU hosts several events in the fall for local high school seniors. It's a great way to meet current students, find out about the academic programs as well as other campus activities."

"Sounds pretty cool," I admit. For people who are into that kind of thing.

"See?" My dad grins. So proud of… Wait, why is he proud?

Kristy takes pity on me, clearly realizing I checked out of the conversation and have no idea what is going on.

"We like to have a mix of FLU students as well as high school seniors to run the events. I'd love to have you participate. You would be paid for your time, of course, but hopefully it'll allow you a more in-depth look at university life while you plan for college."

"That's really nice of you, but with soccer starting and then school, I'm not sure I'll have the time. And I meant what I said earlier," I say, looking at my dad. "I'm not sure about FLU or even that I want to go to college."

"What do you mean?" My dad lets out a small laugh. "Of course you'll go to college."

My mom reaches across the table and places her hand over mine, squeezing ever so gently. "This is your future, honey, and it's important."

Kristy gives me a reassuring smile. I want to say no.

Actually, I want to say, "Hell no," but my parents are both looking at me with so much hope and love. The last thing I want is to disappoint them on a rare occasion that they're paying me any attention. So I nod. "I guess I can help out at a few of the events."

"I'll send you a list of everything on the calendar, and you can let me know which work with your schedule." Kristy smiles, and I do my best to return it.

After that's decided, my parents and Kristy largely ignore me to talk about other things. I give my excuses after I've eaten, thanking Kristy and hugging my mom.

"We're heading out tomorrow morning," Dad says.

"Already?" I can't hide the surprise in my tone. "You just got back."

"There's a dealership in Grand Rapids that is struggling. The guy is a friend, so I promised we'd go check things out and see if we can help," he says.

"We assumed you'd be wanting to spend the last week of summer with your friends." Mom smiles in a way that tells me she honestly believes that. Maybe she needs to in order to feel okay about jetting off again so soon.

"Yeah. You're right." I clear the emotion from my throat. "Well, I guess I'll see you when I see you."

I head out of the restaurant, eager to get to the twins' house. Like most nights with my parents, it's been a mindfuck.

I fire off another text to Amanda.

Me: Still at the party?

I look up from my phone and spot Summer standing at the end of the sidewalk. Her back is to me, but at the sound of my steps, she turns. And frowns.

That pulls a laugh from me. She really hates my guts.

"Hey." I come to a stop a few feet away from her. "Is your shift over or did you spill another drink on someone?"

"Hilarious." Her scowl intensifies and she turns back to face the parking lot.

"Need a ride?" I go to stand beside her. The wind blows the end of her ponytail into her face, and she hides behind it like it's a shield.

"No."

"Waiting for someone?" I don't know why I can't leave well enough alone, but there's something about her cool indifference that makes me want to poke.

She doesn't disappoint, sighing and turning to look at me. "My boyfriend is on his way."

Boyfriend. Interesting.

"Does he go to Oakley?"

"Yes." She grits out the word.

"What's his name? Maybe I know him."

"Doubtful."

"Why? I know lots of people at Oakley."

"He doesn't play soccer or hang out at the country club."

"I don't usually hang out here either." I pull at the neck of my polo shirt.

The look she gives me says she doesn't believe me, but she works here so she must know I'm not a frequent visitor.

"So why the switch of schools senior year?" I ask.

"Believe me, it was not my idea."

I could have guessed that. "Did you get expelled? Were you vaping in the locker room? Leading a gambling ring?"

I have at least a dozen more plausible explanations, but she cuts me off before I can get to them.

"Why are you so interested?" She crosses her arms over her chest, chin tilted as she waits for my answer.

"I'm just trying to get to know you."

"For what purpose?"

My gaze narrows and I crack a smile at her outrage over me...gasp...talking to her. "Did I do something to piss you off?"

"You mean besides breaking my brother's foot and being a giant prick to him over the last few years?"

"*I* was a prick to *him*?" That's news to me. "And his foot was an accident."

She scoffs. "That would be easier to believe if I hadn't gotten a firsthand look at your style of play today. You like to rile people up and push them until they can't take it anymore."

No, that's her brother's style. Okay, fine, it's a little bit mine too, but he's way worse.

"I wasn't the only one talking shit on the field. Your brother wasn't exactly an angel."

She faces the parking lot again, ignoring me and effectively shutting down this conversation.

I can't believe this. Silas finally graduated and now I have his sister fighting his battles. I step off the sidewalk into the parking lot, but two paces in, I turn back. "Are you sure you don't need a ride?"

Her brows lift as if she can't believe the nerve of me. I can't either, honestly.

"I don't want to leave you stranded here. I can drop you off wherever you need. I won't even try to make small talk."

Her expression softens and, for a second, I think she's going to accept, but then the roar of an engine cuts through the quiet night. I step out of the way as a shiny red sports car pulls into the parking lot, makes a quick turn, and stops at the curb next to Summer. The windows are down on the Mustang and the music is loud, though the bass is so loud I can't make out anything except the rattle of the speakers. It's too nice of a car for such a shit sound system.

I take in the guy driving—short brown hair, T-shirt, and jeans. He looks about as average as can be. He's a cardboard cutout of hundreds of other guys. She's so far out of his league I can't even begin to imagine them together. Maybe he's only a friend.

"Hey, babe." He gives Summer a chin jut, then picks up his phone from the console.

She stares at me over the top of the car. "Looks like you're off the hook."

CHAPTER FOUR

Summer

"How was the first day of practice?" Dad asks as I walk into the house on Sunday afternoon. He's standing at the edge of the kitchen, leaning on his cane.

"Terrible," I mutter as I toss my bag on the floor.

His grin doesn't waver as I shut the door and walk toward the kitchen, the smell of pizza drawing me in. Sure enough, there's a warm, uncut veggie pizza on top of the stove.

"Pity pizza?"

He chuckles. "I could just eat it all myself."

I side-eye him as I put myself between him and the pizza.

"That's what I thought," he grumbles with a grin.

I grab plates, then divvy us each up two slices.

"Wanna talk about it?" he asks as I sit at the table across from him.

"They hate me."

"Who?"

"The Frost Lake girls."

"Aren't *you* a Frost Lake girl now?"

I grunt around the bite of hot, cheesy goodness in my

mouth. He smiles, point happily made, and digs into his first slice. He looks good today. And he only makes pizza when he's feeling up to the task of standing and kneading the dough.

My dad was diagnosed with MS about five years ago. He has good days and bad days. And good weeks and bad weeks.

We eat in silence for the time it takes me to eat my first slice. Once the edges of my hunger fade, I finally look at him. He's waiting expectantly. Dad never forces me to talk, but he's always ready.

"I'm not sure they're ever going to fully accept me. And if they don't, then what chance do I have to play well this season?" And I need to play well this season. A soccer scholarship is my best chance at not only going to college but also continuing my soccer career.

"They will," he says with so much certainty that it's hard to argue.

But I still do, of course.

"But what if they don't? How will I get into a college program if I'm sitting on the bench during every game because they hate me and won't pass me the ball?"

"I don't think your coach is going to let that happen."

Again, so rational. It's infuriating.

I huff a disbelieving scoff. "She probably hates me too."

This time he says nothing, just lifts both brows. I glance away and finish my pizza, stewing in my own thoughts. Okay, maybe Coach doesn't hate me, but she's going to do whatever is best for the team. And if I can't mesh with the other girls, then I won't be what's best, now will I?

Dad finishes his food before I do, but he sits with me until I'm done.

"Where's Mom?" I ask as I push my plate back.

"Resting. She worked late last night."

I nod. She does that often. Her main job is at an insurance company, but at least a few nights a week, she picks up jobs with an office cleaning service. More often lately.

Dad owns a commercial and residential paint business. He used to employ three other guys, and they'd take big painting jobs all over the county, but he's had to cut way back since his diagnosis and now mostly does the bids and payment-side of things, which means they're down a person and can't take on as much work.

I know things are tight despite how they try to shield it from me. They never outright say they can't afford something, but I can see it in the strain on their faces when Silas calls to ask for more money for food or soccer gear or whatever he needs at college. And the way Mom fidgets in line while we pick up Dad's prescriptions at the pharmacy.

Someday when I'm playing soccer professionally and big-name brands want to sponsor me, I'm going to pay off their house and send them on a month-long beach vacation. Or that's the dream anyway.

I can't do any of that if I don't figure out how to make the most of playing my last high school season at Frost Lake.

Dad stands from the table, grimacing slightly as he does. He leans on his cane with one hand, then rests his other on my shoulder.

"No one can hate my shortcake."

I huff a small laugh. He hasn't called me that in a while.

"They can and they do," I tell him, but I lean into his touch and it's soothing me despite the uncertainty I feel.

"Nonsense. They just need to get to know you."

"I cannot believe I'm not starting school with you guys tomorrow." I fling myself back on Jill's bed later that night. It's covered in clothing and school supplies.

Charlotte is sitting on the floor in front of the full-length mirror trying out new lipsticks, and Jill is lost in her closet looking for the perfect back-to-school outfit.

"At least you get another week of vacation," Jill says as she reemerges with a yellow floral dress that she wore to our ninth-grade homecoming dance.

"Aww. I loved that dress on you," Charlotte says, staring at Jill in the reflection.

"But maybe too much for the first day of school?" I ask hopefully. We've really gotten off course here. She started with cutoff jean shorts and a tube top, and now she's considering formal dresses. It's a cry for help if I've ever seen one.

She groans and tosses the dress onto the bed, then flings herself on top of it. "I don't have anything to wear."

Jill could wear a plain white T-shirt and jean shorts and still look gorgeous.

I stand and walk over to the side of the bed, then take her hands and pull her to her feet.

"Maybe there's still time to run to the mall?"

"You don't need more clothes," I tell her.

"I could always buy more clothes," Charlotte says, pursing her lips and admiring the dark-red shade.

"Same," Jill adds.

I stay silent because clothes aren't really my thing. I like jewelry, especially rings, but that's it for anything close to personal style. And most of my rings are cheap, funky ones. The mood ring on my left pointer finger cost three dollars at the pharmacy.

All the rest of my money goes toward my college savings. Maybe once I've graduated with a degree and am playing professional soccer, I'll focus on buying a new wardrobe.

"Close your eyes," I say to Jill, placing my hands on her shoulders.

She arches one brow.

"Just do it," I demand.

Her lips quirk into a small smile and her eyes shut.

"You arrive at school. The sun is shining, and the birds are chirping happily around you like Cinderella."

"Birds kind of freak me out," she says, eyes still closed.

I continue, undeterred. "The parking lot is already half-full, but you find the perfect spot. You get out of your car and flip your hair over your shoulder. You are having the best hair day and your makeup is on point."

Her lips curve into a smile and Charlotte lets out a quiet chuckle.

"People are standing in groups next to their vehicles. You make your way through the crowd and up the stairs to the front doors. And as you go, everyone is looking at you. You are the goddamn queen of Oakley High."

She snorts a laugh.

"Okay, now what are you wearing?"

There's a pause and then slowly her eyes open and she aims a wide smile at me.

"Sum, you're a genius!" She hugs me quick, then goes to the bed and digs through the heap of clothing until she finds a black skirt and white tank top.

"Now if only I could visualize myself there," I mutter and walk over to the collage of photos on the wall.

There are pictures of the three of us over the years. School dances, soccer, weekend hangouts, days at the lake.

But my gaze is continually pulled to all the ones taken at Oakley High. The two of them are going to make so many more memories there without me this year, and it sucks.

"How was the first day of official practice with the evil teammates?" Jill asks from the closet where she's disappeared again to change into her perfect outfit.

"Same. They still hate me."

"They're lucky to have you." Charlotte has abandoned her makeup and lies on a corner of the bed to scroll her phone.

"She's right." Jill reemerges, pulling down the white tank top over her dark-brown stomach. "We are so missing you at midfield. Coach moved Bree there, but she's no Summer Lindsey."

I make a noncommittal hum. They'll manage without me. They have six seniors returning and several underclassmen with enough talent and experience to step up.

"You know the thing that really gets me about the Frost Lake team is they could be so good. There are moments of brilliance. Take Sophie Cook. I've never seen anyone so calm and patient on defense. And Amanda Jones is one of the best in the state for sure."

"Too bad she's such a terrible human," Jill adds.

I can't deny that. We've always hated playing against her. And in the two days since I've been part of the team, she's barely acknowledged my existence. I get that she doesn't want me there. I don't want to be there either, but I'm not giving up soccer even if I have to play for Frost Lake.

"Umm…" Charlotte sits up on the bed, staring at her phone. "Sum, why is Kevin hanging out with Lizzy Thompson?"

Jill gasps and looks to me. Her outrage on my behalf is touching. And normally this news would be worthy of it, but I'm not all that surprised. Or at least I shouldn't be.

My face heats and I can't look either of them in the eyes as I say, "We broke up."

"When?" They shriek the question at me in perfect, screechy unison.

"This morning over text."

My friends gape at me with a mixture of disbelief, shock, and pity.

"He said that since we aren't going to be at the same school this year, it was in both of our best interests to have some space and see where things go without the pressure of a label."

"Oh my god, is that actually what he said?" Charlotte asks, lip snarling. That shade is nice on her.

"Almost verbatim. I'm pretty sure he used ChatGPT to write it for him."

"'See where things go'? And twelve hours later he's conveniently hanging out with Lizzy." Charlotte lets out a disgusted huff. "What an asshole."

Jill's expression softens. "I'm so sorry."

"It's fine." I'm not as sad as I thought I'd be, though I am irritated he's already moved on to Lizzy. I knew she liked him. I even told him that this summer when we all went to the lake. I said, "I think Lizzy is checking you out." And he laughed and said something like, "Nah, but even if she were, I'm not interested in anyone but you." Gah. I was such a sucker.

"You can do so much better," Charlotte insists. She never liked him that much anyway. That should have been my first sign.

Jill nods. "She's right. And the Frost Lake High guys are fiiiine."

"Oh my god. I can't believe we didn't get a chance to talk about it yet, but I saw Rowan Blakenship at the club last night." Charlotte looks at me with big eyes, waiting for my surprise.

"I know. I saw him too," I admit. "His table is the one I…"

She sucks in an audible breath. "Nooooo!"

I nod. We didn't have time to talk about the incident last night because the pool was so busy, so she got the short version: I spilled a drink and Jackie banished me back outside. I fill her in on the details at the same time I tell Jill the whole story.

When I'm done, they're both giggling hysterically.

"Just one more reason I'm dreading school next week," I say. Rowan's smirk flashes in my head.

I was worried I'd run into him at the soccer field again today, but I overheard some other girls saying the boys don't start their practices until tomorrow.

"I would have died. He's so hot," Jill says.

"He really is." Charlotte nods.

They look at me like they expect me to agree.

"He is good at soccer. I'll give him that."

"Oh come on, Sum, you don't think Rowan Blakenship is hot?"

"He was such an asshole to Silas." I shake my head. "When I look at him, that's all I can think about."

"How is your brother?" Charlotte asks. She tries for casual, but Jill and I see right through her. We burst into laughter. Charlotte has had a crush on my brother for as long as I can remember.

Her cheeks turn pink. "What? I'm only curious."

"Suuure. I bet you're curious about all the newly graduated Oakley High alumni."

She tosses a stuffed bear at me, grinning. "Shut up."

"Let's take five!" Coach Bradley yells.

The team lets out a collective sigh of relief as we jog off the field. We've been doing shooting drills for the last hour.

I grab my water bottle and take a seat off to the side. Amanda and Sophie are sitting to my right—not that they're acknowledging me in any way.

"Hey." Marta, Frost Lake's senior goalie, takes a seat beside me. "Nice work out there."

"Thanks."

"I'm Marta, but everyone calls me MJ."

"Summer."

"You came from Oakley. I remember you. You scored twice on me last year."

"Sorry?"

She huffs a laugh. "It's cool. At least now you'll be on our side."

"Will she though?" Amanda asks.

My body stiffens. I look over to see her and Sophie watching us intently.

It's Amanda who speaks first. "If you think you're going to come in here, steal all our plays and secrets, and hand them over to Oakley, then you have another think coming."

"I'm not..." I let my voice trail off, confused by the implication. Why the hell would I do that? I can't seem to form an answer, but it doesn't matter.

Amanda gets up and walks off to take a seat farther away

from me. Sophie flashes a timid smile my way, then follows her. We've attracted the attention of most of the team, and my cheeks heat with anger and embarrassment.

"Save your breath," MJ says. "Amanda's just cranky because she's having boy problems."

"Something we have in common," I mutter, fiddling with the top of my water bottle while ignoring the stares from everyone around us.

"You got stood up by Rowan Blakenship too?" MJ's blond eyebrows lift. They're so light they almost blend into her fair skin.

"No. I..." It takes me a second to process this new information. Of course, Amanda and Rowan are together; that makes perfect sense.

MJ laughs softly. "I was kidding. Relax."

I nod in understanding. "My boyfriend broke up with me yesterday."

"That sucks. I'm sorry."

I shrug, then find myself wondering about Rowan and Amanda. "How do you know he stood her up?"

"The teams had a party after our scrimmage Saturday, and she was waiting on him to show up, but he didn't, I guess. I'm not really sure, honestly. They have this dramatic back-and-forth that they play off like neither of them cares. Only it's obvious they do, or Amanda wouldn't be so pissy two days later." She stops, seeming to realize she's told me more than she should about Amanda, or maybe she's just recognized that not everyone on the team was invited—namely, me.

"It's okay," I assure her. "I get it. This whole thing is weird. I'm the enemy, right?"

She shrugs. "Not to me. Whatever your reason for being here, you're one of us now."

The rest of the week, practice goes by much the same way. I don't have another confrontation with Amanda, but she isn't acknowledging me either. I have no idea how I'm going to survive the season with her.

As we're leaving the field on Friday, a few of the guys on the boys' team are waiting to take the field for their practice, including Rowan. He stands on the sideline, holding a soccer ball in one hand. His light-brown hair is pulled back in a stubby ponytail at the nape of his neck and a few long strands hang forward.

When I meet his gaze, he's looking at me. I break eye contact first and walk over to get my stuff.

"Hey!" I hear Amanda's voice, far bubblier than it's been all morning, talking to him. "I haven't seen you all week. First you stand me up at the twins' party, and last night you were a no-show at the bonfire."

Rowan's voice replies. "I didn't stand you up. I was at dinner with my parents. I even texted you that I'd be late."

"Yeah, but I didn't realize you'd be *that* late. And what about last night?"

"I didn't get your text about the bonfire until after I was already at Austin's house."

There's a beat of silence, then Rowan says, "I'm sorry."

I roll my eyes. Why the hell is he sorry? She's the one who can't read and tries to make plans at the last minute.

"You can make it up to me tonight by hanging out with me at Boone's house. Are you going?" She doesn't wait for his answer. "You have to come. Everyone is going. The entire team. Tell the boys."

I usually change my shoes before I leave, but I'm so

eager to get away that I grab my bag and start toward the parking lot.

I'm not even mad that no one told me about the party (again). I'm grateful. The last thing I want to do is spend more time with people who can't stand my presence.

I purposely walk around Amanda and Rowan, but he turns and calls out to me.

"Hey, Summer."

I glance up, expecting a mocking smirk, but if he's trying to taunt me, I can't tell. The only thing I see in his expression is friendliness.

"Hi," I mutter.

"Are you going to Boone's party tonight?" he asks me.

I make the mistake of glancing at Amanda. If looks could kill, I'd be very, very dead.

"No." I clutch the strap of my bag tighter.

"Why not? I thought the entire team was going," Rowan says.

"Everyone who matters," Amanda corrects herself.

Rowan's brows lift, and if I didn't know any better I'd think he hasn't seen this side of Amanda before.

He looks to me and says, "You should come. Boone throws the best parties. He lives out in the Sweet Haven area by the lake. You won't be able to miss it with all the cars."

I have no idea what game he's playing, but I'm not interested. "I have plans."

Those plans mostly include sitting at home, since both Charlotte and Jill will be at the Oakley back-to-school dance. Mom's working and Dad's been poring over the accounting books for his business all week. Maybe I could help him. Real riveting stuff. But still better than willingly hanging out with anyone here.

"See? She has plans," Amanda says. She smiles sweetly. "Too bad. Maybe next time."

"Yeah," I mutter, wishing I could kick a soccer ball right at her head. "Next time."

If I survive at Frost Lake that long.

CHAPTER FIVE

Rowan

"I DIDN'T KNOW AMANDA AND RONNIE WERE BACK together," Vaughn says, taking a drink of his soda and looking across Boone's backyard.

I don't need to look to know exactly what or who he's seeing. Amanda and Ronnie have been all over each other all night.

"Me either," I mutter and steal another quick glance. I can't help but feel a little salty. Maybe I misread the conversation earlier. I thought her asking me to come meant she'd stopped talking to him.

"You gonna do something about that?" Eli asks me, quirking one brow.

"Nah." I shake my head. "Why would I?"

The guys all look at me, some unnamed expression on their faces. Pity, maybe. Do they feel sorry for me? They shouldn't. Amanda and I aren't together. We haven't been for months.

"Whoa, whoa, whoa." Eddie nudges me with an elbow to the ribs. "Look who showed up."

"Hmm?" I ask only half paying attention. My gaze is back on Amanda across the yard. Why the hell did she ask me to come and pretend like she missed me? It isn't like her to play games. I thought things were going to be cool between us and, yes, hoped we might start talking again. People like to give us shit about going back and forth, but it never felt that messy. Not until now. She asked me to come but hasn't so much as acknowledged my presence. And when the hell did she and Ronnie start talking again?

"Holy shit. Is that Silas's sister?" Eli asks, then mutters, "Daaaaamn."

That finally gets my attention. I turn in time to watch Summer Lindsey step off the back patio steps. She's wearing a light-blue dress that hangs mid-thigh. It has tiny little straps that cut into her shoulders. It's the first time I've seen her with her hair down, and the dark-red ringlets fall nearly to her waist. Her discomfort at being here is obvious, but she looks amazing. *Damn* is correct.

She pauses and glances around like she's looking for someone. Everyone is watching her, but no one moves toward her or says hello. She stands there frozen, like she's seconds away from turning around and bolting.

My gut tightens and the hair on my arms stands up. I don't know why she's here, but I can't help but feel like I might have had something to do with it.

"I feel bad for her," Vaughn says.

I pull my gaze from Summer long enough to shoot my buddy a questioning look.

"They changed up the school district lines her senior year. That has to suck."

"That's why she's at Frost Lake," I say, mostly to myself.

Without thinking, I start across the yard. She makes eye contact with me as I approach but still doesn't move.

"Hey." I stop in front of her, even more taken with her up close. Her lips are painted a shiny pink and her eyes have some sort of makeup that make them look twice as big. She is stunning. "Planning on moving from that spot?"

"Yes, but only to go back out to my car and leave," she says only loud enough for me to hear.

"Nah, don't do that. The worst part is over. You came, everyone stared, now they'll go back to minding their own business." I wave around, meeting a few curious stares as I do, but everyone else is falling back into conversations.

"This was a mistake."

"Maybe, but you've already made it so…"

Despite my encouragement, she still doesn't budge.

"Your girlfriend is shooting daggers at me."

"Girlfriend?"

"Amanda."

"We're not together."

"Not right now."

The implication is there.

"Where do you get your gossip? Keeping tabs on me?"

"I hear things and I see things. Whatever dramatic situation you two have going on doesn't interest me."

"Should I just leave you to the wolves then?"

She looks like she can't decide.

"Come on, Lindsey. Let's get you a drink and see if we can't find a person or two who is happy you're here."

She lets out a laugh but follows me across the yard. Eddie and Eli still look like they're about to swallow their tongues. They don't usually go for the same kind of girls, but it looks like Summer is both their type. Hard to imagine whose type she isn't.

"Summer Lindsey, meet the Whitlock twins." I motion with my head toward them. "Eddie. Eli."

"Nice to meet you," she says, far friendlier than she's ever greeted me.

"Hey. I'm Eddie." His voice sounds twice as deep as usual. Real smooth, bro. Then Eli steps in front of him. "And I'm Eli."

They're grinning at her like idiots, but she doesn't seem to notice.

I step over to the next group, pointing as I introduce them. "This is Vaughn, Lacey, Claire, and Austin—though I call him 'Disco' because he showed up to practice once wearing so much glitter he glistened in the sun."

"Glitter?" Summer asks, left brow rising.

"Long story." Austin shoots me a playful glare, then tips his head to Summer. "Hey. Welcome to Frost Lake."

The girls wave and say their hellos and Vaughn gives her a small smile.

She seems to be relaxing the tiniest bit as she realizes we're not all bad—just me, I guess.

MJ, from the girls' soccer team, comes up to Summer. "Hey! I'm glad you came."

"You might be the only one on the team who feels that way," she says, glancing over at where Amanda is glowering at her.

"Nah. They're just afraid of Amanda," MJ says, then looks at me with a small sheepish grin. "Sorry. I know you two are...whatever."

Someone yells out for MJ and she stands tall, then scans

the yard until she finds the source—a group of girls' soccer players on the far side.

"I'm being summoned." MJ turns back to Summer. "Do you want to come play blob tag?"

"I don't know what that is," Summer says.

"It's like tag but once you're tagged, you become part of the blob and you move together to tag the rest of the people. Sounds simple but it's hard and a little silly, but it's fun." MJ's eyes light up. I've seen the girls play it before and they are usually smiling and having a good time with it.

"Umm..." Summer hesitates as MJ takes a step back from us.

I lightly nudge Summer forward.

She side-eyes me like she knows damn well what I'm doing, but she relents anyway. "Yeah. Okay."

"Cool." MJ grabs Summer's arm and pulls her with her.

Summer glances back at me—something a little like fear in her expression—as she's hauled way.

I give her a thumbs-up and she flips me off in return. There she is.

I watch only long enough to see MJ take Summer into the group and the other girls offer small waves and timid smiles.

"What's up with you two?" Austin asks me as I step into the circle with my friends.

"What do you mean?" I grab a cold beer from the cooler and crack it open.

"You seem chummy."

"We had a little run-in at the country club last week."

He nods slowly like he expects me to elaborate. Except I'm too busy watching Summer across the yard. More people have joined in, including Sophie, Eli and Eddie, and a couple guys from the football team.

I'm still watching when Amanda steps in front of me.

"Hey," she says with a hint of apprehension in her tone.

"Hey," I parrot back.

She looks good tonight. She always does, but I can tell she put some effort into it. Effort that wasn't for my benefit.

"Having fun?" I ask.

"Yeah," she says in a way that isn't all that convincing. "Not as much fun as you though."

My brows lift as I try to decipher her meaning.

She looks past me for a moment, then returns my stare. "What's up with you and Summer Lindsey?"

I glance over my shoulder, and sure enough Summer is in view.

"Nothing's up. Everyone was staring at her and I felt bad."

"I don't like her."

"Yeah." I chuckle. "You've made that pretty obvious."

She keeps that pinched, unwavering expression on her face. "Figure she's talking shit."

"She didn't say anything. You did today at practice. And even if you hadn't, it's obvious from the way everyone else is treating her. Like they're terrified to smile at her in case you're watching."

"What do you care? You hate her brother."

"I don't hate him." I don't like him, but that isn't the point. "This isn't like you. You've always been so welcoming to new girls on the team."

"Underclassmen, sure, but she's from Oakley."

"So?"

"I don't trust her. She's probably not even going to Frost Lake this year. I bet she's a spy, doing recon and feeding them all our plays."

"No." I shake my head, amazed at the level of subterfuge she thinks someone would go to for the playbook. The girls' team isn't even that good. "Trust me. She isn't doing any of that. She doesn't want to be at Frost Lake any more than you want her to be, but she got fucked by some school border law."

Amanda's face softens slightly.

"You didn't know?" I ask, but I can tell she didn't. It makes me feel a little better about how awful she's been treating Summer.

"She isn't a spy. She's just trying to make the best of a crappy situation."

"For someone who says there isn't anything going on between you, you seem to know a lot about her." Amanda's head tips side to side as she tosses the accusation at me. It's so unlike her, I can't even comprehend what's happening.

"Just do your team a favor and stop treating her like the enemy. She's here whether either of you like it or not. And she's good. You don't have to be besties, just do what's best for the team."

A little of her irritation fades.

"Back with Ronnie, I see." I motion with my head to where he stands with some of the football guys.

Amanda doesn't look back at him. "Don't tell me you're jealous?"

"Nah." I shake my head. "Just surprised."

"I'm not sure what will happen when school starts back next week."

"Why would that change things?"

"His dad doesn't like him to have a girlfriend during football season."

I could say a lot of things—like I think it's a bullshit excuse or that she could do better (namely with me)—but I'm not sure there's a way to say anything without sounding like a jealous prick.

"I'm sure you two will figure it out," I say instead.

She shrugs. No matter how much she tries to play it off like she doesn't care, I know she does. That's the thing about Amanda. She acts tougher than she is.

"And you?" she asks. "Are you talking to anyone?"

"No." I find myself glancing back at Summer again. She's in a big circle of soccer girls. She's not quite as animated as before, but she hasn't left, so it must not be going too badly.

"Doesn't seem that way," Amanda says, her gaze narrowing again.

"Don't tell me *you're* jealous," I say, using her words.

"Just be careful. I don't want to see you get hurt."

With that, she turns and walks away. She doesn't want to see me get hurt? Then maybe she should stop making out with Ronnie in front of me.

CHAPTER SIX

Summer

Tag is fun...or at least more fun than I expected. Coming here tonight was a risk, but the only thing I could think of that would be worse is letting Amanda and the rest of the team talk shit and think they can walk all over me. I'm here at Frost Lake whether they like it or not. Whether I like it or not. They aren't ruining my senior year or my chances at a soccer scholarship. So I didn't really have much of a choice but to come and show them that I'm not going to back down easily. Still, I spend most of the night wishing I could make a smooth exit without anyone noticing.

Standing in the middle of a yard filled with people I don't know is intimidating. MJ is nice, and a few of the other girls have been polite, if not friendly. But it's clear no one except MJ is ready to welcome me to the team. I don't blame them. I can feel Amanda's wrath even from twenty feet away.

Currently I'm in a circle of soccer girls, which used to be a circle I thrived in. MJ is talking to Rina, a sophomore, about a guy I don't know, so I'm off to the side trying to look like I'm perfectly content to smile and nod and be on the outside.

"Look at you making friends," Rowan says as he steps up in front of me, holding a red cup. His smile is all charm and confidence, and I don't detect even a hint of irony in his statement. He truly believes I'm fitting right in.

Try as I might not to, I've been aware of him all night. He's a popular guy. No one is avoiding him like they are me.

"I wouldn't go that far, but no one has tossed a drink in my face like I expected."

He huffs a laugh like that idea is ludicrous. Is it though?

"Do you guys want to play washers?" Rina asks. She looks to Rowan and then me.

"Yeah, let's do it," Rowan answers before I can, then shoots me a wink.

As we make our way over to where the washers game is set up, Rowan stays by my side. I can't get a good read on him. Why is he being so nice to me? He hates my brother, and his ex hates me. There's no world in which it makes sense that he wants to be my friend.

Rowan and I end up on opposite teams. Me and MJ versus him and Rina, but we're standing together behind one of the boxes.

Two guys wearing Frost Lake High hockey T-shirts stop by to say hi to Rowan, and he introduces me.

"Brandon and Mark, this is Summer. She's new." Rowan takes a drink from his cup.

"You're the Oakley chick." Brandon grins as he shakes a finger at me like he's heard plenty about me already and is finally putting a face to the name.

"That's right," I say, guarding myself against whatever

response might come next, but Brandon just smiles. "We killed your hockey team last season."

"We killed your...every other sport last season," I say in response. Oakley has a great sports program across the board. But it's true, our hockey team has been in a slump for as long as I can remember.

"Not boys' soccer," Rowan says with that signature playful smile.

"You barely beat us and it took two overtimes," I say, thinking back to that game. Silas was pissed. He always wanted to win, but never more than when playing Frost Lake.

"But we still won." Rowan practically beams. I fight an eye roll.

"It's your turn," MJ calls from the other side.

I wave in acknowledgment to her and Rina.

"I'll catch you around," Brandon says to Rowan, then tips his head to me. "Later, Oakley."

I laugh off the nickname. I could think of worse things, though I doubt it's going to make my teammates feel any better about me with the constant reminder from other people that I'm not one of them.

Rowan and I take our turns, then he says, "See? People like you. You just have to hang out more."

"People are nicer to me when you're around." Which is true. "Well, everyone but Amanda."

"Yeah, I noticed there's some friction there. Do you two have bad blood or something?"

I shrug. "We beat them last season, but it never felt like a rivalry or anything."

In fact, I think she was nicer to me then.

"She's one of the most competitive people I know, but she's not usually like that." Rowan glances across the party. I follow his gaze to Amanda. She's standing with some other guy, looking chummy. I glance back at Rowan in time to see his jaw harden and his brows furrow.

We finish washers, then another group is waiting. Rowan and I stay standing together a few feet away, watching the next game. He glances toward Amanda again. It's so obvious he has it bad for her.

"What's the deal with you two?" I ask.

"Who?" He looks away from her and takes a drink from his cup.

"Don't play dumb. Amanda. You've been staring at her nonstop."

"I have not," he says and frowns.

"You have."

He grunts.

"So?" I prompt him again.

"We hung out last year."

"Hung out as in *dated*?"

"It wasn't that serious."

"But you wanted it to be?"

He opens his mouth but then closes it like maybe he's second-guessing his words. When he finally speaks, he says, "I don't know."

I almost feel sorry for him, but it's hard to see him with Amanda after how awful she's treated me. What am I saying? They deserve each other. Or that's what I thought. The more time I spend with him, the less I believe that.

"What about you? Does your boyfriend know you're here tonight?" Rowan asks.

Now it's my turn to look away.

Stupid Kevin. "We broke up."

"Shit. I'm sorry."

I shrug it off. I'm more upset that he immediately started hanging out with Lizzy than I am that he ended things. We'd grown apart. I felt it. He, obviously, felt it. I guess I liked the idea of having him while I transitioned to life at another school.

"How long were you two together?" Rowan asks.

I start to answer, then pause. "Do you really care, or are you just standing here talking to me in some heroic attempt at saving me from public humiliation?"

"Come on. You're not that sad of a case, Lindsey." He bumps his shoulder against mine.

"Debatable," I murmur, then add, "six months."

"That's a long time."

"Is it?"

Rowan laughs. "It is to me."

"I take it you're not much of a relationship guy?"

"I get the concept, and I've seen my friends all fall into things, and they seem happy enough..."

"But?"

"We're in high school." He aims a sheepish, mischief-filled smile my way. "We should be having fun and not taking things too seriously."

I huff a laugh. "That is exactly the kind of thing I would expect someone like you to say."

"What does that mean?"

I debate ignoring the question, but I'm fired up and on edge enough to blow off my better instinct. I face him and study his handsome features and the ease with which he holds himself.

"It means that guys like you from rich families with lots

of friends and zero cares couldn't possibly understand what it's like for anyone who needs to be serious and can't blow everything off for fun."

Rowan Blakenship is a guy who has never known struggle. Maybe I'm not an expert, and certainly people have it worse than I do, but I have watched my dad battle with his health and cling to the good days while gritting his teeth through the bad. And I've seen my parents fight to keep up with bills and life. You can't see things like that and still view the world the same way. I know Silas saw it too. He was eager to graduate and go off to college, the same way I am. My brother was fortunate to get a full-ride scholarship. I saw the relief that brought my parents. I want that too. For them and for me. Having fun, being carefree, and not stressing about the future is a privilege.

"I never said I have zero cares," he says. His brows tug together slightly in the center. "And I can't help that my family is rich. Trust me, it isn't all roses like you think."

I wonder if he means that or is just arguing to feel better about his stance on high school relationships. It isn't like I think money solves everything, but it certainly helps.

"I'm sorry," I say because regardless of his situation, my feelings are just that—my own. I don't make a habit of chastising people for their opinions and choices. "I'm not usually such a buzzkill at parties."

He cracks a smile with one side pulling higher. "Breakup blues?"

"No." I find myself smiling back at him. "More like Frost Lake blues."

"We're not so bad."

"You've all been friends forever and now I'm coming in with one year left. It isn't how I pictured it."

"I'm sorry about the district line bullshit. That has to suck."

I glance at him with surprise.

"Vaughn told me," he says, then his eyes crinkle with amusement. "I was a little disappointed to learn you didn't get expelled for vaping."

I huff a laugh.

"Disco just transferred here last year and look at him." Rowan waves a hand over to where the friends he introduced me to earlier are hanging out.

"Did he really have glitter all over his face during practice?"

"Alllll over."

"How does that happen?"

The wind picks up and I cross my arms at my waist to savor a little heat.

Rowan steps into the path of the wind, blocking me from the brunt of it. "Something to do with Claire, glitter tubes, and Lacey's locker. Lacey is head cheerleader, and the girl loves a glittery sign. You'll see. They deck out the school for games."

Oh my gosh, I'm going to be there, inside the school, walking the halls. It hits me full force. There's no more denying the inevitable.

"I can't believe I'm going to be a Frost Lake student next week," I say as much to myself as to him.

"You'll be fine, Lindsey. I promise."

"Lindsey!" Amanda calls at the end of practice on Wednesday. Today was better. Not good, but almost tolerable. A few of the girls on the team actually talked to me (and passed to me).

I pause with my bag over my shoulder as Amanda walks toward me. I look behind me to see if there's someone else with that name near me.

When I find no one, I look back to her. "Yeah?"

She stops and studies me for a beat before she says, "Rowan told me about the school border thing. And Coach confirmed it this morning."

"Okay."

More silence.

"Look, I know you still have friends at Oakley, but if you're going to be a part of this team, then you need to keep the things we do here to yourself."

My brows pinch together. She can't be serious.

"They would never ask me to spy on you guys. That's not—" I stop myself from saying *our* in time. "Their style."

"Good."

It isn't exactly the welcome I might have hoped for from my new team captain, but I accept the olive branch anyway. I'm ready to turn and walk off, but she's still standing here and making some sort of effort, so I don't move either.

When she speaks again, I wish I had taken my opportunity to go.

"You and Rowan..." Amanda's voice trails off. It's the closest to discomfort I've seen from her.

"There is no me and Rowan," I clarify. The last thing I want is to get mixed up in their drama.

"It's fine if there is. We aren't together. I'm talking to Ronnie First. He's quarterback for the football team."

"Good for him." I nod a few times, unsure what else to say.

"He's fun and definitely cute, but he doesn't really do serious."

"Ronnie?"

"No, Rowan."

"Oh." I open and close my mouth several times.

"I just thought you should know."

"Thanks," I say, still feeling very uncomfortable.

"Okay, well, see you tomorrow," Amanda says, and relief shoots through me as she steps away.

"See you," I say, watching as she walks off.

I'm still staring, a little dumbfounded, when MJ jogs up.

"Hey. Nice job today," she says.

"Thanks." I let out a breath. There's something about MJ that makes it hard to be anything but relaxed. She glances back at Amanda. "What was that about?"

"I'm not sure," I admit. "I think she might have been warning me away from Rowan. Or welcoming me to the team. It's hard to say."

She laughs softly. "She can't have all the guys at Frost Lake High. Besides, if she cared so much about Rowan she shouldn't have cheated on him."

My brows lift. "For real?"

She nods but looks like maybe she wishes she hadn't shared that. "I've probably said more than I should, but it isn't a secret or anything."

We walk slowly toward the parking lot behind the soccer field. My mind spins as I stew on this new information. I knew that Rowan was still pining after her and she was with someone else, but why the hell would he still want to be with her if she cheated on him?

"I don't know exactly what happened, but rumor is that

she started hooking up with Ronnie while she and Rowan were still hanging out."

"Wow." I didn't see that coming. I saw Ronnie, and he didn't seem all that impressive to me.

"Amanda and Rowan were talking at Boone's party last night, so I'm sure they'll be back together again as soon as she and Ronnie end things." MJ looks at me, gaze narrowing slightly.

"Sounds tiring," I say of the back-and-forth.

"There's really nothing going on between you and Rowan?"

"Is that so surprising? I barely know the guy."

She shrugs one shoulder. "He talks to you a lot for someone he's not interested in."

My cheeks heat, and I do my best not to think too hard about if she's right or not. It doesn't matter. "Trust me. There is nothing going on between me and Rowan Blakenship."

I have a shift at the club on Saturday afternoon. Charlotte isn't working today, but we're slammed anyway. It's a gorgeous day, and it seems like everyone is trying to enjoy one last day of summer.

We have our first break in two hours just before I'm about to clock out.

"Go ahead and go," Brent says.

"Are you sure?"

"Yeah. Next shift will be here soon."

Grateful, I grab my stuff before he can change his mind. There's just enough of the day left that I might be able to get in a long run. I'm not where I want to be conditioning-wise yet. The Frost Lake girls, Amanda in particular, have that advantage on me. I should have gotten in a few more running days over the summer.

As I'm crossing the grassy area between the pool and the clubhouse, someone calls out to me.

"Lindsey!" someone shouts, which is uncommon for the golf course.

I look in the direction of the voice to find Rowan behind a table on the first tee box. He waves as my stare falls on him.

There isn't anyone at the tee box currently besides him, so I walk over.

"What are you doing here?" I ask.

"Holding down the fort." He waves to the Frost Lake University banner on the front of the table. Then he picks up a navy foam finger. "Can I interest you in some merch?"

"I can see *what* you're doing, but why?"

"I got roped into helping out. Some sort of admission fair thing," he says. "My parents are friends with the head of admissions. You met her, actually. Well, sort of."

"The woman at dinner," I say, perfectly picturing her. I groan. "Of course I would make the worst impression ever in front of FLU's head of admission."

"So what?"

"I'm applying there."

"Really?"

"They just got a new coach for the women's soccer team two years ago, and she's amazing. They made it to the Sweet Sixteen last season, and this year they're going to be even better."

His lips tip up at the corners. "Well, I guess I don't need to sell you on FLU."

"They're my top choice," I say and then mutter quietly,

"I almost got fired in front of the head of admissions at my number one school."

"On the plus side, I doubt she remembers you."

I scowl at him, and he laughs.

A group of golfers walk up to the tee box.

"Afternoon," Rowan says to them.

The guys tip their heads to him.

"Good school," one of them says, then touches the brim of his hat. He's wearing an FLU hat. "Do you go there?"

"No, sir," Rowan says. "I'm still in high school, but I hear great things. My parents are alumni."

"You're Lee Blakenship's son," the other says.

Rowan nods.

"You play soccer for Frost Lake. You all had a great season. I hope you win state this year."

I try to find an easy way to slip away while they're talking but can't seem to manage it. Especially when Rowan slings an arm around my shoulder and says, "That's right. And this is Summer Lindsey. She's a transfer to the girls' team. They're looking good too. Might have two teams making a run for that state championship this year."

The two men give me polite smiles, then exchange a few more words before heading up to the tees.

Rowan moves his arm from around my shoulders like this is all perfectly normal. What must it be like to be this comfortable in your own skin?

"Are you on a break?" he asks.

"No, actually I'm done for the day."

"That's great. You can keep me company."

I arch a brow. "Why would I do that?"

He bats his eyes at me and attempts to pout, but he's too

playful and happy to pull it off. "Because I have FLU merch and the other two left me to go to lunch."

"I need to get a run in before it gets too late."

He scoffs. "On your last Saturday of summer break?"

"Yeah? And possibly look for other colleges to apply to now."

He sits and pulls out the chair next to him for me. "If you're so worried about what Kristy thinks, then stick around. She'll be back in thirty minutes."

I gape.

"She went to lunch with the other person working the booth, Val. She's on the soccer team." He beams at me like he knows he has me. "You can fangirl all over both of them."

"It would be cruel to joke with me right now."

He holds my gaze. "Only one way to find out."

CHAPTER SEVEN

Rowan

"Here, put this on." I hand Summer an emerald FLU T-shirt.

"Why?" She looks down at her country club uniform shirt.

"You look like you work here."

"I do."

"Not right now you don't."

She rolls her eyes but takes the shirt and pulls it on over the polo, then does some weird shifting around to take the polo off underneath. I watch unabashedly, almost as impressed by this party trick as I am intrigued by her. *Almost.*

Despite her best efforts, both shirts ride up on her stomach, flashing me a few inches of fair, smooth skin. My gaze drops, holding there, until she pulls off the polo and the green shirt falls into place.

"Impressive."

"Years of changing on the sidelines," she says by way of explanation. She balls up her work shirt and glances down. "Better?"

The shirt is two sizes too big for her and hangs loose around her neck. Her collarbone and part of her shoulder are visible.

"You look great."

She huffs, like my comment is bullshit, and takes her seat with me again.

"Has anyone ever told you that you are shit at taking compliments?"

"Maybe," she says, with a timid smile. "What are we supposed to be doing exactly?"

"Man the table. Answer questions about FLU."

"Do you know a lot about FLU?" she asks me.

I point to the brochures. "Most people just want the free merch, or that's what I'm told. It's my first day on the job."

"Not a bad gig." She leans back in the chair. "Beats cooking hot dogs and cleaning out the popcorn machine."

I drop a hand to my stomach. "You're making me hungry."

She laughs and stares out at the golf course. It's not an uncomfortable silence, but there's still so much I don't know about her. I'm not even sure where to begin.

"How's practice going?" I ask because I know she likes talking about soccer. It's the one topic she doesn't seem guarded about.

"Better, I think, since Amanda stopped openly hating me so much." She looks over at me. "She told me you talked to her about me."

"I only told her to lay off. She had ideas about you being a spy for Oakley."

"Well, whatever you said, thank you. She's including me at practice now, so it's a vast improvement."

"Good."

"She thinks there's something going on between us. I told her there isn't, but I'm not sure if she believes me."

I cringe, thinking about what Amanda might have said to her. "She can believe whatever she wants."

Summer studies me, gaze narrowed.

"What?" I ask.

"I'm trying to figure out if you really mean that or if you're deflecting. You both said there isn't anything going on, but everyone else seems to think you'll get back together."

I shrug. I don't know either.

Our conversation is cut short when Kristy and Val come back from lunch. I make the introductions.

"Summer Lindsey. She's a senior at Frost Lake High too. I asked her to help me out. She knows a ton about FLU."

Summer blushes. "I toured it with my brother when he was choosing a school. He ended up taking a soccer scholarship out of state, but I fell in love with the campus."

"She's also a killer soccer player," I add.

"No way," Val says. "I play on the women's team. What position are you?"

"Midfielder." Summer is blushing but beaming.

"I'm a striker," Val says.

"I know. I'm a big fan. I came to a couple of games last year. That last-second goal you made against Colorado is forever imprinted in my brain. And that game against Grand Rapids in the conference tournament where you went into the penalty kick shoot-out."

"You really are a fan," Val says, grin widening.

"That's great," Kristy says. "Are you applying next fall?"

"Yes, of course. I've already started working on my application letter."

We're interrupted by groups of golfers and high school kids looking for free shirts and Frisbees for the next couple hours. Summer and Val chat on the side and it's fun to see her excited and animated. It makes me think I'm seeing the real Summer for the first time.

When it finally dies down, Val is the first to go.

"I have to get to practice," she says, then smiles at Summer. "Good luck this season. Hope to see you next year."

"Thank you and same." Summer is beaming and I'm beaming right back like a proud brother. Except I'm not sure my feelings for her are very familial. There's something about her. She's intriguing as hell.

"Oh wow. I didn't realize how late it is." Summer's eyes widen at the time on her phone, and she stands. "Thank you so much for letting me hang out."

I let out a quiet snort. She's such a nerd, thanking us like she wasn't doing us a favor.

"Thank *you*," Kristy says. "I appreciate the help."

"You're welcome." Summer shifts and then looks at me again. "I guess I'll see you at school Monday."

"Yeah, guess so."

I can't wait.

She takes a step backward and then turns and heads toward the parking lot. When she's ten feet or so away, she glances back. And I'm still smiling at her like an idiot. I wave, and then she swivels around and steps out of view.

Kristy stands and starts placing the leftover merch in plastic tubs. "You're on the schedule next week for the career fair, right?"

"Yes." I nod.

"You should ask Summer if she'd like to join as well."

"I'm sure she'd love that," I tell her, and I would too.

"You two are cute together." Kristy's smile is knowing, except whatever she thinks she knows isn't correct.

I open my mouth to tell Kristy we aren't a couple, but before I can, her phone rings. Kristy looks down at it and frowns. "I have to get this," she says as she takes a step back. "You're free to go. Thanks for your help today, Rowan. See you next week."

Monday morning, the halls of Frost Lake are filled with first-day excitement. Lacey and the other cheerleaders have the halls decked out in glittery signs.

"Seniors. Finally," Vaughn says as we stop in front of our lockers. The letters S-E-N-I-O-R-S are spelled out in big, white letters down the row of lockers that have historically been reserved for the seniors at Frost Lake. And now I guess that's us.

"Yeah. Finally," I say, but it doesn't feel real.

"We have to take a photo," Lacey says, sliding in next to Vaughn. She's dressed in her cheerleading outfit and even more smiley than normal.

"Another?" Vaughn asks.

"Yes." She elbows him in the side. "This is our last first day of school."

Lacey holds her phone out as the three of us squeeze together. She takes two or three, then darts off to another group of seniors, presumably to make them pose with her as well.

"Do you think she's going to be like this all year?" Vaughn asks, but instead of his old grumpiness, he sounds like the thought amuses him.

"Definitely." I open my locker and put my backpack inside.

"Hey." Claire comes to stand next to me and opens the locker to the right of mine. "We're locker neighbors this year."

She proceeds to hang up a mirror and a pencil box. I love the shit girls put in their lockers.

"Nice." I duck in front of her and check out my reflection, pretending to smooth out my hair.

She laughs. "You look good."

"I know. I know. Just wanted to stare at my handsome mug for a sec."

Claire pushes me out of the way. "Excited?"

"Eh..." I bob my head side to side. "Kind of."

Today's a trip. I'm happy to be a senior this year. Stupid or not, I feel a little more important walking the halls today. It's just that I don't have any idea what's next. Everyone else is soaking up the beginning of the end, but they're so clear on what they want that it seems to leave them free to enjoy today all the more. I'm not sad, but it's definitely bittersweet. High school is cool, and I'm excited to graduate and do other things. I just don't know what that something is yet.

"What about you? Ready to crush senior year?" I ask her.

"Hell yeah." As she answers, Austin wraps his arms around her waist from behind. She squeals and then leans back in to him. He drops a kiss to her cheek.

I look to my left where Vaughn and Lacey are holding hands in front of his locker. Well, shit. I'm between the two couples. Getting to my locker this year is going to be tricky.

I look down the hallway. A flash of red catches my eye.

"I'll catch you guys later," I say to the couples, who likely aren't listening to me anyway, and head toward Summer.

Her back is to me as I approach. She stares into the empty locker. I can feel the nerves practically radiating off her.

I lean against the locker next to hers. "Ready to do this thing?"

She startles, then closes her locker. "*This thing* being school?"

I nod.

"Yeah. It'll help me focus on something other than how weird it is." Her gaze lifts and roams over the halls. I try to see it from her point of view. If I were to walk into Oakley today, I'm sure I'd feel uncertain too.

"What do you have for first period?" I ask.

She takes her phone out of her front shorts pocket and unlocks the screen.

"First period psychology in Room 301."

"With Mr. Hayes. Me too." I grin at her. "What else?"

She holds her phone out and I slide over to read from it as she does, "anatomy, literature and composition, academic prep, calculus, and, finally, photography."

"Tough schedule."

She hums. "You?"

"My schedule isn't nearly that rigorous, but we have psych and academic prep together."

"Two hours of the day that I'll know someone."

"I'm sure you'll know a few other people." Like the entirety of the girls' soccer team. I'm surprised none of them are here making sure she's finding her way.

Summer lets out a long breath like she's steeling herself for battle.

"Do you want me to show you around?" I offer. "I'm going the same way anyway."

She hesitates a beat before nodding, almost like she wants to say no even though it'll make her life easier. It makes me laugh how stubborn she is.

"Come on. I'll point out your other classes on the way."

CHAPTER EIGHT

Summer

Rowan stops in front of Room 301 and waves a hand for me to enter. "Period one."

He's already shown me all my other classrooms for the day. It's unlikely that I'm going to remember how to get to them, but I have a little better understanding of the layout of the school.

When I hesitate, Rowan quirks a brow.

"Come on, Lindsey. It won't be so bad." He steps into the room, and I clutch my notebook to my chest and follow him into my first period class.

"Rowan!" someone calls from the back of the room.

I'm staring straight ahead and not looking around at my classmates, but I can see people waving and looking at him as we pass. He goes all the way to the last row and takes a seat. I finally glance up at one of the twins. He smiles back at me.

"Summer, right?" he asks.

"Yeah."

"Eli." He leans back in his chair and kicks one foot out and keeps grinning at me.

Rowan takes the seat next to him, and I take the one in front of Rowan. I don't look at anyone else, but I can feel their stares. I have a big ole "New Kid" sign taped to my forehead.

"Hello, everyone. Welcome. Find a seat and we'll get started shortly." The teacher greets us as the time on the clock above his desk indicates one minute until the hour.

It's then that I finally let myself look up from my notebook, just in time to see Amanda and Sophie walk into the room. Amanda's expression tells me everything about how she feels seeing me here. She might have started including me at practice, but I've been under no illusion that we were going to be friends. This pretty much confirms it.

My stomach sinks as she looks away and takes a seat in the front row. Sophie's mouth pulls into a tight line as she pauses, looking right at me, then sits beside her friend.

The air around me is thick with tension. I glance down at my mood ring, unsurprised to find it a mixture of green and blue. Confused and anxious. That sums it up nicely.

I have no idea why Amanda insists on hating me so much. Does she really think I'm going to give my old teammates all the Frost Lake strategies and set plays? And even if I did, would it really matter? So much of soccer comes down to skills and decisions during the game. One opportunity leads to another and another. Or the same thing for mistakes. One mistake can cost a possession and then a goal. You can only plan so much. She knows that as well as I do.

Mr. Hayes is talking and I've blanked out. Great way to start the new academic year. He grabs a stack of papers off his desk and hands them to the people sitting at the front of each row. The papers move back as he continues to go over what the class will cover this semester.

The papers stop three seats in front of me when the guy looks back and realizes the seat is empty.

There's no one in front or on either side of me. Maybe it wasn't intentional, but it feels as if everyone is giving me a wide berth.

My face heats. The last thing I want to do is draw attention to myself by raising my hand, but I need a paper. Ugh.

I start to lift my right arm at the same time Rowan taps me on the shoulder. I swivel around and he's holding out a paper to me. Relief washes over me.

"Thanks," I whisper and turn back around.

"Mr. Hayes, I didn't get one," Rowan calls from behind me.

I glance back and he winks.

The rest of the class goes by without incident. Mr. Hayes is a fun teacher. He cracks jokes and doesn't mind when people talk without raising their hands. I don't add to the conversation, but the jovial mood around me loosens up some of the nerves I'm feeling.

When the bell rings, I let everyone else head for the door first. Rowan takes his time, lingering with me.

"You survived," he says. His notebook is tucked in his hand at his side. He is the picture of casual, academic indifference.

"Barely."

"Do you remember where your anatomy class is for next period?" he asks.

"Yes," I say, far more confidently than I feel.

"Are you just saying that so I won't be tempted to walk with you across school?"

"What? No."

He narrows his gaze and his smile pulls wider. An unexpected laugh leaves my lips.

"Good, because I'm going the opposite direction," he says.

We stop outside the classroom, off to one side of the busy hallway.

"I'm not going to thank you again," I say to him. He keeps saving me. It's starting to feel redundant.

"Not necessary. I like being your Frost Lake High tour guide." He takes a step away. "See you at lunch?"

"Yeah." I nod, then turn in a half circle trying to get my bearings.

Rowan fights a laugh, then points in the direction I need to go. I lift a hand in a wave and then head off, hopefully toward my second period.

Anatomy has a completely different vibe than my first class. Mrs. Gideon is like seventy years old and talks quietly and in a monotone voice as she reads the syllabus word for word.

My third period is literature and composition. It's a small class of about thirteen people, including MJ. We have assigned seats and aren't together, but knowing she's here puts me at ease.

Next is lunch. MJ walks with me and I drop off my stuff at my locker, then we do the same at hers.

"Fair warning that most of the food is terrible," she says as we get in the back of the line.

"I'm not very hungry anyway," I admit.

It's the same sort of stations we had at Oakley. A salad bar, hot food—which today is a choice of hamburger or veggie burger with soggy-looking fries, and then a variety of purchase options like chips or cookies. I grab a veggie burger and fries and snag a bag of Doritos for later.

"Most of the soccer girls sit together," MJ says once we have our trays of food. She leads the way as I'm wondering what the Oakley lunchroom looks like this year. I text with Charlotte and Jill every day, but we haven't had a chance to really talk. I bet they're sitting together right now. What I wouldn't give to be there with them.

The table is right next to a table filled with boys' soccer players. Not surprising, but I'm still startled to see Rowan again. He waves, and I smile despite myself. He's kind of impossible not to like—and I should know because I'm trying my best to dislike him.

MJ sets her tray down and tells people to scoot to make room for me.

"Hi," I say tentatively as I slide into the bench seat. Across from me are two juniors, Posey and Regina. And to their left, Amanda and Sophie.

The table is already filled with chatter. MJ joins their conversation in that effortless way only she seems to do. Girl cliques are tricky. Most of the girls on the team have one or two friends they stick to. Everyone except MJ. She bounces from person to person and gets along with everyone. She's a little like Rowan in that regard.

I look over to his table. He's sitting with Vaughn and Austin, plus their girlfriends, and either Eli or Eddie. I still can't tell them apart.

Rowan looks up like he can feel me staring at him. He says something to Vaughn next to him as he stands and then he's coming my way. He sets his tray down next to mine.

"Are you eating for two?" I ask, eyeing up the extra

servings. Two hamburgers, lots of fries, two bags of chips, and a cookie.

He lets out a laugh as he sits. "The lunch ladies love me."

"Why does that not surprise me?" I ask with an eye roll.

We're close, his arm and leg brushing against mine, as he settles in next to me.

"How were the rest of your classes this morning?" he asks.

"Fine. Yours?"

"Good. Or, you know, as good as school gets." He opens a second chocolate milk carton on his tray.

It's unnerving having him this close. He's so comfortable in his skin. Or maybe it's just that all of this is new for me, but he's known this place and these people for years.

"I like your rings," he says as I try one of the fries. It's as cold and soggy as it looked.

"Thanks."

I flex my fingers out in front of me and try to see them like he does. My mood ring on my left pointer finger, a gold band on my left thumb, a pink heart on my right middle finger that Charlotte got me and Jill last year for Christmas, another gold band—this one smaller—on my right ring finger, and an S ring on my pinky finger.

"Are you going to Rieger's party tonight?"

I drop my hands back to the table. "Who is Rieger?"

Rowan sits tall and glances around the lunchroom. "Mariah Rieger. She's a senior basketball player. I don't see her, but she's great. You'll like her."

I nod. The problem, in general, isn't that I won't like her. It's that people aren't really liking me so far.

"So you're going?"

"Probably not."

"Why not? Everyone will be there."

"Not if I don't go." Although I doubt I'm considered "everyone" by most people's standards.

"You should at least stop by and say hi."

"I guess that means you're going."

"Rowan never misses a party," Amanda says from my right side. The conversation at the table has died off without me realizing it, and everyone is looking at me and Rowan.

"That's true," he says, but I feel the shift in him. He's tensed up under Amanda's scrutiny.

"You should come, Summer." Amanda smiles at me so genuinely—or at least it appears that way.

"Yeah, maybe."

She stands with her tray, still aiming that smile at me. "See you at practice."

She leaves, followed quickly by Sophie.

"Yikes," MJ mutters under her breath. "That was awkward."

"Awkward?" I ask in reply. She seemed...nice.

MJ tips her head to the left, her gaze darting toward Rowan.

It's only then I realize Amanda totally snubbed Rowan. Oh god. It hadn't even occurred to me. No wonder he came over here to sit. He was probably hoping she'd talk to him, and instead she ignored him.

When I look over at him, he's staring down at his lunch. A pang of pity hits me square in the chest. For a guy who looks so happy and carefree 99 percent of the time, the moments he doesn't are hard to witness.

"Are you okay?" I ask him as conversation around the table picks up again.

"Yeah. Fine." His lips curve into a smile that isn't all that convincing.

"You're not fine. Or if you are, then you're a robot with no emotion."

"Beep. Beep. I am Rowan," he says in a mechanical voice while moving his arms like a Ken doll. He's smiling again—a real one.

"Why don't you just talk to her and tell her you want to get back together?"

"She's talking to Ronnie."

"Maybe, but she's obviously jealous."

"How do you get that?"

"Please. Why else would she talk to me when you're sitting right next to me? She's acting like she doesn't care, but that's twice now she's basically given me the green light to date you."

Rowan quirks a brow. I already told him she thought we were talking, but not the complete story.

"At practice last week, she asked if we were talking and said it was fine if we were. I told her there wasn't anything going on between us," I clarify quickly. "But I'm not sure she believed me."

"Made worse by my coming over here." He groans like he's just realized how it must look that he keeps hanging out with me.

I'm still not sure why he does either, but it feels like a bad time to pile on by asking him.

"She also mentioned that you weren't really into relationships."

He huffs a laugh. "Yeah, well, that part is true."

"I'm not sure I believe you."

"We were never official, Amanda and me."

"But you wanted to be?"

Instead of answering my question, he poses one of his own. "You know who else thought you and I were a couple?"

While he waits for my answer, he picks up a fry and tosses it in his mouth.

"Who?"

He finishes chewing and then says, "Kristy from FLU."

"Oh my gosh, why?"

Rowan shrugs. "I guess she assumed that was why I asked you to hang out and why you stayed even though you weren't being paid."

I stayed because talking to Val was the single most exciting thing that's happened to me in weeks…maybe months.

"She asked me to invite you to work at the next event. It's at the Frost Lake career center. Same sort of thing. Four hours, a hundred bucks, not a bad gig."

"Really?" I try and fail to contain my excitement. Getting paid will be nice, but it's more time with Kristy that has me giddy. If I can impress her, surely that will help my chances at getting into FLU.

He shoots me an amused grin. "I'm guessing by your reaction that you're in?"

"Yes. Definitely."

"Cool, I'll send you the details."

"Wait. Do I have to pretend to be your girlfriend while we're there?"

"Nah. Unless you want to. That could be fun." He winks.

I roll my eyes, and he chuckles softly under his breath.

This is great. I need to check the schedule at the club and make sure I'm not working that day or find someone to switch.

When I look back at Rowan, he's glancing around the cafeteria. I follow his line of sight to Amanda sitting next to Ronnie at another table.

"If you want her back, then you should just ask someone out for real," I say.

He blinks like he didn't realize he was staring and looks back at me. "Why would I do that?"

"If she's this jealous that you're hanging out with someone, imagine if you were really talking to someone else."

"I don't know." He's skeptical. Bless his clueless boy heart. It isn't his fault. The complicated workings of the teenage girl brain should be studied.

"I promise you. She cares." She only talked to me at practice after he hung out with me at Boone's party and then today when he's sitting next to me. "She wants her cake and to eat it too."

He squints. "I never understood that saying. Who has cake and doesn't want to eat it?"

I laugh softly. "My point is, she wants you to want her even if she's with Ronnie."

"But she could be with me if she just stopped talking to him."

"I didn't say it was logical."

He laughs again. "She wouldn't buy it. I've never dated anyone else. Not like that."

"Which would only make her more jealous," I argue. "Just ask someone out and see what happens. I agree it isn't the most mature plan, but it'd be a quick way to see how she really feels. And in the meantime, maybe going out with someone else will help you realize that she isn't that great."

Seriously, Amanda is pretty and she's a good soccer player but otherwise, I don't see the appeal.

He doesn't look convinced at first, but he shoves in three more fries and looks around contemplatively as he chews.

Finally he bobs his head. "Yeah. You're right."

He's still staring off into space like he's deep in scheming thoughts.

"That's a great idea."

"It is?" Now I'm surprised. "Great" might be a stretch, but I have no doubt it'll work.

"Yes."

"Glad I could help."

He looks at me now. His smile slowly stretches wide until he's grinning at me. It's a little unnerving having his complete focus on me while he looks so happy. My stomach flips and warmth pools low in my belly.

And he keeps on smiling at me.

He's looking at me like a man with a plan. A man with a plan that involves me in a way I'm not going to like. That happy, light feeling vanishes and dread takes its place. "Oh no."

"Why not? Everyone thinks we're talking anyway."

"But we aren't. I barely know you."

"Then you can get to know me." Rowan shrugs like this is a great bonus to an already amazing plan.

"You're asking me out to make your ex jealous. Gee. I feel so special." I let out a short, dry laugh. "Why would I want to get to know you?"

"I don't know, maybe we could be friends or something."

"Friends?"

"Why not? I'm a good friend. All my friends say so."

"My brother hates you, for one."

"Do you hate everything and everyone your brother does?"

I consider that, but only to make a point. "Everyone, yes, but I refuse to hate peanut butter just because he thinks the texture is 'icky.'" I air quote the last word, and as I do, I picture Silas shuddering as he watches me take a spoonful of peanut butter from the jar.

Rowan laughs. He's back to looking like a happy, carefree guy. This version is hard to resist. His expression shifts and he regards me seriously. "It's only for a little while, and when we break up, it'll give you and your brother more ammunition to talk shit."

His logic, while perhaps true, doesn't make this scenario any less bizarre.

"This is absurd."

"Is it? You get to spend time chatting up Kristy at all the FLU events your heart desires, and I can show Amanda that I'm the kind of guy who can be in a relationship and find out how she feels about me."

My mind whirls with too many thoughts to articulate a single one. I do want to spend more time with Kristy, and I was the one to suggest he ask someone out. I just didn't mean me.

"And I will introduce you to everyone else at FLH. If what you say is true, that people are nicer to you when I'm around, then six weeks should be plenty of time to introduce you to everyone I know and make them like you."

"Six weeks?" I was picturing a single date. Maybe a week of sitting together at lunch.

"That spans the recruitment events this fall, and it's plenty of time to introduce you to people at school, games, and parties."

"I don't know. What if she takes her jealousy out on me and starts being a jerk in practice again?"

"Fair point. That would suck." He seems to consider that for a moment. "I don't think that will happen, but if it does, then we'll stage a breakup immediately and call it good." He tips his head to my teammates around the table and lowers his voice even more. "Hopefully by then the rest of the team will have had a chance to see how awesome you are."

I wonder if he means that or if he's just trying to convince me to go along with his plan. I don't get the feeling that the other girls on the team think Amanda and Rowan are good together, so I doubt they'd think it was weird. Plus, it isn't like Amanda and I are friends. Still, dating a teammate's ex is a weird line.

"If for any reason one of us wants to stop sooner, we call it," he reiterates. "I've got your back."

My throat is thick and my heart rate increases. I can't believe I'm even considering it.

"How awful could it be? You get to hang out with me. I'm awesome." His cocky charm only makes me more hesitant.

He wants to win Amanda back, and I want to survive this year without everyone looking at me like the enemy. Is it possible this will get us both what we want? I look around at MJ, talking and laughing with Rina. I think I could be friends with these girls. And more importantly, I think we could be a good team.

When I glance at Rowan again, he's still smiling at me, brows raised slightly. He looks so hopeful that I can't help but feel some of it too.

"Okay. I'm in."

CHAPTER NINE

Rowan

"Ready?" I ask Summer as I hold a hand out to her. She's sitting in the passenger side of my truck looking like she'd rather be anywhere else.

"Definitely not." Looking reluctant enough that it has my ego in check, she places her hand in mine and steps down. "I think I might throw up."

"Don't do that." I shut the door behind her with one hand and appreciate how good she looks tonight. She's in jeans and a light-pink tank top. Her hair is always the real showstopper though. Tonight it's pulled back in a low ponytail, but a few strands fall free. Little perfect spiral curls that hang around her neck and face.

"No promises," she mutters.

"It's a party, Lindsey. Try not to look so miserable."

She hums a reply that might be her agreement to try and attempts to pull her hand away from mine. I hold tighter and when my intent is clear—I'm not letting go—Summer groans.

"Oh no."

I bark out a short laugh. "Not the reaction I'm used to, but I guess it's the best I can hope for under the circumstances."

I'm still surprised she said yes to this wild scheme. Though the longer I thought about it today, the more I was certain it would work. That is, assuming Summer is right and Amanda is jealous. I guess we're about to find out.

"Wow, this house is even bigger than I remember," Summer notes as we walk toward the front. "My friends and I used to trick-or-treat here when were younger because they give out the best candy."

"Yeah, same," I say, which is true. But I decide to leave out that I live two houses down.

As we get closer to the door, Summer's steps slow considerably. I stop at the bottom of the porch and face her.

"Take a breath," I instruct.

"I'm fine." She fidgets and pulls at the hem of her shirt.

I keep watching her to make sure she really is okay, then nod. "Here goes nothing, Lindsey."

I turn and take a step, but Summer latches onto my upper arm.

"Wait," she says, panic laced in her tone.

"What's wrong?" I ask, facing her once more.

"What do we tell people?" she asks.

"Are you expecting an interrogation?"

"Humor me. I do better with a plan."

My lips twist into a smile. "You want a plan for going to a party with me?"

"Are we talking? Together? Casual? What's our label?"

"We're together."

"Why?" Her face scrunches up in what might be disgust at the idea.

"Well, usually it's because two people like each other."

She smacks me lightly on the chest. I really love riling her up. But I won't pretend her shock at picturing us together doesn't make me second-guess everything. It's been so long since I talked to anyone but Amanda. Maybe I'm not as good at this as I thought.

"I mean, why would you want to be with me?" she asks, then adds, "in case people ask."

"No one is going to ask me why I want to be with you. It's obvious."

She cocks her head to the side, waiting for a real answer.

"You're hot, Lindsey."

She's quiet for a beat and then bursts into laughter.

"You asked," I say, not the least bit sorry for saying it. She is hot. Really hot. Lots of guys would be thrilled to be here with her tonight.

"That's a terrible reason."

"What would *you* like me to tell all these people who aren't going to ask? Your fiery personality? Your smart brain?" I taunt her just a little.

"I'm not that smart," she says with a sigh. "B+ average."

"Above average." Better than my grades. "I'll tell them I like your above-average brain then."

She groans and turns away from me and stares at the front door like it's the enemy. "Just tell them you think I'm hot."

"You *are* hot," I say as I take a step onto the porch. This time she lets me pull her with me.

The music hits us as soon as we step through the front door. There are already a lot of people here, and they're grouped off in the same sort of cliques at school. Basketball girls, hockey guys, cheerleaders, honor students, band kids, etc. I continue through the house and go outside where I know I'll find my teammates and hers.

Summer's grip on my hand tightens with every step.

As we reach the back patio, I pause and look at her. She looks so nervous that it's going to be hard for people to believe she came with me willingly.

I lean down, a hit of her soap or perfume invades my nostrils, and one of those perfect curls tickles my jaw.

"Relax," I tell her at the same time my nerves ramp up. I know this is for show. She knows it's for show, but my body doesn't seem to be getting the memo. It's been a long time since I was out with a girl, and the number of times I walked into a party holding hands with one is...never. I don't hate it.

The backyard is a mirror copy of a dozen other parties I've been to here. And the soccer teams are exactly where I expected. I clock Amanda and Ronnie, but I don't let my stare linger.

"Hey, you made it," Eli says as we finally stop next to him, Hunter, and Blake. Vaughn, Lacey, Austin, and Claire are in their own little group. They do that more and more now. How adorable.

"Of course. I just had to pick up Summer first," I say.

It's then that all their gazes drop to my and Summer's joined hands.

I feel her tense in those seconds when no one says anything. Eli looks like his brain might explode. Summer has her own group of guys who are going to be very jealous to see her with me. And Eli is number one on the list.

"You guys do remember Summer, right?" I ask, quirking a brow at them and hopefully communicating that they're acting weird. If I really had brought her on a date tonight, I'd want my friends to make her comfortable. Which coincidentally is exactly how I feel. It's cruel that she had to switch schools senior year. I can't imagine starting all over.

"Yeah, of course." He recovers and smiles at Summer. "Eli."

"And that's Hunter and Blake," I tell her.

She offers them a small wave and a smile. "Hi."

"You want something to drink?" I ask her. She's so stiff you'd think I brought her here against her will. Which okay, I kind of did. But we're in this together now. I squeeze her hand and that prompts her to finally respond.

"Yes."

"Catch you guys later," I say to the guys and drag Summer along with me.

She lets out a shaky breath that has another laugh slipping free. There's a giant cooler on the back patio. I drop her hand and flip open the lid.

"What do you like?" I ask her, then hold up a water and a Sprite. "Someone around here probably has booze too."

"Alcohol is the last thing I need." She takes the water and twists off the cap. "Did they buy it?"

I glance over her head to my teammates. "They're staring this way and talking, so either they're on to us or we just became the newest couple gossip."

She sips the water and ducks her head like that's going to keep people from seeing her or talking about us.

"If you're having second thoughts—" I start, but she shakes her head immediately.

"No." Her eyes close briefly. "I'm sorry. I'm screwing this up."

"You're not screwing anything up." I reach out and take

her hand again, this time to comfort her and not for show. "But if this is too much, let's call it now."

"Maybe if we set some rules, that would help."

I let go of her hand again and pop the tab on the Sprite. "Rules, huh?"

"I can't relax when I'm worried you're going to kiss me or something."

"The ego hits just keep coming," I mutter under my breath and then take a long sip of the lemon-lime soda. "All right. Hit me. What are the rules?"

"Holding hands is fine, but I'm not kissing you."

"Yes, noted. But just so you know, you're missing out. I'm an excellent kisser."

She doesn't look convinced.

"I won't kiss you," I promise. Geez. This girl. "But we need a thing."

"A thing?"

"Something couple-y we do."

"Were you and Amanda into PDA?"

I give that some thought. "We weren't *not* into it."

We didn't walk around parties holding hands, but she'd sit on my lap or I'd wrap my arms around her from behind. And I can remember more than one make-out session in random dark corners or, fine, even out in the center of the party. We just kind of went with whatever we were feeling—often fueled by the late night and party atmosphere. We were less touchy at school.

"Rowan?" Summer arches a brow like maybe she said something I missed.

"Sorry, what?"

"Can't we just hold hands?"

"That's so boring and so junior high."

"Gee, thanks."

"Oh, please. You were counting down the seconds until I freed your hand," I point out.

"Okay. Then what?"

I glance around at the couples around the party, calling out what I see, "Kissing. Hand up the shirt. Hand on the butt." A few couples are straight up making out. Little early in the night for that, but to each their own.

"No, no, no," she replies in quick succession.

"I'm only doing recon, not suggesting I cop a feel."

This time when I turn my attention back to the couples at the party, she does the same.

"Lots of girls sitting in laps," she notes.

"Yeah." She's right—it's as common and cliché as hand-holding.

"Were you and…what's the ex's name again?" I glance at her.

"Kevin."

"I'm guessing the two of you weren't into PDA."

"Kevin liked to put his hand in my back pocket. He was a butt guy."

This makes me laugh. Actually, I'm cackling. She says it so nonchalantly. I may have misjudged her as a prude.

"He said I have a nice ass," she says matter-of-factly, but her face is turning red.

I can't stop laughing.

"What about you and Amanda? What was your *thing*?" she asks, her voice full of challenge.

"We didn't have a thing. We were too on and off again to ever have a rhythm. I mean, sure, at the end of the night we'd go off and make out or something, but when we were at parties, we'd usually hang with other people. She had her friends and I had mine. We'd just kind of meet up at the end of the night I guess."

"That's…" Her voice trails off and I hang on, waiting for her thoughts. Pathetic? A red flag? I'm starting to question a lot of things about my relationship with Amanda. I really fucked things up.

She shakes her head as if deciding not to share whatever she's thinking. "What about an arm grab?"

"What the hell is that?" It doesn't sound nearly as cool as a butt grab, which is all I can think about since she mentioned her ass. It is nice; Kevin was right. Now seems like a bad time to tell her that though.

Summer takes a step closer to me and links her arm through mine, then grabs my bicep. The movement puts our…everything close, including our faces. I peer down at her, gaze briefly roaming over her face and the light freckles that dot the bridge of her nose and fan out over her cheekbones. She smells like oranges and vanilla.

She lifts her brows in silent question.

I clear my throat, which is suddenly very dry. "Not bad. I think we can do better though."

She unhooks her arm and moves back. "I'm open to ideas."

"It'll come to me." I wave her off. "For now, I don't think we need to sweat it. People might be more suspicious if we overdo it."

"Okay."

"Any other rules?" I ask with a hint of taunting in my tone.

"Don't kiss me or grope me or call me 'babe' or 'baby' or 'baby doll.'"

"Got it." My lips twitch with amusement.

She looks like she's still thinking, so I wait.

"No talking shit about my brother," she adds.

"No problem. He's the one who—"

"Ahhh..." She puts up a hand to stop me from saying more.

"All right, all right. No talking about Silas."

She seems to relax a fraction, and it's just in time. MJ and Rina approach. I open my stance and take a small step closer to Summer.

"I was hoping you'd be here," Rina says to Summer.

"You were?" Summer asks her.

"Yes, you have to show me how you did that Ronaldo chop. I've been working on it since last season, and I can't get it."

I feel Summer relax beside me. Reminder: Soccer talk is the key to making her comfortable.

"Oh, it's not hard at all. I can show you."

"Really?" Rina eyes widen.

"Yeah, of course. Before practice tomorrow, I'll—"

She doesn't get to finish the sentence. Rina grabs her arm and pulls her with her.

"Show me now. I saw some of the guys with a ball. They'll let us borrow it."

"Oh. Umm..." Summer looks back at me almost like she's asking permission.

"Don't keep her away too long," I say to them, then toss a wink at Summer. Predictably, she rolls her eyes so only I can see.

With Summer preoccupied, I head over to the guys. Vaughn and Austin have disentangled themselves from their girlfriends and are hanging out.

"Where are the wives?" I ask.

"Lacey is comforting a freshman cheerleader who locked herself in the bathroom and Claire went as backup," Austin says.

"Yikes. Little early in the night for drama," I say.

"Yeah, speaking of..." Vaughn turns his captain-like, smug, inquisitive gaze on me. "I guess congrats are in order."

The statement comes out more like a question. I expected this.

I steal a page out of Summer's book and roll my eyes. "Let's hear it. Give me all your jokes now and let's get them out of the way."

"We're just confused. You barely know this chick, and you show up holding hands." Austin arches a brow. "When did this happen?"

"We've hung out a few times. Parties and the country club—she works there." I add the last part for authenticity. *See, guys? I know things about her.* They don't look any more convinced. I point between them. "Maybe if you two weren't sucking face with your girls twenty-four/seven you'd have noticed sooner."

"Noticed what?" Vaughn asks like he needs me to spell it out.

"That Summer and I are into each other." It feels weird to say the words. Especially to these guys. I've never lied to them before. I rationalize it by telling myself I do like hanging out with her.

"You don't do relationships," Vaughn says.

"What are you talking about? I dated Amanda last year."

"You and Amanda don't count."

"Why the hell not?" The question comes out with more bite than intended.

"For starters because neither of you would commit," Vaughn says. "It was a constant back-and-forth based on boredom and wanting someone to hook up with at parties."

"That is not true."

"All he means to say is that you and Amanda were never a true couple. You talked on and off, hooked up sometimes, but you both hung out with other people too," Austin says.

"Which was fine because as long as I've known you, you've said people were far too serious in high school and you didn't want to miss out on all the fun and experiences by being tied to one person," Vaughn says. "And now you show up here with Summer Lindsey, of all fucking people, and say you're together even though you've known her for five seconds."

"Jesus. You two need to lighten up. We're dating, not getting engaged." I laugh it off and avoid direct eye contact. I really didn't expect them to have such strong opinions on my dating life.

"She's Silas Lindsey's sister," Vaughn adds.

"So?"

"You don't think it's suspect?"

"What, like he's trying to fuck with me through her?" That pulls a genuine laugh from me. The thought that Summer concocted this whole scheme is ironic, considering I talked her into it. "I don't think even Silas is that manipulative."

"So you two are really together then?" Austin asks. He sounds far less skeptical than Vaughn.

"Yeah." I take another drink of my Sprite and try to appear calm. I am in a relationship with Summer Lindsey. Telling my friends and having this very painful conversation makes it all the more real. Except not real because Summer and I aren't really together. Wow. This is a mindfuck already. No wonder I've never dated before.

My buddies are quiet and share some secret look that I can't and don't even try to decipher. Is it hot out here? I pull at the collar of my T-shirt.

"Then we're happy for you," Austin says.

Vaughn nods along and gives me a small smile. I wouldn't say he's convinced, but the fact he isn't calling bullshit says he at least partially believes me. "At least it's not Amanda."

I don't know what the fuck that means, but I'm ready for this conversation to be over.

I'm relieved when Summer finds me a little later. I'm still standing around with Vaughn and Austin, but their girlfriends have joined us. I'm back to being the fifth wheel but I care a lot less because they've stopped grilling me.

"Hey." The smile I give her is genuine. She's my only ally in this weird fake-dating thing. "Done already?"

"I tried to tell Rina it wasn't that hard. She got it on like the fourth try."

"Or maybe you're just a good teacher." I bump my shoulder against hers.

She laughs softly and then she must feel my friends staring at us because she glances around the circle and flushes.

"Oh my gosh." Lacey steps forward and reaches for Summer's left hand. "Is this a mood ring?"

"Yeah." Summer graciously lets Lacey pull her hand so she can get a better look at it.

"I had one of these in middle school, and I loved it. Except it was always stuck on blue."

"Because you are always happy." Claire laughs.

"Really?" I ask, staring a little harder at the circle ring on Summer's finger. It has a gold band and the center is purple. "Like it reads your mood?"

I think I remember the girls wearing these years ago, but I'd forgotten about them too.

Summer nods. "Allegedly. Really, I think it's just reading body temperature."

"What does purple mean?" I ask.

"Love," Lacey answers for her. "Purple is love. Which makes sense because she's next to you."

Summer flushes brighter. "I was also just playing soccer."

My brows lift and I cover a laugh with a cough. "You love soccer more than me, huh?"

"Definitely," she says back and everyone around us laughs.

I hook a finger through one of her belt loops and tug her to me. The movement catches her off balance and she falls into me. That citrus-sweet scent hits me again, and my pulse races.

Lacey and Claire start reminiscing about other nostalgic things from middle school, and the conversation and attention shifts from me and Summer. But she stays close to me, and I keep my finger looped in her jeans.

This pretending thing isn't so bad.

CHAPTER TEN

Summer

Rowan's friends are nice. Vaughn is a legend, primarily because of his father, but I've seen him play and he's more than proven himself to be on the same track. He'll definitely go pro at some point. He's quiet and more reserved than Rowan or Austin, but his girlfriend Lacey is bubbly and sweet. I love her. She reminds me of Charlotte.

Claire and I are more alike, neither of us shy but not as outgoing as Lacey either. It's easy to see how Rowan fits in with these people. He's the funny guy, the one always looking to make them laugh or start the conversation. It's almost like everyone is more at ease when he's around.

It's hard to believe this is the same guy that Silas hates so much. The guy *I* hated so much.

As people start to leave, Rowan shows no sign of going anywhere. Vaughn and Lacey left quite a while ago and Austin and Claire are saying their goodbyes now. I stifle a yawn as Claire hugs me and says she'll see me tomorrow.

"What is that?" Rowan asks, catching me with my hand over my mouth and my eyes watering.

"Sorry. It's late."

"Late?" He scoffs.

"Rowan usually closes these things down," Claire warns me.

"Not me. I'm a morning person."

Rowan gasps dramatically, pulling an instant smile to my lips.

"That's it. That's a deal-breaker, Lindsey."

I shrug one shoulder. "Oh well."

Teasing him and giving him shit has become our bit for the night, and his friends think it's hilarious. If they only knew. Or wait, maybe they do.

My skin pricks as the idea settles in. Did he tell them that we're faking? They were so nice to me tonight, but maybe they would have been either way.

"Good luck getting him out of here before dawn," Austin says with a wave as he and Claire walk away.

I turn to Rowan, who sighs.

"We can go if you want," he says, sounding like he's making a big sacrifice by leaving.

"One more lap around the party?"

His eyes light up. "Yeah. My girlfriend is a party animal."

His palm finds mine as a laugh slips from my lips.

"No one has ever accused me of being a party animal," I tell him.

"You were just hanging out with the wrong people. I'm a blast, therefore you're more compelled to stay. It's a common problem. You'll see."

I shake my head at him like I think he's full of shit, but the truth is, he's probably right. As tired as I am, and as reluctant as I was to come, tonight was fun.

I let him guide me around the backyard one last time. I

can't relax with his fingers intertwined with mine, but I do my best to smile and look natural. People are excited to see Rowan. All of them. He's so universally liked and by extension, so am I. It's an odd feeling. Kevin was popular and I had great friends at Oakley, but I wasn't part of the in crowd.

We stop and chat with every group that's still here. I meet a bunch more people, only remembering about a quarter of their names. Every single person glances at our joined hands. Some register their surprise openly, a few guys even comment on it, but everyone seems to accept we're a couple. It's mind-boggling to me that anyone believes it. From what I've witnessed, Rowan is one of the most popular guys in school, and I'm nobody.

"You and Amanda are done for good then?" a guy named Troy asks. I can smell the booze on him, but I don't know if he's drunk or just oblivious to the faux pas of asking about Rowan's ex in front of his current girlfriend.

Not that I really care, but I know I should be offended.

His smile stays intact, but Rowan's fingers tighten around mine. "Amanda who?"

The guys laugh and Rowan plays it off like he's completely unaffected, but he pulls me away right after.

Unfortunately, the next group we encounter as we're circling around is the football guys. Amanda sits on Ronnie's lap. He's talking to his friends and mostly ignoring her except for a hand draped over her upper thigh.

She spots us first as we approach. Her stare drops only for a second to our hands and then quickly lifts to our faces. She smiles.

Rowan is walking at a pace that suggests he has no intention of stopping so I wave at her and hope she isn't going to come tackle me from behind.

"She didn't look jealous," Rowan whispers when we're a few feet away.

I glance back. She's still watching us. She doesn't look pissed at me, so that's good news. In fact, she isn't looking at me at all. She's watching him.

"Don't worry. She is."

He pauses and looks back the same way I did, but she's already looked away.

"Thank you for doing this," he says when he meets my gaze again. He's still holding my left hand, and he's standing so close I can smell the mixture of his laundry detergent or body wash and the minty gum in his mouth.

"Did everyone buy it?"

"I think so."

"Do your friends know the truth?"

"Nah." He shakes his head. "No way."

"Why not? They must know how you feel about Amanda. I'm sure they'd understand."

"Would they though?" he asks, squinting slightly.

"Okay. Fine. It's sort of a wild idea."

He laughs. "Understatement of the year."

"But I can tell how much they care about you."

"They're good people," he says.

We're still standing close. Still staring at each other. It's easier to be around him now, minus the hand-holding and the warmth radiating off him.

The wind blows my hair into my face. He reaches out and brushes it back with the hand not attached to mine.

"I like your hair," he says.

"It has a mind of its own." Especially in the current humidity.

"I still like it."

I make a noncommittal hum. Sometimes I wish I had easy hair. Straight, not as red, not as out of control. It isn't that I don't like it; it's just loud in a way that I'm not.

"I think the appropriate response is, 'Thank you, Rowan. You're the sweetest boyfriend.'" He makes his voice high-pitched and nasally as he says the last part.

"I do not sound like that." I swat at his chest playfully.

"Oh, you so do."

"And I would never call you 'the sweetest boyfriend.'"

"Why the hell not? I'm sweet."

"There are a lot of adjectives I'd use to describe you, but that isn't one of them."

"Fine." He huffs. "Is 'hot' one of them at least?"

I laugh.

"If you keep fueling my ego like this, Lindsey, I'm going to get a big head."

"I'm sure you'll be just fine." I don't think his ego is hurting one bit.

He's shaking his head at me again as he pulls his phone out of his front jean pocket. He unlocks the screen and goes to the camera app. When he puts the phone out in front of us, I ask, "What are you doing?"

"Taking a photo with my hot girlfriend. I'm going to make it my wallpaper."

I arch a brow.

"See? I'm sweet."

I laugh and he snaps the photo. He holds it out for me to see.

"Not bad."

"Right? We actually look like a couple."

He does exactly what he said and makes it his phone wallpaper. It's too weird. All of it.

"Now your turn," he says.

"I am not making you my wallpaper."

"Why not?"

"It's too…" I search for the right word. Cliché? Cutesy?

"What is it right now?"

I take out my phone and show him. It's a photo from last year of me, Charlotte, and Jill on the bus to an away game.

He takes it from me and studies it closer. "These are your friends?"

"Yeah. Charlotte is the one on the left and Jill is on the right." My chest tightens. "I miss them. Everything about this year feels wrong without them here."

He stares at it a moment longer and then hands it back. "It sucks that you had to switch schools senior year. I'm sorry."

"Thanks." I put the phone back in my pocket.

"I'd like to meet them."

"I don't think that's a good idea."

"Because they don't know you're fake dating me?"

"And because you're so hot they'd try to steal you away from me," I say dramatically.

"All right, wiseass." He huffs another small laugh.

The next morning, after less than six hours of sleep, I don't want to get out of bed. But as tired as I am, I can't help but smile. I had more fun than I expected. And today at practice we're getting our uniforms and doing a scrimmage. Our first game is this Thursday and I'm itching to play.

I'm just out of the shower when my phone starts ringing. I wrap a towel around me quickly and drip across the floor to get my phone from the vanity.

I was expecting Charlotte or Jill, but it's Silas who's calling. A smile pulls at my face. I've barely talked to him since he left for college. His love language is sending funny videos, but as far as real communication, there's been very little.

"Hey," I answer on speaker as I try to dry off enough that I don't make a huge puddle.

"What the fuck, Sum?"

I make a face at the screen like he can see me. "Well, hello to you too."

"Have you completely lost your mind?" he asks, still sounding pissed.

"What the hell has crawled up your ass?" He's making me as agitated as he sounds.

He scoffs, deep and rough. It sounds like he's walking in a crowd, maybe on campus to his next class or at the cafeteria. I try to picture him sometimes, what his life is like there. And what mine could be next year.

"I'm talking about you and Rowan Blakenship."

My stomach drops. *Oh shit.*

My silence is all the confirmation he seems to need.

"What the fuck?" he asks again.

"How do you already know about that?"

"That's what you have to say to me? Not an explanation for why you're suddenly dating the biggest asshole at Frost Lake High on week one?"

"It isn't what it seems," I say.

"Well, good, because it seems like you're hooking up with that rich prick behind my back."

I roll my eyes. "First of all, I'm not doing anything behind your back. I've barely heard from you in weeks, so it isn't my fault that you don't know what's going on in my life."

He's quiet now, silently fuming, if I had to guess.

"Are you seeing him or not, Sum?"

"It's complicated."

He groans, then mutters softly, "What the actual fucking fuck?"

"You didn't answer my question. How did you find out about this? No one at Oakley even knows."

"If that's true, they will shortly."

My skin pricks with an uneasy feeling. "Meaning?"

"He posted a picture of the two of you on his Instagram, and I woke up to a bunch of texts from my old teammates asking me if I knew."

I navigate to Instagram and search Rowan. I'm not following him, but his profile is public. And sure enough, there's the photo of us from last night. There's no caption, but plenty of people have commented things like "You two are so cute" and "Lucky girl." I roll my eyes at that one.

"Are you going to tell me what the fuck is going on or not?" Silas asks.

"We aren't really together. We're pretending."

"What does that mean?" I can't see it, but I can picture my brother's face all twisted up in disgust.

I do my best to explain the situation. How his ex-girlfriend is on my team and thought I was out to sabotage her and all of Frost Lake. And how Rowan wants her back. The connections he has at FLU.

Silas goes quiet again for so long I worry he's plotting my death. Or maybe Rowan's. Should I be texting him to warn him?

"That's the dumbest thing I've ever heard, Sum. The guy is clearly using you or trying to get in your pants."

"Gross. And don't be a jerk. Maybe I'm trying to get in his pants."

Silas groans.

Serves him right.

"I know you think he's an asshole—"

"He *is* an asshole." Another rough scoff. "I should have punched him when I had the chance."

"What is your deal with him?" I ask. "And don't say he broke your ankle, because you hated him long before that."

"He walks around like he's the shit just because his parents have money. He's got this blasé attitude like nothing matters. Probably because he knows Mommy and Daddy can bail him out of trouble. He isn't like us, Sum."

My stomach twists. I'm not sure how much of Silas's assessment is true, but he's right that we're different.

"Fine, fine. He's an asshole. A joke. A rich prick. It doesn't matter. We aren't really together."

"I don't like it," Silas says. "That guy is trouble. If something happens, it'll blow back on you. Stay away from him."

"I can handle myself."

Another rough scoff. "Fake dating. What a fucking prick."

"You cannot tell anyone about that, Si. You're the only one who knows."

"I don't owe him shit."

"Please? For me."

"I don't like it. It feels super shady. What possible reason does he have for wanting to date you?"

"Ouch." I may have thought it a dozen times, but it isn't great to hear someone else say it.

"You know what I mean. We hate him. He hates us."

"You," I correct him. "He hates you."

He lets out another annoyed groan.

"You know, he doesn't seem so terrible."

"Right. Good one." He laughs. "Were you not listening to anything I just said?"

I can see we are never going to see eye to eye on Rowan or my pretending to date him, so I change the topic.

"How's college? I miss you."

"It's great."

I clear my throat loudly.

"I miss you too," he says, and I can practically see the eye roll that goes along with his annoyed tone.

I smile. "When are you coming home next?"

"I'm not sure. Maybe not until Christmas."

"Really? That long? That sucks."

"I figured you'd already turned my room into your own personal soccer field."

"I tried. Mom and Dad wouldn't let me."

"How is Dad?"

"You haven't talked to him?"

"No, I have, but you know how he is. He says he's fine even when he's not."

It's true. Dad always puts on a smile for us. Or maybe for himself too.

"He seems good. A few rough days, but they've been fewer and farther between since he went on this new medicine."

"That's great."

I can hear the relief in my brother's tone. As happy as he was to leave, I know it must be hard to be away and not know what's going on here.

"Listen, I just walked into class, so I have to go."

"All right." My chest squeezes. I really do miss him.

"I'll text you later."

"Okay. Sounds good."

"And Sum?"

"Yeah?"

"Be careful. I don't fucking trust Rowan Blakenship as far as I can throw his bitch ass."

CHAPTER ELEVEN

Rowan

"Your dad is trying to kill us," I tell Vaughn in the locker room after practice. Every muscle in my body hurts. We did conditioning, followed by weight training, and then an hour of defensive drills.

He laughs softly. "Yeah. You and everyone else who didn't work out all summer."

I flip him off, then look to Austin for some solidarity, but he doesn't look like he's in as rough shape as me either.

"Are you going to be ready for Friday?" Austin asks. He looks nervous or worried on my behalf.

"I'll be fine." I wave off his concern.

"Good. Because we're going to need you," Vaughn says. He has his captain stare on point.

"Question. Do you think I can borrow a new pair of lungs for the game?" I ask no one in particular.

It does the trick of making him laugh and stopping him from spiraling. It's too early in the week to start worrying about our game.

I finish changing, grab my bag, and shut my locker. "I'll see you boys tomorrow."

As I'm leaving out the back doors, I spot Summer still out on the soccer field. The girls' practice ended an hour ago, so why is she still here?

I walk out toward her. She's dribbling the ball down the field, practicing her footwork. I smile when she attempts the Cruyff turn. She does it, sort of, but not seamlessly enough, and she stumbles over the ball. She lets out a grunt of annoyance and slows her pace to regain control.

"Give it up, Lindsey. It's almost dark," I call out to her.

Her head pops up and she pauses and turns to face me.

"I thought you already left," she says as I walk out onto the field.

"Same. Weren't you done like an hour ago?"

She nods. "I don't work tonight, and I wanted to get some more practice in before our game."

"You guys play Thursday, right?"

She smiles. "Yeah. We got our uniforms today."

I'm just noticing she's wearing it. The blue color looks good on her. I bet she hates it.

"I know. I know," she says as if reading my thoughts. "My friends are never going to forgive me."

"Sure they will."

She grunts, then looks down at her jersey. "It's more comfortable than the ones we had at Oakley. We had these super old hand-me-downs from the nineties."

"I vaguely remember them."

"Are you heading home?" she asks, shifting uncomfortably like it just occurred to her to feel awkward in front of me. We had first and fourth period together and she sat with me at lunch, but I get the feeling she still isn't quite sure how to exist around me.

"That was the plan." I jut my chin toward the ball. "What's yours? Stay until they kick you off the field?"

"Will they do that?" Her eyes widen.

A chuckle loosens in my chest. "What are you working on?"

"Dribbling under pressure."

I look around like I'm searching for the pressure.

She rolls her eyes. "I'm trying to add some new stuff to help me on offense. I need to contribute more if I'm going to catch the eye of scouts."

I nod slowly. She talks like Vaughn and Austin. And Amanda.

"Right. FLU bound."

"Maybe. Their roster is so good, and Coach Endrews is incredible."

"Yeah, you mentioned that."

She looks a bit sheepish but just shrugs.

"Soccer means a lot to you."

"It's everything."

"Did you start playing because of Silas?"

"No. He started playing because of me," she says, sounding a little smug. "We each got to pick one summer camp each year and we both attended. I picked soccer."

"What'd Silas pick?"

She scrunches up her face in disgust. "Golf."

"I cannot picture him playing golf." He's such a hothead, and golf is so quiet and a little pretentious.

"That's probably the last time he did." She smiles again. "We both ended up loving soccer, and that was that."

It's still hard for me to wrap my brain around her and Silas being related.

"I talked to him this morning," she says.

"Yeah? He went to Arizona for college, right?" Valley U has a good soccer team, and it's blessedly a long way from Frost Lake.

"That's right. Surprised you know that, given your deep hatred and rivalry."

"I don't hate your brother." I don't like him very much either, but I keep that to myself.

"Well, he hates you. Even more now that he knows we're dating."

My jaw drops. Summer nods, brows lifted as she lets the knowledge that her brother found out about us sink in.

"How?"

"Someone sent him the photo you posted," she says.

"Oh shit. I wasn't thinking." I run a hand through my hair. "I'm sorry."

A shiver works its way down my spine. No wonder I've felt off all day. I bet he's plotting my demise right now.

"It's fine. I told him the truth."

"The truth?"

"Yes. It was the only way to keep him from completely losing his shit."

"Fuck." My mind spins. It figures that the only person who knows Summer and I are fake dating is the person who dislikes me the most. "He's going to tell everyone."

"He won't. I made him promise."

I must not look convinced because she says it again. "He won't tell anyone. He might not like you, but he loves me. Outing you would make me look bad too."

I fall quiet and she gives me a second to think it

through. I don't trust him as much as she does, but there isn't much I can do but hope he's more loyal to his sister than I'd expect.

"Well, fuck. I think I've aged ten years." I let out a long breath.

Summer gives me a small smile.

"Do you want some defense?" I ask. I'm not sure why. Maybe because it's better than going home and sitting alone. My parents are gone on some business trip again.

"Really?" Her eyes light up.

"Yeah, but you have to take it easy on me. Practice was brutal today. Coach C has it out for us."

"Coach Collins is a genius. I'd kill to have someone like him giving me tips."

"Of course you would." I keep forgetting how hardcore she is. I toss my bag toward the sideline and move in front of her.

She's practically giddy with excitement as she rests her right foot on top of the ball. She waits, like she's giving me time to prepare, then she breaks toward the goal.

Maybe I should have better prepared because my muscles protest as I fight to keep in front of her. She has that forearm pressed against me and her ponytail whips into my face. I get a mouthful and she elbows me in the gut.

"You're as mean as your brother on the field."

"Awww. Thank you," she says sweetly, then tries a step over. I'm a hair faster and kick it away.

She grunts as she fights for possession. She doesn't have to try that hard because I'm using all my energy to keep between her and the goal.

This time, I give her a little more space to see what she can do. She's quick, dribbling and pushing me down the field. When I think she's in range of the goal, I tighten up my defense.

"Whatcha got, Lindsey?" I ask, invading her space. When she tries to push me away, I push right back. "That's it. Get mad."

She doesn't meet my gaze, but she glares anyway. It makes me chuckle.

"Sell the fake. It's all in your acting skills."

She considers that for a second, then does it.

"Nice. Do it again."

I stay right with her, but I try not to anticipate and react as if I don't know what's coming next.

"Take your time but try not to telegraph so much. If you have control, then you have all the time in the world. Make the defenders come to you and it'll create openings."

She keeps at it. We move from one side of the field to the other and back. I'm not sure how long we're at it, but I've forgotten about the ache of my muscles and the sun has set. The only lights are coming from around the school and the parking lot.

I kick the ball from her again. She lets out a growl of frustration.

"I think we should call it, Lindsey. You're tired."

"I'm fine."

"Then I'm tired."

She relents, though she doesn't look happy about it. She kicks the ball up and catches it.

"What?" she asks when she realizes I'm staring at her.

"Nothing."

She gives me a look that calls bullshit.

"You're good. Maybe better than your brother."

"What do you mean 'maybe'?"

"Your brother was all-state. I'm sure he had his pick of colleges trying to recruit him."

She still looks annoyed by the comparison. "Just because I'm a girl doesn't mean he's better."

"I didn't say that."

"He didn't have to switch schools his senior year or have teammates who think he's a spy." She takes a breath and then opens her mouth like she's going to keep going.

I hold up a hand. "I know. I was trying to pay you a compliment. You're good. Great even."

"But?" She cocks her head to the side.

A laugh bursts out of me. "No but, Lindsey."

She studies me for a beat then smiles, lifting her chin.

"Thanks, Rowan. You're great too," I mock in a higher pitched voice.

"You're not terrible."

"That was hard to admit, wasn't it?"

"*So* painful."

Laughing, we walk off the field side by side.

"Thank you," she says as I reach down to pick up my bag. The scream of my muscles is back. I'm going to pay for the bonus workout.

"Don't mention it."

"Heading home?" she asks.

"Yeah. You?"

"Yeah, my mom is probably pissed I missed dinner. Every night six thirty on the dot."

"That sounds nice." I can't remember the last time my family had dinner together at home. And we certainly never had a routine that etched in stone.

"You don't have family dinners?"

"My parents work a lot," I admit. "I'm sure they left something for me."

And by "they" I mean the chef who drops off food twice a week.

"Okay, well..." She looks at me like she doesn't know what to say again. "See you tomorrow?"

"See you tomorrow, girlfriend." I wink at her.

"That is so weird," she mutters.

—

"Pssst." I lean forward to get Summer's attention.

We're in fourth period, academic prep. I typically use the time to catch up on sleep or finish any last-minute homework, but Summer is head down, studying for a test that isn't until next week.

"Yeah?" she asks without looking up.

"Pick a color."

"Excuse me?" She finally looks back over her shoulder.

I'm holding out the fortune catcher with a grin.

"No way. How retro are you?"

"Says the girl who wears a mood ring." I shake my paper creation at her. "Pick a color."

"Green."

I spell it off, moving the paper in my hands in and out with each letter. When I'm done, it reveals four numbers. I hold it out for her to see.

"Seven," she says.

Again I move my hands, this time counting to seven as I do.

"Pick wisely, Lindsey," I say as I hold it for her to select one last number. "Your fortune depends on it."

She smirks like maybe she thinks I'm ridiculous. "One."

Slowly, I pull the fortune catcher back and lift open the flap for number one.

"What does it say?" she asks, peering closer and looking eager. It makes me want to draw out the moment longer. I like seeing her like this—playful and happy.

"Someone is thinking of you," I read from the paper.

"*That's* my fortune?"

I lean back in my chair. "That's what it says."

"I want a new fortune."

"Yeah?" I arch a brow. "Someone thinking about you is a pretty good fortune."

"Not it isn't," she fires back. "They could be thinking I'm dumb or ugly or bad at soccer."

"It's the last one that would really pain you, isn't it?"

"Totally." Her smile widens. "Give me that thing."

I hand over the fortune catcher and she puts her fingers and thumbs in it, then holds it out for me.

"You know I know all the fortunes, right?"

She nods, giving me a "Duh, I'm not an idiot" look. "Are you going to pick a color or what?"

"Red."

"R-E-D." She moves the fortune catcher in and out, stopping and then tipping it down so I can see the four numbers.

"Three."

She counts it out and then waits for me to pick my fortune.

"Two." I fight a smile.

She hesitates like she knows I'm up to no good but then gives in and looks under flap number two. "Seriously?"

"What's it say?" I play dumb.

"Your butt looks good today," she says in a dry, bored tone.

"Oh wow, that's so nice of you, Lindsey. A little forward but—"

She throws the fortune catcher at me before I can finish.

"You aren't even a little curious what the other fortunes are?" I ask.

"No," she says immediately, then laughs.

"Fine. Fine. You'll just have to get a new fortune tomorrow."

She finally lets out a small laugh as MJ leans over from the aisle across from us.

"Are you going to the game on Friday?" MJ asks her.

"You mean our game on *Thursday*?" Summer quirks a single brow as she stares at her teammate. "Of course."

"No. The boys' game."

It's clear that Summer had no idea about it and MJ stares at her with confusion.

"I assumed you were going to cheer on Rowan."

"Right. Yes." Summer shoots me a side glance.

"Yeah, babe. Don't you want to cheer me on?" I ask in a sweet, hopeful voice.

Her gaze narrows at my question and possibly the endearment. Oops, I forgot about her hatred of the babe/baby nicknames, but her reaction is almost reason enough to keep calling her that.

"I forgot," she says, turning her attention back to MJ. "Yeah. I'll be there."

"Great. A bunch of us are going to Sophie's house after practice and then to the game."

Summer nods slowly but doesn't say anything.

"It's totally cool if you come," MJ assures her. "I promise."

Summer's shoulders loosen a fraction. "Okay. Sure. Sounds fun."

MJ lets out a little happy squeal and Summer looks back at me.

I wink at her. "I can't wait to see you wearing my jersey."

"Wait. What?"

I laugh, then shrug. "You'll see."

On Thursday after school I pull into the driveway at the same time my parents are arriving home from…wherever they were.

"You're back," I say, grinning as I hop out of my truck. I wasn't expecting them. Though to be fair, I never expect them.

Dad stretches and groans. His dress shirt is wrinkled, and his hair looks like he's been running his fingers through it.

"Things wrapped up faster than we thought," Mom says.

"Grab a bag, will ya?" Dad tips his head toward the back seat.

We take their luggage into the house and linger in the kitchen.

"How's the first week of school?" Mom asks as she flips through the stack of mail on the counter.

"Not bad." Good, actually. I smile to myself as I think about everything that's happened to kick off senior year. What a ride it's been already.

"And soccer?" Dad stares into the fridge, pushing around containers and food until he finally pulls out a bottle of white wine.

"Coach C is pushing us hard, but we're all pumped for the season to start. One last state championship run."

He nods, a little absently as he grabs a glass from a cabinet and uncorks the wine.

"We have a game tomorrow night." I look at the glass he's filling instead of directly at him. "Since you're back early, maybe you could come watch. It's been a while."

Understatement of the decade. It's been years since they watched me play. I wouldn't say they don't care about me or soccer, but they've never been the kind of parents who come to games to show their support.

"Oh yeah? Do you play at home?" Mom looks up from the mail with a smile.

I nod excitedly as the image of them in the crowd lights a flame of hope inside of me. "Yup. First home game of the year."

"I can practically smell the burnt popcorn and hot dogs." Dad winks playfully.

"Ooh. Maybe we should grill burgers and hot dogs for dinner," Mom says. "I'm starving."

"Good idea." Dad moves back to the fridge, presumably to pull out the stuff needed for dinner.

"So you'll come?" I ask, trying and failing to keep the anticipation from my voice.

My parents share a look that I can't decipher. All the while my emotions bounce around. I rarely ask them anymore because I know it will interfere with something work-related, but I always secretly want them there.

"It's been a long few weeks," Dad says, sounding regretful as he smiles sheepishly. "I was kind of hoping for a quiet couple of nights between trips."

"Right. Of course." Disappointment settles heavily in my stomach. I'm sure it's written all over my face.

"It's only the first game of the season," Dad says. "You

boys have a long road ahead of you. Best team in the state." He's grinning widely like he's proud of me or the team, or maybe it's all just bullshit.

"We'll make it to another one," Mom adds.

Somehow I doubt that very much.

CHAPTER TWELVE

Summer

"Congrats!" Charlotte says as soon as the video call connects.

"Thank you." I smile back at her. I'm on the bus back to Frost Lake from our first game. We won, easily beating Stoutland. I didn't start, but I did end up subbing in quite a bit, and I think I played pretty well.

"It's still so weird to see you in blue." Her gaze drifts down to the team warm-up jacket.

I do the same. "I know. For me too."

"How's everything else? School? *Boys*?" She says the last word very pointedly.

"I was going to tell you."

"So it's true?" Her jaw drops.

"Sort of." I glance around the bus. I'm sitting alone but there are people in front and behind me. Most have headphones but I still don't want to risk it. "I'll explain later."

"Explain now."

"It's true, but it isn't real."

She studies me carefully. I can almost see the gears working as she tries to figure it out. "I don't understand."

I look around again. "We're faking."

"Why would you do that?"

"Later," I promise.

"By later you better mean as soon as you get home. And I'm conferencing in Jill."

"Fine." I let out a small laugh. "How are you? How's school? And soccer? And…everything?"

"Okay. The same." She shrugs.

"I miss you."

"We miss you too."

I scooch down farther in my seat and settle in for the long bus ride back. "You play Springfield Monday?"

"Yeah. And Coach is freaking out because we're still not playing that well in practice."

"What's the problem?"

Charlotte laughs. "You really want to talk about soccer team drama right now?"

"Uhh…yeah?"

She must not because she launches into her own questions. "Tell me more about Frost Lake. Is everything way nicer? Are there lots of cute boys?"

"Yes and yes," I admit. The last one pains me to admit, almost like I'm shit talking my old classmates.

"Maybe I need to come with you to an FLH party."

"You should probably wait until they stop calling me Oakley."

She snorts. "I'm okay with them calling me Oakley if they're cute enough."

"I'll let you know the next time I'm invited to one."

"Good. Maybe your new boyfriend can introduce me."

He absolutely could and would. "He does know everyone."

Her stare narrows again, and I know she's trying to figure out why in the world we're together. "As far as fake boyfriends go, you could do worse. He's hot."

My cheeks heat. Yes, yes he is.

"You look hot," MJ says as I stare at my reflection in the mirror.

Half the team is piled into Sophie's bedroom, and there are clothes strewn around everywhere. It's exactly like so many other nights with Charlotte and Jill with one big difference—I'm wearing Rowan Blakenship's number on my chest.

When Rowan told me he couldn't wait to see me in his jersey, I thought he was kidding. Little did I know that the player's girlfriends make shirts for each game and some even paint the guys' numbers on their faces. I'm certain girls at Oakley did these things too; it just never occurred to me that I'd be one of them. Or that it'd ever be Rowan's name and number I'd be rocking.

The blue T-shirt is three times too big and hangs off one shoulder. On the back, I (unfortunately) wrote BLAKENSHIP with a white fabric marker and drew a large number ten. From the front, I could almost pass as a regular person who isn't dating my brother's rival. Except I also have a blue ten on my right cheek with a soccer ball shaped like a heart.

If Silas could see me now, he would die.

"Are you sure this isn't too much?" I ask her. "We've only been dating for a week."

"Are you kidding? He's going to love it," she assures

me. "What guy wouldn't want you sitting in the bleachers cheering for him? You're seriously hot, and you and Rowan are cute together."

The girls around us murmur their agreement. My stomach dips as I turn and look at the back of my shirt again. I hold in the groan, but I feel it deep in my bones.

"She's right," Amanda pipes in. The room goes quiet like everyone just realized she was here too. My entire body clenches. Is this the moment she finally punches me for dating her ex? She's continued being nicer to me, but I still maintain she has feelings for Rowan.

Instead of coming at me, she smiles. "Since his parents never come, he loves having people in the crowd there for him."

My brows pinch together as I decipher her words.

Before I can ask any follow-up questions, Sophie says, "Okay, we need to go or we're going to be late."

She's wearing one of the twins' names and numbers. They aren't officially together but they've been talking. MJ is supporting Hunter, who she claims is just a friend, and four other girls are either talking to or dating a guy on the team. There wasn't this much intra-sport dating at Oakley.

Then again, the guys at Oakley weren't as hot. Or maybe that's just because I haven't known the Frost Lake guys my entire life.

We pile back into the cars we rode over in. I'm with MJ and Rina. The two of them talk back and forth in the front, while I sit in the back feeling anxious and a little excited.

It feels like since the game yesterday, the team has accepted me a little more. MJ is still the only one who I'd consider a friend—or a potential friend at least—but the others are talking to me more and more.

Between trying to find my place with them and pretending to be dating Rowan, my emotions are bouncing all over the place. I knew it was going to be hard switching schools, but it's even trickier than I imagined. In part because I'm finding I want to make friends. I don't just want to exist here. Charlotte and Jill will always be my besties, but they have their own things going on. I want friends here too.

When we pull up to the school, my stomach has worked itself into knots. The outdoor bleachers are packed with parents and students. I follow MJ and Rina, and we meet up with the rest of the girls, taking up two rows in the bleachers directly behind the Frost Lake bench.

The guys are just coming in from warm-ups. When I find Rowan, he's staring this way like he's looking for someone. When his gaze lands on me and he smiles, I realize that someone is me. My pulse quickens. Oh god. I look ridiculous, and I'm certain he's going to have a good laugh at me all decked out like I'm really his girlfriend.

"Stand up." MJ does and motions me up. The other girlfriends are doing the same and then turning around to show off the back of their shirts as the announcer welcomes everyone and introduces the other team.

Slowly, I get to my feet and turn so Rowan and everyone else can see that I'm wearing his name and number. Every second feels like an eternity. But when the announcer switches to the starters for Frost Lake, I get lost in the screams and excitement around me. MJ grabs my hand and lifts it into the air. We shake our arms and yell. And when Rowan is called, I turn in time to catch his expression.

I wait for the mocking smirk, but instead his smile is almost tender. Small and subdued—especially for him.

Ralley is terrible. I don't think they were this bad last year. I remember the game at Oakley, watching Silas play. But they lost a lot of seniors in May and their young team is making a lot of sloppy mistakes that Frost Lake is punishing them for.

Rina leans over MJ ten minutes into the game, which is coincidentally when most people have lost interest. The score is already two to zero and it would be worse if Coach Collins hadn't subbed in for half the starters.

"What's Rowan like as a boyfriend?" she asks.

"Excuse me?"

"He hasn't really dated anyone, unless you count Amanda, which…" Her eyes widen and I really wish she'd fill in the blanks for me. Instead, she says, "Whatever. The point is, we're all dying to know what he's like. Does he do sweet things? Does he text? Is he a dry texter? I can picture him sending funny videos and I'll bet your parents love him. The teachers do, so I expect all adults like him." She finally stops talking and looks to me with rapt interest.

I open my mouth and then shut it. I quickly file through everything that's happened in the past five days we've been a fake couple for an appropriate answer. "We don't text a lot, but that's probably because we're together all day. My parents haven't met him yet. And yeah, he's funny and sweet."

I think back to the fortune catcher and to him staying after practice to help me with soccer and the way he held my hand and introduced me around the party. He's been a great fake boyfriend. And suddenly, I'm not so sure I've been a great fake girlfriend in return. Sure, I'm here and cheering him on, but that's only because of peer pressure. Would I have if the girls hadn't dragged me? Not likely.

I need to step up my game.

Rina is still watching me like she's hopeful for any other tidbits, but a whistle on the field pulls all our attention. There's a flag on Ralley, and Frost Lake sets up for a corner kick.

Coach Collins is yelling out instructions from the sideline. He is almost as impressive to watch now as he was as a player. I spent one summer watching his rookie season videos on repeat. The man is a legend.

Vaughn has a similar style and skill. He's improved a lot since last season. Silas will be pissed to hear that. He always hated playing against Vaughn but would reluctantly admit he was good.

He never admitted as much about Rowan, but I think that's just because he hates him so much. My stomach tightens at the reminder. He would really freak out if he saw me right now.

As the game continues, everyone else loses focus but I can't stop watching. There's so much talent on Frost Lake. Vaughn and Austin and the twins. The more I watch, the more I'm drawn to Rowan though.

I could blame it on the fact that I'm pretending to be his girlfriend or needing to cheer for him so the girls aren't suspicious, but in reality, he's just fun to watch.

He takes risks more often than I would, attempts tougher passes, gets more looks at the net. I'm more aggressive on defense than offense. It's where I feel more comfortable. Rowan seems to transition between the two with equal ease. And his risks pay off more often than they don't. In his final minutes on the field, he makes a crazy back-heel-flick goal. I'm on my feet and yelling with zero thought of anyone else. Adrenaline courses through me.

The goal puts Frost Lake up by four and Coach Collins subs him out. After Rowan accepts congratulations from his teammates and coach, he looks up at the bleachers. I smile as big as I can at him. Wearing his number might be for show, but I'm so genuinely giddy about the goal, I don't even need to fake it.

Rowan flashes me the cocky grin I expected earlier and then winks. With the shake of my head, I sit back down. With Frost Lake trampling Ralley, more people are moving around. Half the team gets up to hit the concession stand one last time or head to Freddie's Pizza, which is apparently where everyone is going tonight after the game.

Amanda is among the few left. She's been sitting a bleacher down and far enough to the right that we haven't interacted, but now she eyes the empty space and moves to sit next to me. MJ is on my other side, but she's talking to another teammate and can't save me.

"Hey," Amanda says as she places her feet up on the bleacher in front of us.

"Hi," I reply.

"Rowan's having a good game." She's looking at the field, but I still flush hot.

"He is."

"You must be his lucky charm." She side-eyes me and smiles. I try and fail to detect any hidden animosity. Is it possible for her to want him back and not hate me for dating him?

"Or he's just really freaking talented."

She laughs. "He is, but I know having people here for him is a big deal."

I contemplate my next words carefully, trying to decide if I can ask the thing I want without giving too much away.

Will she know Rowan and I are faking it if it's clear I have no idea what his family situation is like?

I rationalize that even if we were dating, it would be new.

"His parents really never come?" I ask her.

"Not once as far as I know."

My brows lift and I feel the weight of that knowledge heavy on my chest. "Wow. I can't imagine."

"I know. Me either," she says. "Sometimes I wish my parents would stay home, but they're always there. Dad yelling at the refs and Mom cheering at all the wrong times." She looks at me again. "She is clueless about soccer, but she tries."

We share a small laugh. My parents know enough, and they don't yell inappropriately, but I still get it.

"Have you met them?" she asks.

"Rowan's parents?" My question comes out like *why in the world would I have met his parents?*

She nods and glances back at the field. I look back at Rowan. He's on the sideline next to Vaughn. The two of them are laughing and smiling.

"Yeah. Briefly." It isn't a lie exactly but perhaps a wild exaggeration. I'm not about to tell her I was their server and dumped water in his dad's lap.

"Really?" She gives me her full attention again and I wish I'd been more exact in my language. Something like, "I was in their presence once" or "I ran into them at the country club."

"Barely," I say, and it feels like it's the right thing to make her feel better because I'm almost certain there's a flash of hurt in her expression. "You?"

"No. Never." Her body language stiffens. She smiles but

it feels like it's for my benefit. "We weren't that serious. We mostly hung out at parties and stuff."

"Really?"

"I thought we could be more briefly but…" She lifts one shoulder in a shrug. "You know how he is."

I get the impression that was a dig, but whether at me or Rowan, I'm not sure.

—

As soon as the game is over, MJ grabs my hand and pulls me down to the field.

"Maybe we should just wait in the parking lot or meet them at the pizza place," I suggest.

She laughs in response and keeps tugging me with her. She has a strong grip.

The guys shake hands with the other team and then start toward the locker rooms. MJ pulls me to the exact spot where they cross the field to get into the school.

I don't know why I'm so nervous, but when Rowan spots me waiting for him, it dissipates.

"Congrats," MJ says to him.

"Thanks."

She lets go of my hand and then rushes to Hunter and throws her arms around his neck.

I hesitate, uncertain what I'm supposed to do, but Rowan answers it by stepping forward and hugging me. His hands slide around my waist, and I loop mine over his shoulders.

"Nice game." My words come out a little breathless.

"Thanks, Lindsey." He squeezes me, lifting me onto my toes.

A surprised laugh slips from my lips.

"How much are you hating wearing my number?" he asks quietly, then sets me back down.

"Less after that back heel flick."

His smirk lifts higher on one side.

"You were really good."

"Thanks."

The rest of the team is trickling away. He takes a step that direction but keeps staring at me.

"Are you coming to Freddie's, babe?"

I glower at him, and he smiles wider. "Not if you're going to keep calling me that."

"But you're such a babe."

I keep glowering and he laughs.

"Fine, Summer, will you please come to Freddie's tonight?"

He hardly ever calls me by my first name. I can't decide if it's nice or weird. Maybe a little of both.

I nod. "Meet you there, *babe*."

He picks up his pace, walking backward faster now. "Doesn't work. I like it when you call me that."

With a wink, he turns and jogs into the school.

CHAPTER THIRTEEN

Rowan

"EVERYBODY, SCOOT DOWN!" EDDIE CALLS FROM THE OTHER end of the table.

Summer inches down the bench. I don't know where she thinks she's going to go, as she's already in danger of falling off.

I circle one arm around her waist to steady her and then glance down at the row of people trying to squeeze together. "There is no more room. Stop pushing."

We needed another table, but Freddie's is packed tonight.

"I can go sit with the girls," Summer suggests. I don't like the idea any more now than I did the two other times she suggested it.

"There's no world in which I'm making my girlfriend go sit somewhere else."

She gives me that playful glare she's so fond of, and my pulse picks up speed. "You should celebrate with your teammates. It's not a big deal."

I shake my head and bop her on the nose just for fun.

I feel so happy and light. The game was a blowout and the crowd was great, and I'm not going to lie, looking over to see Summer rocking my name on her back and my number on her face had me smiling all night long.

"It's fine. We got this," I say when Vaughn on my other side presses into me again. He's a big guy, and I am not enjoying being this close. I use the arm around Summer's waist to pull her onto my lap.

She squeaks in surprise. "What are you doing?"

"Making room." I spread out and put some distance between me and Vaughn. "Much better."

"This is not better," she hisses. Her ass is on my thigh and she's sitting sideways with her profile to me. The number ten on her face is in perfect view.

"Relax."

Her entire body is rigid, and her eyes are wide. "How?"

"I don't know. Maybe act like you don't mind sitting on my lap so much though."

Her features relax, but her cheeks take on a pinkish hue.

I don't mind nearly as much as she seems to, but maybe that's just because she's a hot girl with her ass rubbing against me. "If you're really uncomfortable, we can go sit somewhere else together."

She seems to consider that, then shakes her head. "This is fine, but if you try to feed me..." She gives me a warning glare.

The idea makes me laugh. "Got it. No feeding you and no babe."

"Thank you," she says with a fake sweetness and relaxes a fraction more.

"Speaking of food, though. What do you want?" I ask.

"Umm...pizza?"

"Yes, but what toppings?" I study her closely. "You aren't a fan of vegetables on pizza are you?"

"I am, but I'm guessing by the grossed-out look on your face that you aren't."

"Vegetables are fine…just not on pizza." I shudder.

"Seriously?"

"It doesn't make any sense. Pizza isn't healthy. Stop trying to make it healthy…" I shake my head.

"Okay, so all the veggies for me." She smiles all smug.

"Brat." I reach over and tug her ponytail.

"I like everything except black olives."

I keep my hand in her hair. The thick, red strands are smoother than they look. I wrap my finger around one curl and then let it spring free. When I meet Summer's gaze again, she's looking at me expectantly.

"Sorry, your hair distracted me."

She laughs again and drops one hand to my leg to steady herself. "That's one I haven't heard before."

"Really? I love your hair." I move my arm back to her waist and curl two fingers through the belt loop.

For a second she stiffens again like she thinks I'm about to cop a feel, but then her body goes slack. "I like yours too."

"Yeah?" I shake my head to let the long strands fly around my face. "I need a haircut."

"I could cut it for you."

"Really?" I look at her skeptically.

"Yeah. I used to cut Silas's sometimes. My mom taught me."

"Is she a hair stylist?"

"No." She laughs. "She's an office manager for an insurance company."

"That's cool. And your dad?"

"He owns a painting business, but he's had to take a step back the past few years."

I nod like I understand. My relationship with my own parents and their dedication to business above all else makes it hard for me to know what's normal and what isn't when it comes to this kind of thing.

"He has MS," she says finally. "It makes it hard to work sometimes."

"I'm sorry."

"Thanks." She gives me a small smile. "He's on a new medicine that's helping a lot and..." She stops. "Sorry, boring."

"Nah, not at all. I don't really know that much about you."

She leans in like she's telling me a secret. "That's because we just met."

"Lucky me."

Her small responding laugh makes warmth spread through my chest.

Vaughn elbows me. I tear my gaze away from Summer and look at him.

"You know what you want?" he asks.

The server is waiting to take my order.

"Coke, a large pizza with pepperoni and sausage, and..." I glance at Summer.

"Water," she says.

"Anything else?" I ask her.

"No, I'm not really hungry."

I make sure the server heard that and then give her my full attention. "You have to try the pizza here. It's the best."

"No. The best pizza is at Momma Vi's."

"Let me guess, in Oakley?"

She flashes me a smug smile. "Of course."

I hum and narrow my gaze. "I'm doubtful, but you're on."

"I'm on?"

"We'll try the pizza here and at this Momma Vi's place and then we can cast our votes."

I can see her considering it carefully, as if I suggested we get matching tattoos or play seven minutes in heaven. Now there's an idea. My gaze inadvertently drops to her mouth. Her bottom lip is fuller than the top, but the smaller one has a cute little bow that makes it stick out a tiny bit. Very kissable. Aaaaand now that's all I can think about.

"Fine. Deal," she says, bringing me back to the moment. "But we have to get Momma Vi's veggie lover on thin crust."

She makes a small moan, which does nothing to stop me from thinking about kissing her.

The following day, I meet Summer at the career center. She's already at the front doors waiting for me.

"Morning." I hold out a paper bag to her. She eyes it suspiciously.

"It's a doughnut," I say, taking a bite of the strawberry frosted with sprinkles in my other hand.

"Oh."

"Take it, Lindsey. I've already had two. Save me from myself."

With a small laugh, she accepts the bag. "Thank you."

"You're welcome." I open the door for her. "Have you been here before?"

"The Frost Lake Career Center?" she asks like the idea is ludicrous. "No, have you?"

"No, but you seem like the type."

"To need a job?"

"To plan your future."

She steps ahead of me into the center without reply. There are already a few other businesses set up for the fair and I spot Kristy in the back corner.

"This way." I grab Summer's hand and lead the way.

Kristy is placing the emerald FLU runner over the table as we reach her. I drop Summer's hand in order to help straighten the cloth on the other side.

"Thanks," Kristy says, then smiles at both of us. "Good morning. Sorry to get you out of bed early on a Saturday."

"Sum's been awake for hours by now. Already done her homework and ran two miles." I'm guessing, but I doubt I'm far off.

"Well, I appreciate it," Kristy says, then glances to the plastic tubs behind the table. "I'm going to help you set up, and then I need to run back to campus for another event. Are you two good to handle things here?"

A whole day with Summer? Hell yeah. I grin. "Absolutely. We have everything under control."

"Does FLU have a women's studies program?" the guy standing in front of the table asks. He's maybe mid-forties, in a gray sweat suit complete with a headband and carrying a pickleball paddle like he's on his way to the court. I really hope there's one next door and he doesn't just walk around everywhere with the paddle attached to his hand.

So far, he's asked about premed, computer science,

marketing, and now women's studies. He's either trying to solve the answer to his midlife crisis or making a list of every program at FLU.

I open my mouth to attempt to answer his twelfth question, but as with all the others, I have no idea.

"Yes. And there's a list of courses on the website to give you an idea of what's required to complete the degree," Summer answers like she memorized the handbook. Actually, she might have.

Before he can ask anything else, I shove a pamphlet at him.

"Here you go. There's a list of all the programs and links to all the department websites. You can scan the QR code."

He stares at it, then hesitantly takes it, glances at Summer one last time, and walks off.

"Rowan," she admonishes when he's a few feet away. "He wasn't done asking questions."

"He can Google." Plus, I'm fairly certain he just wanted an excuse to talk to Summer.

To my surprise, Summer smiles. "I'm going to tell Kristy on you."

"She would have shoved a pamphlet at him too." Probably sooner than I did.

I lean back in my chair and Summer does as well. Aside from Mr. Pickleball, it's been quiet today. A few people came by and picked up free swag or asked about the admissions process (I also couldn't answer those questions, but Summer, unsurprisingly, could). Otherwise we've been sitting here, smiling and saying hello when a random person walks by.

Summer absently picks up one of the pamphlets and reads the back. "Do you know what you're going to study in college?"

"Business, maybe, or finance. I haven't given it a lot of thought."

"FLU has a good business program."

"Yes, so I've heard," I say dryly.

She eyes me like she's trying to make sense of my tone.

I let out a sigh. "The *Blakenship* College of Business."

Her mouth falls open.

"Yeah." I nod. "Weird, right?"

"No." She shakes her head. "I mean, yes, but that's so impressive. You should be proud."

"Why? I didn't do anything."

She tips her chin down to give me a pointed look.

"Well, I didn't."

"Did your parents go to FLU?"

"Yeah."

"My parents didn't go to college. Well, my mom did two years, but she quit when she got pregnant with my brother. And my dad says it wasn't for him."

"If I'm honest, I'm not sure it's for me either."

"What do you want to do instead?" she asks like it's no big deal. It's the first time I've said the words and not gotten push back.

"I don't know."

"You don't have any ideas? What about soccer?"

I shrug. "I like playing, but it isn't like I'm going to make a career out of it."

"Why not?" she asks, voice defensive like I said she couldn't.

"I'm not hardcore like you or Vaughn or Austin." Or Amanda, but it doesn't feel like a good time to mention her.

"Are you kidding me?" Her smile turns into a wide grin, and she laughs.

My brows lift while I wait for her to explain what's so funny.

"Rowan, you are..." Her voice trails off and she shakes her head again.

I keep staring and waiting.

"You really have no idea," she says with another small chuckle. Summer shifts in her chair, angling her body toward mine. The movement makes her knees press into my thigh. "You have so much natural talent, it's unbelievable."

"Yeah. I've heard that before. It's the nice way of saying I play well for someone who doesn't put in a lot of effort."

"No. That isn't what I meant," she says in a firm tone that doesn't leave room for arguing. Her hand drops to the top of my leg now, and a pleasant tingle spreads through me from her touch. "The things you can do on a soccer field can't be taught. You see things others don't and move your body in ways that shouldn't be possible. And the risks you take... I could never pull them off. You have something that is rare and special. You don't have to want to do anything with that natural ability, but you should at least acknowledge it. Why do you think Silas hates you so much?"

My body hums with pride and a twinge of embarrassment. I'm not sure anyone has ever delivered me so many compliments in a row. And she's the last person I expected to do it.

My lips curve into a goofy, happy smile. "Because I'm a prick who shit talks on the field?"

Her laugh is quick but heady. "Because you're good and he knows it."

"He is too," I admit freely. I've never had a problem giving him his props when it comes to talent. It's his attitude that sucks.

"Don't worry. I won't tell him you said that." Summer grins.

"Hey, I'm back." Kristy comes to a stop in front of us, breathless like she ran here. It takes a beat for me to remove my gaze from Summer, but when I do, a slow smile tips up the corners of Kristy's mouth, and her stare is locked on Summer's hand draped over my thigh. When Summer realizes it, she pulls back and faces forward.

"Hi!" Summer quips, voice a little too high to sound natural.

"How's it been?" Kristy asks.

I sit forward and scan the mostly empty career fair. "Slow."

"Yeah, I was afraid of that. There is a pickleball tournament next door at the YMCA, and parking is a nightmare. Plus, it's gorgeous out. Everyone is enjoying the weather."

"We handed out quite a few brochures and the key-chain flashlights were a hit," Summer adds like she thinks her ability to drive people to the table is going to impact her performance review.

"Great. Thank you." Kristy smiles in that endearing way teachers sometimes do with their star pupil. "Well…I think we should call it and enjoy the rest of the day. I appreciate both your help."

"No problem," I tell her.

"I can stay and help clean up," Summer says.

"No. I got it. I'm going to put my audiobook on and savor the next hour of me time before I get home and my kids start asking what's for dinner." She pulls out her AirPod case as if to prove the point. "I'll see you both in a few weeks at the next event."

Summer and I stand and say our goodbyes, then walk

through the empty career center. Most of the other vendors are packing up too. Outside, the sun is high in the sky, and I squint as my eyes adjust from being inside for so long.

"What are you doing later?" I ask as we cross the parking lot to our vehicles. "Some of the guys were planning to go out to the lake."

"I have to work this evening."

"Double shift today, yikes." I can't believe she agreed to help today. No, actually I can. She works harder than anyone I know.

"What about tomorrow?" I ask.

"I have some homework."

"There is no fun in your weekend, Lindsey."

She laughs and I get the feeling this is just the standard for her. Work, work, work. Good thing she met me.

"Meet me at the soccer field at two."

"Why?" she asks, shooting me a skeptical glance.

"Just do it. I promise I'll make it worth your while." I wink and then get in my truck.

CHAPTER FOURTEEN

Summer

I HAVEN'T STOPPED SMILING IN TWO HOURS. MY FACE actually hurts from it.

"Nice job." Vaughn holds his hand up to me and I slap my palm against his.

"I'm going to need you to step up your game," Austin says with a grimace as he side-eyes Rowan.

"You try to guard her," Rowan tells him. "She has bony elbows."

I fight a laugh and lose.

"One more game?" Rowan asks. We've been playing two on two. Me and Vaughn vs. Austin and Rowan. I never dreamed of playing with Vaughn, but if I had, this would have exceeded my expectations for it.

"I have to meet Lacey and her dad for dinner," Vaughn says.

"My parents are expecting me." Austin shakes his head.

I should go home too, but I'd skip all my meals to play with these guys a little longer. They're so good. Playing with them is surreal. Although despite what Rowan said, he was not guarding me as hard as he could. I know it, and I'm sure his friends do too. I've seen these guys in a game, and they're more relaxed out here than they were in a real situation. Still, I kept up with them, and I am going to be on a weeklong high because of it.

"This was fun," Austin says to me with a flick of his head. "You might be the secret weapon the girls' team has needed to get into the playoffs this season."

A warm flush creeps up my neck and onto my cheeks. Rowan slings an arm around my shoulders.

"'Might be'?" he scoffs.

Austin and Vaughn chuckle. I'm too aware of Rowan's fingers brushing against my arm and his body pressed up against mine to do anything as natural as laugh. You'd think I would have gotten used to it by now—the little touches and the easy way he flirts with me in front of his friends—but instead it's like each time adds to the building tension between us. Except I'm the only one who seems to be affected.

"See you guys tomorrow," Vaughn calls, and he and Austin head off the field.

Rowan pulls back, taking his heat and a little more of my sanity with him. He hits me with a wide grin. He's all playful and charming right now, and I am struggling to remember he's not, in fact, my boyfriend but only a guy who I'm pretending to date so he can get back with his ex.

The thought of Amanda does the trick of reining in my emotions, and I glance away from him.

"I should go too."

"What? No. Stay a little longer." He kicks the ball up and catches it.

When I force my gaze back to his face, he's giving me a hopeful and boyish puppy-dog stare.

"Fine." I laugh. "But I need water first." I should probably dump it over my head. I cannot lose sight of what this is between us. No matter how fun it is to be with him or how nice he's being to me, it's not real.

We sit in the middle of the field. He leans back, propping himself up with his elbows, and I sit, legs crossed, next to him.

I guzzle my water and refrain from the cold shower I really need. Rowan is quiet, staring out at the empty field. I stare at him. His dark hair is thick and shiny and a little too long, but I find myself wanting to reach out and touch it. He's in an old, faded Frost Lake High soccer T-shirt and black shorts. They've ridden up slightly due to the way he's sitting, and part of a tattoo peeks out.

"What is it?" I ask before I think to stop myself.

"Hmm?" Rowan asks and glances back at me. When he turns his focus to my line of sight, he sits up and lifts the hem of his shorts higher. The linework is simple and the tattoo itself isn't colored in. It looks like a paper bird.

"Is it a bird?" I ask, tilting my head to get a better look.

"A crane." He nods.

"Why?"

"I got really into origami one year. I learned how to make all sorts of things. Frogs, boxes, ninja stars, flowers, and—"

"Birds," I finish for him.

"Yeah."

"Is this how your fortune catcher obsession started?"

"I'm not *obsessed*. They're fun."

It was fun, and somehow I can picture Rowan sitting in class folding paper into all sorts of creations. Probably instead of studying.

"Do you still do origami?" I ask, then add, "outside of fortune catchers obviously."

"No, not really. What weird hobbies do you have?" he asks me.

"Soccer is my only hobby."

"Come on. Seriously?"

I nod, feeling a small bit of embarrassment admitting it.

"What about when you were younger?"

Glancing up, I think for a moment. "I wanted to be a pop star for a hot minute."

He barks out a laugh.

I glare at him.

"I'm sorry. It isn't funny. I'm just surprised. I'm sure you would be a great pop star. I'm just imagining you onstage with that hair all big and sexy. I'd have bought tickets to watch you."

The word *sexy* settles like a hammer in my stomach. "You have a weird obsession with my hair."

"That I do." He lets out another small laugh. "What else?"

"Umm..." I bite the corner of my lip and go back farther in my memories. "Silas and I tried basketball one summer, and then there was swimming."

"You didn't like either of those?"

"Not enough to do them on my own. Not like soccer. I could play all day every day."

"I've gathered that." His eyes crinkle with another big smile.

"Not you though?"

"I like soccer, but it's fun to me because I get to do it with my friends."

"That's true of most team sports."

"Yeah, but I'm good at this one."

That he is.

His gaze drops to my ring. "Purple again. Every time we're together, it's purple. I think your mood ring is broken."

"Every time we're together, it revolves around soccer, and we've already established my love of that." My cheeks burn hotter.

"Not yesterday," he says. "At the career fair it was purple too."

"How do you know that?"

He shrugs. "I notice things."

I pull my hand back so he can't see the bright purple color on my ring.

Rowan gets to his feet, talking so low I almost miss it when he says, "Especially when it comes to you, Lindsey."

CHAPTER FIFTEEN

Rowan

I STAND AND PLACE BOTH HANDS AROUND MY MOUTH AS I yell, "Go Summer!"

She doesn't look over, but her lips pull at the corners like she's fighting a smile as she jogs down the field. Frost Lake is now up by two and my girl just scored the last goal.

"She's fire, right?" I glance back at my friends still sitting on the bleacher. I have no idea how they're so calm. Ralley is good and the girls are about to beat them for the first time in years.

I shout a few more "Nice job's" and "Woooo's" before I take my seat with the rest of the crowd.

"You really like this girl," Austin says from beside me. It's not a question, but the surprise in his expression is clear.

I open my mouth to say something, only I'm not sure what. I do like her but not the way he thinks. Or...do I? I'm not even sure anymore.

"I think it's cute. And I like her for you." Claire gives me a smile as she snuggles closer to Austin's other side.

"Yeah, she's great." I'm hesitant to say more. I don't love

hiding the truth from them about Summer and me, but I do think she's fantastic, so that isn't a lie.

After the game, I wait for her in the parking lot. We're going to Austin's house with a handful of other people. A chill get-together because the boys and I are traveling tomorrow morning for our game in Stoutland.

I'm scrolling my phone and leaning against the side of my truck. I look up when the next person comes out of the school doors and almost immediately glance down again when it isn't red hair I see but blond. Amanda's familiar face makes me pause.

We haven't spoken much. A polite hello at school when we pass in the hallway but that's it.

I stand tall and give her a small smile as she gets closer. "Hey, nice game."

"Thanks." She doesn't look as happy as I'd expect given the outcome.

"That was a big win over Ralley. They're tough."

"Yeah. Coach is really happy. The girls too."

But not her.

"Is everything okay?"

A moment passes where I think she's going to blow me off or shrug and continue to her car, but then she says, "Ronnie and I had a fight, and I was in my head all game because of it. That's why I played like shit."

"I didn't notice."

She lets out a rough, disbelieving chuckle like there's no way anyone couldn't have noticed her terrible game. I don't know if she's exaggerating or if I was too busy pretending to be a good boyfriend.

"I'm really sorry," I tell her. I don't know if I mean about Ronnie or the game.

"Thanks." She shifts her weight and pushes her backpack up higher on her shoulder. "Things with you seem good."

I nod and swallow around the lump forming in my throat.

Amanda watches me like she wants me to say more, but I'm lost in my thoughts. She and Ronnie are fighting. Does that mean they're over? Or will be soon? And if so, what does that mean for us?

"Are you going to Keller's house?" she asks.

"Yeah." I find my voice. "You?"

"I think so."

"Cool. I'll see you there."

"Probably not." She takes a step away. "You'll be busy being all cute and cozy with your *girlfriend*."

I run her words and tone through the jealousy filter, but she's so damn hard to read.

"I'm never too busy for you."

One side of her mouth lifts into a pleased smile. "See you, Rowan."

"See you," I say quietly.

I watch as Amanda disappears into the rows of cars. A pit forms in my stomach as I replay our conversation. Did I really not notice she had a bad game? I can't think of a single example where I saw her screw up. Maybe a couple instances she dribbled too far into the defense when she should have passed to Summer, but other than that… nothing comes to mind. In fact, as I run the game back, it's mostly Summer I remember. Summer being a total badass. She really came into her own out there tonight. The other girls were passing and looking for her, and she worked hard on defense, razzing the other team and winning possessions back.

I'm lost to the world around me when that flash of red I was looking for earlier finally comes into my periphery. I've no sooner blinked away my thoughts than Summer throws her arms over my shoulders.

"We won!" She squeals and hugs me around the neck.

I'm slow to hug her back, but a happy *zing* pulses over my skin as she presses against me and bounces. "I can't believe it. Did you see my goal?"

I squeeze her around the waist and push away the cloud of weirdness hanging over me from the talk with Amanda.

She pulls back while she waits for my answer, but her hands still rest on my chest.

"You know I did. I was screaming so loud the people in the next county heard me."

She jumps in place a few more times. She's so damn happy that it loosens a smile from my lips.

"Congratulations," I say to her.

"Thank you." Summer steps back but continues beaming at me. She looks around like she expected more people. "You waited for me."

"Yeah, of course."

"I could have met you at Austin's house."

"No way. I'm the kind of boyfriend who likes to chauffeur his awesome girlfriend after she scores the game-winning goal." I go around my truck and open the passenger side door for her. "I'll bring you back to your car later."

"Okay." Without protest, she hops into the truck, and I shut her in. As I'm circling the front to get to the driver's seat, I can't help but wonder if this whole faking-it thing is messing with my head more than I expected.

CHAPTER SIXTEEN

Summer

Something is off with Rowan.

We're sitting outside at the Kellers' house. It isn't a big party, maybe twenty people and most of them couples. I guess that includes me. We've pulled outdoor furniture together in a large circle around the firepit.

I'm sitting on Rowan's lap to free up a chair, and he has his thumb hooked in the belt loop of my jeans and a flask in the other hand. The alcohol was my second clue that something was wrong. The first was the quiet ride over. Anytime I speak, he smiles and responds, but he keeps falling into these silences where he gets a contemplative look on his face. Look, it isn't that Rowan isn't a deep thinker, but he usually says what's on his mind.

He's acting like a wallflower instead of the life of the party.

Lacey and Vaughn are sitting next to us. She's talking about a new dance routine they're working on for homecoming, but I'm only half listening. My body is tense as I keep stealing glances at Rowan. He's smiling, but even that doesn't look very convincing. What the hell could be wrong with him?

"I wish I could dance," I say to Lacey. "Those routines always look so fun."

"I could teach you."

"I don't think I'm teachable. The only rhythm I have is dribbling a ball down the field."

Rowan lets out a small chuckle. "I doubt that's true."

"Me too," Lacey says and then looks at him. "You on the other hand would make a great cheerleader. The lungs on you tonight were truly impressive."

"I had to cheer my girl," he says, a little bashful, then takes another drink from the flask. Whatever it is, it smells strong.

My girl.

Goose bumps race up my arms.

Vaughn swipes the flask from him. "I think you're done. I need you not to throw up on the side of the field tomorrow."

"We should probably go," Lacey tells her boyfriend.

He nods his head. "Yeah, maybe if I go, the rest of the team will take the cue."

"Or the party can finally start," Rowan says and tries to get his flask back.

"I'm holding on to this." Vaughn tucks it in his pocket and stands. He looks to me. "You got him?"

"Yeah. I'll drive him home."

"I'll pick you up in the morning so I know you won't be late to the bus," Vaughn tells him.

"I'm fine, Cap. Don't worry about me."

Vaughn looks like he believes him as much as I do, but he and Lacey say their goodbyes and head out. A few more people go at the same time, and since it's going to take some time to get Rowan home, get my car, and head home, I figure we should do the same.

"You were amazing!" MJ hugs me when I tell her and the rest of the team that's left at the party that I'm going.

"Thanks. You too."

She grins big and happy.

I wave and smile at the others as I scan the group. When I reach Amanda, she's looking past me to the guy at my back. My cheeks heat and jealousy hits me so swiftly that I have to remind myself that this was the point.

"Bye, Amanda," I say to draw her attention to me.

She blinks and drops her gaze. A small, sad smile curves her mouth. "Bye. Nice game tonight."

Rowan continues his broody silence on the walk to his truck.

"You don't have to take me home. I can get an Uber," he says when I hold my hand out for the keys.

"I don't mind."

He reaches in his pocket and then drops his keys in my outstretched palm. His truck is an older model Ford instead of the fancy, new vehicle I'd expect from him. Even the cheap car my parents let me drive is nicer than this. Maybe his parents don't want to spoil him or something. It takes me a couple tries to get the engine started.

"I don't know where I'm going," I tell him as I pull out onto the road.

"Crestwood Hills."

"Where Mariah Rieger lives?"

"Yeah. We're neighbors."

I vaguely remember the way, but what is vivid in my mind are the huge houses in that neighborhood. I guess it makes sense, but I'm still surprised he didn't mention it.

We ride in more awkward silence until I can't take it anymore. I need to say something. Anything.

"I noticed Amanda staring at you tonight," I say.

He makes a grunt like he either thinks I'm mistaken or doesn't care.

"A few times while we were at Austin's house and then as we were leaving. I'm pretty certain she's jealous." At least the look she was giving him was how I imagined mine looked while I was being jealous of her jealousy. What a freaking mess. I need to pull it together.

"Nah. She and Ronnie had a fight. She's just bummed about that."

"They did?" I glance over at him. He's staring out the window with his head leaned back.

Another grunt of acknowledgment.

"How do you know?" I didn't hear anyone mention it tonight. Not in the locker room or at the party.

"I talked to her."

That uneasy prickly feeling that may or may not be jealousy is back. "When?"

"After the game." He turns to meet my stare. "I was waiting for you, and she came out, so I talked to her."

That makes sense. It isn't like I expect him to ignore her. Especially since he's trying to win her back.

"Did they break up?" My heart races in my chest and I feel...disappointed, I think. This is what he wanted. What I wanted for him. Make Amanda jealous and get her back. Except now that it's happening, I don't feel as happy as I think I should.

"No. I don't think so."

That's a small relief, but...not to him. He's obviously bummed.

"I'm sorry. Do you want to stop…" I can't bring myself to say *fake dating*. "This and tell her how you feel?"

"No." His brows pinch together. "No. We should stick to the plan."

"But if they're going to break up, don't you want to be there for her?"

Instead of answering me with words, he shakes his head.

We're quiet for the rest of the drive. I pull up in front of Rowan's giant house. The lights are dark but there's a shiny silver truck in the driveway.

"Parents home?" I ask, nodding my head toward the vehicle.

"Nah, that's my other truck."

He must read the question in my raised brows.

"I never drive it. I like this one better. It was my grandpa's, and we rebuilt the engine together one summer before he passed."

"Sentimental." I nod. "I get it."

He unbuckles. "Anyway, thanks for driving me. I feel bad that you have to Uber to your car."

"It's fine. I think that's him there." I glance at the headlights pulling in behind me in the rearview mirror.

"No, it isn't fine, but…" He lets his voice trail off without finishing.

We get out of the truck and he walks me to the waiting car.

"Hey, can I ask you a question?" he says as I open the back passenger door. I bend down to smile at the driver, then look at Rowan.

"Sure."

"Did Amanda have a good game tonight?"

Of all the questions I thought he might ask, that wasn't

anywhere in the top fifty. Though maybe it should have been. He's obviously been thinking about her.

"You were at the game," I say instead of throwing her under the bus. She was a mess tonight, but it happens. Knowing she and Ronnie were fighting, it makes more sense.

He frowns. "Yeah. You're right."

Rowan steps back and clears his throat. "Night, Lindsey."

"So you're hanging out together, holding hands, going to each other's games, but you're only pretending to like each other?" Jill asks on Saturday night.

She and Charlotte cornered me after work and forced me to Charlotte's house to explain everything. (Okay, they didn't force me, but they would have if necessary.)

"Y-yes," I say the word slowly, which only makes the confused expressions on their faces more prominent. "It's complicated."

"Yeah, I'll bet." Jill is the first to crack a smile.

I cover my face with both hands and groan.

"I don't see what the big deal is. You're helping each other out," Charlotte says.

I peek out between my fingers in time to see her shrug one shoulder.

I drop my hands and let my shoulders sag. I'm still in my work clothes and I can smell the popcorn butter and fry grease. "Yes, that's exactly how I was selling it to myself, but it's harder than I thought to keep things separate."

"Harder to keep what separate?" Jill asks.

"Our fake relationship and reality." I'm vague and hope they can read between the lines. I don't think I can bring myself to say exactly what I'm thinking.

"What's he like?" Charlotte hugs her knees and looks at me with rapt interest.

"Oh yeah, same question." Jill's eyes light up.

I take my time, choosing my words carefully. "He's really funny and nice. He's friendly with everyone, but he has a small group of close friends. His relationship with his parents is strained, I think, or at least different than I expected."

"How so?" Jill asks.

"They're gone a lot and don't go to his soccer games."

"But you saw them at the club," Charlotte reminds me.

"Yeah." I nod. "I get the impression they're just doing other things and Rowan's on his own a lot."

"Sometimes I wish my parents were gone...ever. My mom was waiting at the door when I got home from my date last night." Charlotte rolls her eyes.

We're temporarily sidetracked from talking about Rowan while Jill and I pepper Charlotte about her movie date with Charlie. She's said no to him three times over the past two years because of his name. Charlotte and Charlie? The similarities are ripe for jokes. But it went well, and it looks like she's going to overlook his name for now.

"Tell us more about him," Jill says, returning the conversation to Rowan.

"And what it's like to date him," Charlotte adds.

"Fake date," I feel compelled to point out.

"I'd fake date him. He's cute." Jill waggles her brows, and I ignore the little stab of jealousy at the thought. What the hell is wrong with me?

"He's sweet, actually, in a playful kind of way. For a guy who hasn't been in many relationships, he's pretty good at it."

"Maybe he's only a good actor."

"Could be," I agree as a pit forms in my stomach. I don't want to believe that after he was cheering so big and loud for me at the game. Then again, maybe he was only selling the relationship. It's so confusing.

"What else?" Jill prompts me.

"Okay, he does this thing…"

They both lean in.

"When I'm sitting or standing next to him or I'm on his lap—"

"You sit on his lap?" Charlotte's eyes go wide like saucers. "Are you kissing him too?"

My pulse picks up speed. "No, of course not."

Not that I haven't thought about it. I bet he'd be good at it.

"Don't interrupt her. She was going to tell us something good." Jill elbows Charlotte playfully.

I wet my lips and beg my heart rate to normalize. "He sticks his fingers through my belt loops."

My friends stare at me, confusion etched into their features.

Reaching over, I demonstrate on Jill. She and Charlotte both look at where my finger is hooked around a belt loop on the side of her jeans.

"I don't get it," Jill says.

Then I use that finger to tug.

"Oooooh," they say in unison.

"Plus, the angle is different, so it makes his other fingers brush against my hip and waist and…"

They're grinning now, and my stomach feels like I executed a perfect back heel flick.

"We're pretending, but I don't hate it as much as I should."

"To recap." Jill clears her throat. "His parents maybe

suck, and your brother hates him. Oh, and he likes Amanda." Jill makes a face when she mentions my teammate.

"She isn't as bad as we thought," I tell them.

"I'm still holding a grudge for how she treated you at the beginning," Charlotte says.

"Same." Jill nods.

"She is protective of her team."

"Which includes you," Jill points out.

"I know, but we're good now. We probably won't ever be besties, but we want the same thing."

"Rowan?" Charlotte asks with a smirk.

My face heats. "To win and make it to the playoffs this season."

"And Rowan?" Jill's brows lift with the question.

I don't answer outright, but my face is on fire and whatever expression they see makes them both burst out laughing.

"This is baaaaad," I say. "Right? I can't actually like him. Leaving out my brother's feelings and the fact that he's already pissed I'm helping Rowan and would die if he knew I liked him for real, Rowan doesn't feel the same. He's pretending, and now I have to continue to fake it when..."

"You are thinking about jumping him every time he puts his fingers through your jeans' belt loop?" Jill grins again.

I regret telling them that already, but yes.

"Maybe your feelings aren't real. Let's break this down." Charlotte goes into strategy mode. "When did they start?"

I think back. "I don't know. One minute I was performing and the next I was thinking maybe we aren't so bad together."

"Do you think he feels the same?" Jill asks with a sense of hope that I'd love to share.

"No." I shake my head and let the disappointment of that answer really sink in. Maybe it'll help stop me from getting any more attached to the idea of us being a real couple. "He likes Amanda. He wants her back."

"Feelings change. That was then," Charlotte says.

"Before the faking and him seeing how great you are. You vs. Amanda—the choice is easy." Jill waves a hand like it's no contest.

"They have history."

"Not all history is good. Didn't you say she cheated on him?" Jill has a point. What in the world could she have been thinking? And with Ronnie? The guy is cute, for sure, but he's no Rowan.

"He says they were casual." I lift one shoulder and let it fall. If he doesn't hold it against her, how can I?

Jill reaches over and squeezes my leg. "I still say you're the better choice."

"Your brother would seriously lose his shit if you dated Rowan for real." Charlotte's mouth pulls into a grimace.

"Don't I know it," I mutter. "But it doesn't matter. Last night Rowan told me that Amanda and Ronnie are fighting. And the first person she confided in was him."

"You think they're going to get back together then?" Charlotte asks at the same time Jill asks, "She ran to him even though you two are dating?"

I answer Jill first. "I don't think it was like that." Then I look to Charlotte. "Yeah. I do."

Between everything I know about their history and on-and-off-again relationship and Rowan's feelings for her, the longing way she looks at him sometimes, and the weird behavior from Rowan last night, I'd say it's only a matter of time.

"Did you at least get what you wanted out of this thing?" Charlotte asks.

Jill nods. "Yeah. How is it going with the FLU admissions lady?"

"Good. I think she likes me, and I signed up to help with another event."

"But have you asked her about your chances of getting in?"

I shake my head, feeling a little ashamed. I'm usually a person with a plan, but in this instance, I've just gone with the flow.

"Ask her," Charlotte demands. "Before it's too late and you don't have the connection anymore."

"You mean when Rowan and I fake break up?" That pit in my stomach doubles in size.

"If he's getting what he wants out of this, then you should too," Jill says, and honestly, it's a good reminder.

"Thank you. I will. I promise."

There's a beat of silence and then Charlotte laughs.

"What's so funny?" I ask.

Her laughter gets louder, and she stops just long enough to get out, "Holy crap, you're Rowan Blakenship's girlfriend!"

CHAPTER SEVENTEEN

Rowan

"Nice job today, men." Coach Collins stands at the front of the bus and nods his head to each of us as we walk by. "Rest up tomorrow and I'll see you Monday."

Vaughn and I are the last two off the bus. Everyone is excited to be back and eager to enjoy a Saturday night without practice tomorrow.

"Are you going to Boone's party?" Vaughn asks as we walk to our vehicles.

"I'm not sure," I answer honestly.

"Have to check with Summer?" He gives me a lopsided grin.

Like he's one to talk. I saw him texting with Lacey the second we got back on the bus after our win.

"No. I'm just not sure I'm feeling it tonight."

His happy expression morphs to concern. "Everything good?"

"Yeah. Just tired."

"You've never been too tired to party."

He makes a good point.

"Do you ever feel like we're just living the same day over and over and over again?" I ask him.

"No," he says the word slowly and shakes his head side to side. "And now I'm seriously worried. What's going on with you? I thought the drinking and moodiness was weird last night, but then you played great today so I figured you must have fixed whatever was going on with you and Summer."

"Summer and I are fine."

"Fine?" He arches a brow. Okay, that wasn't the right thing to say, apparently.

"We're great."

The intense stare continues.

"I ran into Amanda after the game while I was waiting for Summer, and it just messed with me a bit." It's more than I want to admit to him, or anyone else, but hopefully it'll be enough to send him on his way. "But everything is good now."

"You two have a tendency to bring out the worst in each other."

"Me and Amanda?" I ask, a little defensively.

"Yeah. Listen, I like her fine when you two aren't together, but when you're talking or hooking up, she doesn't seem that into you."

"Ouch."

"I'm sorry." He shrugs his big shoulders. "She wants you to want her, but then you do, and she moves on to wanting someone else. Maybe not intentionally, but that's how it looks."

"We were never exclusive. She could mess around with whoever she wanted."

"And you could have to."

"Your point?"

"You didn't. You wouldn't."

Well, fuck, that stings a little. Maybe I was a lot more into her than she was into me. I don't know, but it's the least of my concerns.

"I appreciate you having my back, but I don't hold anything against Amanda for what happened."

"Either way. I'm glad to see you with Summer. I like her."

"You like her because she's all 'soccer is everything,' just like you."

His grin pulls higher. "Not true. Lacey isn't into soccer and she's my favorite person."

Hearing him call anyone his favorite person would have been mind-boggling a year ago.

"Yeah, but Lacey is into you being into soccer."

"She does like it when I score."

The knot in my chest loosens as I laugh at my buddy. It's good to see him so happy. I unlock my truck and open the door.

"Too much information," I say as I get in.

I go home, shower, change, and then sit in the empty living room and stare at my phone, deciding if I should text Summer. I haven't heard from her since last night. I texted her to make sure she made it home, and she replied to let me know she did and wished me luck today.

I tap out a few messages, asking how her day was and what she's up to tonight, but I don't send any of them. I can't shake the weird feeling that things have shifted between us.

My phone pings and I jump, heart racing, but it's only

Eddie asking if I'm going out tonight. I should go, have a few drinks, enjoy the night, sleep in tomorrow, and let everything else shake out on its own. I briefly wonder if Amanda and Ronnie worked things out, but I don't linger there. Vaughn's words hit me again. I thought what we had was fun and comfortable, but maybe I'm misremembering it.

My head spins and the only thing I can think that would be worse than stewing in thoughts about Amanda is sitting in this house all night by myself.

I grab my keys and head out to my truck. I tell myself I'm going to the party, but when I head toward Oakley, I know I'm not making an appearance at Boone's tonight.

I picked her up and dropped her off the night of Mariah Rieger's back-to-school party, but it still takes me a few wrong turns before I find her house. My pulse quickens when I spot Summer's car in the driveway.

I park along the curb two houses down. The lights are on downstairs, and one window upstairs is illuminated. There's a big tree on the side of the yard that reaches out toward the house, partially blocking my view.

I don't have a plan, and suddenly this feels beyond stupid. Am I really going to ring the front doorbell and ask if Summer's home? I let my head drop against the steering wheel. What the fuck? *Get it together.* I pull back and bang my forehead on the old leather twice, then sit back and rub the spot.

Great, now when I meet her parents, I'm going to look like I was punched. My palms are sweaty as I get out of the truck. I walk so slowly the neighbors probably think I'm casing the place. As I get to the edge of Summer's house, someone walks by the second-floor window. I freeze, then her red hair hits the light.

She's out of view before she notices me creeping outside. One small victory. Looking around, I make a last-minute decision that I hope I live to regret.

With a quick glance around, I walk to the tree and pull myself up to the first branch. It's a large red maple, thick and sturdy.

My thoughts as I pull myself up, testing each branch before I give it my full weight, then moving onto the next, are: *What the actual fuck? You're a goddamn idiot. This girl is going to be the death of you. Or at the very least the death of your pride.*

As I get closer to her window, I seriously consider climbing back down and never thinking of this moment again, but then she comes back into view. I cling to the trunk of the tree as I watch her. She's in a plain white T-shirt and cutoff jean shorts, and her hair is wet, making the color a few shades darker and pulling the curls straighter. I never realized how long her hair was before.

My gaze drops to the notecards in her hands. I should not be surprised she's studying on a Saturday night. Good thing I'm here to save her. I start moving again, faster this time. When I'm eye level with the window, I sidestep away from the trunk and hope like hell the branch can hold me.

My weight shakes the leaves against the window and Summer quickly glances this way, then back to her notecards. Swallowing, I take two bigger steps and clutch onto the windowsill. *Oh, thank fuck.* I let out a breath.

I'm just composing myself to knock when I meet Summer's wide-eyed gaze two feet away. She hurries forward, mouth falling open.

"What are you doing?" she yells as she quickly unlocks and pulls the window open. There's still a screen between us.

"Thought I'd drop by," I joke.

She's still staring at me in shock.

"Think you could let me in before I fall to my death?"

That spurs her to action, and she frees the screen and pulls it in while I lift myself up and over, falling not-so-gracefully onto her floor.

"Ow." I grimace as my knee takes the brunt of my landing.

"Rowan, what the hell?" Summer asks as she bends down and offers me her hand. She looks me over like she expects worse injuries.

"I was going for romantic, but I think maybe I misjudged the creepy factor," I mutter as I take her hand and she pulls me to my feet.

Summer lets out a small laugh that grows as I rise to stand in front of her. I aim a wobbly smile at her.

"Best fake boyfriend of the year," I say, holding my hands out to my sides.

"Vaughn and Coach Collins would have killed me if you fell and got injured."

"No, they'd kill me." I pull my gaze away from her and take in the room. It's very Summer. Soccer posters, framed photos of her with her friends, and one of her and her brother that I choose to ignore. The walls are a light yellow and her comforter is purple.

"I wasn't expecting you," she says and moves quickly to her bed to smooth back the comforter.

"Worried I'm going to find out you don't make your bed every day?" I ask with a chuckle. "Joke's on you; I never make my bed."

"Never?" she asks as she continues to fluff the pillows and pat out the wrinkles.

"Every week the cleaners do, does that count?"

"No." She laughs again though.

"Yeah, I didn't think so."

"I didn't have time this morning. I woke up late," she says like she still needs an excuse.

I walk over to a picture of her with two other girls. "Charlotte and Jill, right?"

"Yes."

There's another with her and a guy that I think might be the ex, Kevin. I don't recognize him outside of his flashy, red sports car.

"What are you doing here?" she asks.

I turn to face her. "Saving you from a night of studying."

She looks like she considers denying it. She shifts uncomfortably, hugging her arms over her chest.

"I can go if you want." I hitch a thumb toward the window. Getting down could be tricky, but what's one more death-defying stunt tonight?

"No." She shakes her head and the wet strands of dark-red hair. "Sorry. I wasn't expecting you to appear at my window."

"I did consider the front door, but I wasn't sure how to explain myself to your parents."

"They don't know about you," she confirms.

"I figured as much."

"Though they were curious about the guy yelling for me so much at the game last night."

A small puff of laughter leaves my lungs, and I walk over to her dresser, examining the things strewn across the top. Rings, her phone, a soccer ball. I pick up the last item and hold it in both hands.

"Are they home?" I ask.

"My dad is, but he's watching baseball so you're safe at least until the game is over."

"Baseball fan, huh?"

"Yes, he's wildly disappointed that neither Silas nor I were interested."

"Somehow I doubt he's disappointed in you." Or her brother, for that matter.

"I heard you beat Pacific."

"Yeah." I dip my chin in a nod.

Summer motions to the bed. "You can sit if you want."

I take the ball and sit on the edge. The frame squeaks under my weight. I scoot until my back is against the wall and my legs dangle over the side.

"This is so weird," she mutters and picks up her notecards. She walks toward me and extends them my way. "Ask me these."

I flip through the first few cards, then glance up at her.

"I have an anatomy test on Monday."

I nod my understanding and stack the cards again. "This is not how I pictured spending my Saturday night."

"Mine either." She laughs like seeing me in her room is the strangest thing ever. Maybe it is.

"What's Silas's room like? Does he have a shrine in there of me?"

Her laugh is louder. "No, but I wouldn't be surprised to find your face in the middle of his dartboard."

I look back at the notecards and lift them in one hand. "If I ask you these, then can we do something else?"

"Like?"

"Boone is having a party."

"I have to work tomorrow."

"So that's a no?"

"If you don't want to help me, then you can climb back down the tree." She smiles smugly.

"Fine, but for every study card, I get to ask a non-school question."

She considers it, then relents with a nod of agreement.

"Define 'proximal,'" I say. I cannot believe this is how I'm spending one of my few free Saturday nights during the season.

I flip the card as she reads the definition, nearly word for word.

"Correct."

Her smile lifts.

"Now my question." I think carefully. There is so much I still don't know about her. I start with an easy one. "Why did you and Kevin break up?"

"He broke up with me because he said it didn't make sense to stay together when we were going to be at different schools."

"Seriously?" Seems like a dumb reason. Oakley and Frost Lake aren't that far apart.

"That's what he said, but I think he was looking for a reason to dump me, because he started hanging out with *Lizzy* the very next day."

"Lizzy, huh?"

"All the guys want to date her. She's beautiful and popular and—"

"Not nearly as good as you, I'm certain."

She flushes. "She's actually really nice and smart. It's hard to hate her. Next question."

I shuffle to the next notecard. "Which terms are used to describe whether a structure is in front or behind another?"

"Anterior and posterior."

"Correct again." I drop the cards into my lap. "Why do I feel certain you know all of these by heart?"

"That's the point."

"My turn again." I mull over a dozen or more questions before I ask, "Do you ever think about getting back with him?"

"Who? Kevin?" She immediately shakes her head.

"Why not?"

She lifts a single finger. "You get one question."

"Fine," I mutter and read from the next card, "what is the sagittal plane?"

Again, she rattles off the answer with no problem.

"You're like Google," I say, impressed.

"Thanks." Her body language is more relaxed now. She walks over and sits on the bed, as far away from me as she can get but still close enough that I can see the smattering of freckles across the bridge of her nose.

"More questions about Kevin?"

I don't really give a shit about her ex. What I really want to know is what kind of guy is she looking for.

"How many other guys have you dated or talked to or..." I let my voice trail off with a flick of my wrist to indicate she should answer it however she wants to define it.

"Is that supposed to be code for 'hooked up with'?" She arches a brow.

"However you want to answer."

"Kevin and I only hooked up once and I've never been with anyone else. I went on a few dates with this guy Oren on the boys' soccer team. He's a senior."

"I know him," I mutter, picturing his stupid face. I never had a problem with him before, but I'm now fairly certain I've always known he was a jerk and never realized it.

"We were better as friends. We just talked about soccer the whole time."

That makes me feel slightly better. I like soccer and all, but it's the last thing on my mind when Summer is around.

"Why are you so curious about my dating history?" she asks, picking at the comforter. "It's a lot less interesting than yours."

"Where'd you get that idea?"

She rolls her eyes. "Come on. I see the way all the girls at school look at you and talk to you. You have your pick."

I let my head fall back against the wall and laugh toward the ceiling.

"I'm serious," she says. "You might have inadvertently made me the most hated girl in school. Except they're nice to me to stay on your good side."

"People are nice to you because they like you. Not because of me."

She hums like she disagrees.

"And I've only hooked up with two people."

"Amanda and…?"

I squint, wondering if this is one of those times I should keep my mouth shut so it doesn't cause more problems down the line.

"It's someone on the girls' soccer team, isn't it?"

Fuck.

"Who?" Summer demands, but she's smiling.

Dread pools in my stomach. I don't want to lie. And I guess some part of me wants to tell her. I want her to know me in a way I haven't shared with other people.

"Sophie."

She leans forward, shoulders hunching and gaze narrowing. "I'm sorry. I must have misheard you. It sounded like you said *Sophie*."

I bite down on the corner of my lip and wait for it to fully sink in.

"As in Amanda's best friend? That Sophie?"

Reluctantly, I nod.

"What the hell? How could you do that to Amanda? How could Sophie do that to Amanda?"

"It was her idea."

She inches closer on the bed. "I need more information."

"It was right after the first time Amanda and I stopped talking. I can't remember now why we stopped, but then she was talking to someone else, and we were all at a party..." My voice trails off. There is no great explanation for doing it, and I know it doesn't look great, but at the time it wasn't a big deal.

"And Amanda said you should hook up with Sophie?"

"Not in those exact words, but she kept saying we'd be cute together, stuff like that."

"Wow." Summer's lashes drop and then pop open as she shakes her head. "I do not get you two at all."

"Me and Sophie?"

"You and Amanda."

"It was a long time ago, and Sophie and I knew immediately that we weren't a good match. She's a great girl. I've gotten to know her from hanging out with Amanda, but there's no chemistry there."

"So little you hooked up with her," she mutters.

"I thought it would help me get over Amanda."

"And did it?"

I consider that. "I talked to a few people after that before Amanda and I sparked things again, so yeah, maybe it did."

"When I first met you, I thought that you and Amanda were perfect together."

One side of my mouth lifts. "Something tells me you didn't mean that as a compliment."

Her responding smile is sheepish. "I didn't know either of you very well, but my first impressions weren't great. But the point is, the more I get to know you, her, the situation..." She pauses and presses her lips together.

"What?" My pulse picks up speed again. Whatever she's going to say next feels important, like she can help me pinpoint the thoughts that have been swirling around since Friday.

"I can't understand why you want to get back with her so badly. There are a lot of girls at Frost Lake who you don't have this toxic history with."

"I know." My stare drops to her lips. "I've thought about that a lot recently."

"You have?"

"Sure. Maybe I'd be better off with someone new." Maybe there was a reason Amanda and I never worked out. Maybe, maybe, maybe.

"Exactly."

"Someone smart and kind, beautiful..." I move my hand along the comforter until the tips of my fingers brush against hers.

Her cheeks flush as she holds my stare.

"Someone I could have fun with and who'd show up for me, cheer me on at games and make sure I get home at night. A real sweetheart."

I mean her. She has to know it, but Summer's expression

is one of confusion or maybe skepticism. Faking with her has been easy and fun. How much different could a real relationship be?

She pulls her hand back and drops her gaze to her lap. "There are lots of girls like that at Frost Lake. You could have your pick."

What I want to say is, *I pick you*. But there's something in the way she won't meet my gaze that tells me it doesn't matter.

CHAPTER EIGHTEEN

Summer

"Whoa, whoa, whoa." My mom calls after me as I hurry to the front door with my backpack hooked over one shoulder. "Where are you going so early?"

I slow my steps but keep moving forward. I turn to look at her only after I've twisted the handle and pulled open the door. The morning chill seeps in through the tiny crack.

"School. I have a test this morning and I want to study a little more."

"At least have breakfast first." She's standing at the stove and the smell of eggs and bacon wafts through the air.

Dad sits at the table with a plate of both in front of him.

I close the door and trek back into the kitchen. I snag a piece of bacon and then kiss my mom on the cheek. "Thank you."

She smiles, but says, "You need a good breakfast. Your brain will thank you later."

"My brain is crammed full of anatomy definitions. It isn't hungry."

That makes her laugh. I move over to Dad and kiss him

on the cheek too. He looks tired this morning and his cane rests against the table.

"Bad morning?" I ask him.

"Little pain. Nothing bacon won't fix." He winks at me.

I linger and he tips his head toward the door. "Go on. We'll see you tonight for dinner."

"Bye. Love you guys." I shove the bacon in my mouth and head out.

When I get to school, I stop by the counselor's office. I do need to study, but the real reason I wanted to get here early was to see her.

She's just arrived and is placing her coffee on her desk next to the keyboard.

"Mrs. Carroll?" I ask, hovering in the doorway.

She looks up as she sets her purse on the bookshelf behind her. "Summer. Hi. Good morning."

"Do you have a minute?"

"Yes, come in." She waves with one hand. "I have five before a staff meeting. What's up?"

"I want to attend FLU next year."

"Great school." She smiles.

I nod. "I have sort of an odd question. I'm working with the head of admissions, Kristy Leigh. A friend introduced us, and I'm helping out at their recruitment table at a few events."

"That's great. Kristy is a friend, and she's lovely."

I nod again. "Do you think..." I start, then rephrase. "Would it be off-putting in any way if I asked her about my application? She's been so nice to me, but I don't want to overstep."

Mrs. Carroll gives me a reassuring smile. "Not at all. She may not be able to give you specifics, and she won't give you assurances until everything has gone through the proper channels, but I think she'd be more surprised if you didn't ask her than if you did."

"Thank you." My shoulders slump with relief.

"Are you applying to other schools as well?" she asks.

"Yes, but FLU is my top choice." By a mile. By ten thousand miles. "They have a great women's soccer team."

She tips her head back and then nods in understanding. "That they do. Go, Cougars!"

We share a stifled laugh, and I back out toward the hallway. "Thanks, Mrs. Carroll."

"You're welcome, Summer. Let me know if I can help as you finish up your applications."

During lunch, I bring my notebook.

"I thought your test was this morning," Rowan says as he takes a seat next to me. He drops a bag of chips in front of me.

I briefly look up at him and then wish I hadn't. At some point since he snuck out of my room Saturday night, he got a haircut. The strands still hang to chin-level, but the ends are neater and his overall appearance is somehow more handsome.

"It was. I'm working on an email to Kristy."

"Kristy at FLU?"

I nod and then cross out the last two sentences I've written.

"Why?" Rowan asks, undeterred by my lack of conversation today. Or really the past thirty-six-ish hours.

Things were weird when he left Saturday night. I had work on Sunday and then studied all night. Rowan didn't text, and I tried not to read too much into that. He seems fine today, normal, like nothing happened. Like he didn't admit that he thinks about us together for real…or, I'm not sure exactly what he admitted if I'm honest, but if I think about it too long, my brain feels like it's going to explode.

"I want to talk to her about my application."

"O-kay," he says slowly like he still doesn't understand.

I stop writing and look at him. My heart squeezes in my chest as I do. This is bad. So incredibly bad. I cannot like him. I can't. We don't make sense. We wouldn't work. I'm not sure he's looking for anything more than casual, despite what he says. The whole Amanda thing, plus Sophie—it's messy. I tell myself anything I can think of to stop from noticing the dark-blue flecks in his eyes and the slight smirk on his lips or remember the way he looked all casual and comfortable in my small bedroom.

"Getting a soccer scholarship is a long shot, but if I can get into FLU with a little academic funding, then I can hopefully walk on to the team, and I'll get a job on the side to pay for the rest." I know student loans are an option too, but if I can get out of college debt-free, that would be the best-case scenario. "I want to see if she has any tips or ideas for me to make my application stand out."

"Why don't you just ask her in person instead of scratching out some formal email?" He glances down at the paper where I've written and crossed off a dozen different attempts.

"I won't see her again until the next recruitment event I signed up for, and the early admissions deadline is before then."

He continues to stare at my paper as he nods absently. "The chips are for you."

"Thank you." I reach for the bag and open it. He's started doing this almost daily, grabbing something extra from the lunch line for me. A cookie, a bag of chips, a Gatorade, an extra serving of fries that I'm sure the lunch lady intended for him.

"What are you doing tomorrow night?" he asks, finally glancing up at me.

"Practice, studying..."

"Have dinner with me and my family."

I choke on the chip and cough several times to dislodge it from my throat. My eyes water and I take a long drink of water before I meet his gaze again.

"Sounds that tempting, huh?" He grins.

"Chip went down the wrong way." My voice is still tight as I speak.

"My parents are back in town this week. I'll ask them to invite Kristy over, and you can ask her your questions then."

"At dinner with your parents?" I reiterate to make sure I'm understanding him correctly.

"Sure."

"Won't that be..."

"Awkward?" he asks, smirk still firmly in place like he's in on a joke that I'm not.

"Do I need to remind you that the last time I saw them, I spilled water all over your dad and nearly got fired?"

"Oh, right. I had forgotten that." Rowan chuckles softly. "They won't remember, and even if they did, they won't care."

It feels too easy. The answer can't be this simple. That might be Rowan's life, but it's not mine.

He pulls out his phone, and while he's scrolling I glance back at my notebook. It would be less intimidating to talk to Kristy in person instead of firing off a stiff email and hoping she doesn't think I've violated some unspoken rule of reaching out to the head of admissions. Or, worse, getting lost in the thousands of emails just like mine from other desperate applicants.

"Done," Rowan says, setting his phone on the table.

I blink out of my thoughts. "What?"

"My mom said yes and she's calling Kristy now." The bell for next period rings and Rowan grins bigger as people start to move around us. "Too late to back out now, Lindsey."

The Blakenship's house is big. Huge. Massive. My shoes echo in the entryway.

"Everyone is in the kitchen," Rowan says as he leads me through the house. His steps are too quick for me to gape too long at anything, but everything is beautiful. Immaculately decorated and organized. Big, flashy artwork and furniture that's perfectly sized for the space. I picture the big sectional at my house that my mom always complains is too big and the old photographs in mismatched frames on the wall.

My stomach is a ball of nerves. Voices greet us as Rowan steps into the room. Their kitchen might be bigger than our entire first floor.

Everyone stops talking at once, and as Rowan moves to my side, all eyes are on me.

I swallow around what feels like a giant cotton ball in my throat.

"Hello." His father is the first to speak. "You must be Summer."

I nod and wave.

"Nice to meet you," his mom says. "We're so glad you could come."

"Summer, these are my parents, Lee and Tonya. And you know Kristy." Rowan waves a hand to motion toward each and then steps forward and snags a carrot off a platter in the middle of the counter.

"Thank you for having me," I say to his parents and hope they don't notice the quiver in my voice. Then I meet Kristy's gaze and smile at her.

"Hi," she says, flashing a friendly smile back at me. If she has any idea that this was a setup to pump her for information, she doesn't show it.

"What can I get you to drink?" Mrs. Blakenship asks, pulling open the fridge. There's a row of neatly organized drinks.

Rowan steps forward and grabs two different kinds of sparkling water, then holds them both out to me. I take the grapefruit flavor, and he grins like he expected that's the one I'd pick.

"Rowan tells us you play soccer as well," his dad says as I take a drink.

I nod until I can speak. "That's right."

"And you're a senior?" his mom asks.

"Yep."

"I'm surprised we haven't met you before," his mom says. "Have you always lived in Frost Lake?"

"Summer switched schools this year from Oakley," Rowan answers for me.

"Your senior year?" His mom has the level of shock and horror that I felt all summer. "That's awful."

"It was, but I'm adjusting." I glance at Rowan.

"More than adjusting. You're killing it," he says, then

looks up at his parents. "The girls' soccer team has a winning record for the first time in a decade because of Summer."

My cheeks heat. "Not only because of me."

"Mostly because of you."

"And you've been helping Rowan and Kristy with the FLU recruitment. Are you planning to attend next fall as well?" His mom continues to smile at me.

I wonder what else Rowan has told them about me. Do they know we're together-ish?

"I hope to, yes, but I haven't been accepted yet." I glance shyly at Kristy.

"Are you applying early or in the new year?" she asks me.

"Early decision." That way if I need to apply other places, I can start looking.

"And you, Rowan?" Kristy asks him.

"I..." He has everyone's attention, and for the first time, I think I see him uncomfortable with it. "I haven't started mine yet, so I guess the new year." He clears his throat and focuses on Kristy. "Speaking of, Summer and I were wondering if you had any tips for our applications?"

"Maybe we could talk about it over dinner," his mom suggests. "So the food doesn't get cold."

We all murmur our agreement, and she leads us into a formal dining room. The table is big enough to seat twelve, but the five of us sit at one end. I'm next to Rowan with his mom and dad across from us, leaving Kristy at the head.

The food smells great. There's roasted chicken and some sort of potato casserole, green beans, and rolls. My mouth waters.

"What are you planning to study?" Rowan's dad asks as he lifts the platter of chicken. He dishes some out onto his plate and then passes it to me.

"I'm not sure yet."

"No?" his mom asks like she expected me to have my entire life planned out. I would if that were possible, but so much depends on the first step. Get into FLU, walk on to the soccer team, work hard, and cross my fingers that I make it professionally.

"I want to play soccer as long as I can."

"College?" His dad's brows lift. "Or professionally?"

"Both."

"That's a big dream," he says in a way that I think he means to be supportive but only reminds me that the odds are against me. Less than 1 percent of female college soccer players make it to the major professional leagues. I know this, but I still want to try. I can't imagine doing anything else.

"I could totally see it." Rowan nudges my leg under the table with his. "You'll be representing Frost Lake in the Olympics or the next World Cup."

"The chances are slim, but I love it, and I've never been able to see myself doing anything else."

"How are your grades?" Kristy asks me.

"Okay. B+ average and I'm working hard this year to bring it up."

"All she does is study, play soccer, and work. She's basically your ideal applicant," Rowan tells Kristy.

My face heats. I know what he's doing. Hell, Kristy probably knows what he's doing. It's sweet he wants to gas me up in front of her, but I don't want him to make me out to be this amazing student only for her to see my transcript and know differently.

"Grades are important, but they aren't everything," she says.

"Good for Rowan." His dad chuckles softly.

"School's never really been my thing," he says with a shrug.

From what I've seen, he pulls decent grades without putting a lot of effort into it.

"You're good enough to play professional soccer too." It's my turn to nudge him under the table.

"Nah. I'm no Vaughn."

"You don't give yourself enough credit."

"Rowan's planning to study business," his dad says as he stabs a piece of chicken with his fork and lifts it to his mouth. "Right, Son?"

Rowan stares down at this plate. "I haven't decided for sure."

"He's been talking about taking over the business since he was little. He used to come with us to our first car lot and sit in the office, tapping away on a calculator like he was making deals and selling cars." His mom looks so proud as she tells me this.

I smile back at her because I can picture it, and it's a cute image. But it's so clearly not what he wants. He's examining the potato casserole like it's the most interesting food he's ever seen.

"What did you study?" I ask the adults, scanning my gaze to each of them.

"Officially I was a history major, but mostly I hung out with my friends and tried not to flunk out," his dad says with a wink. "Then I went back later for my MBA."

"I majored in communications, which back then spanned everything from marketing to writing."

"She was the top salesperson for her company five years running," Mr. Blakenship adds.

"A long time ago," she says, but she looks secretly pleased that he mentioned it.

"Before I stole her away to come work with me," he adds.

We all look to Kristy next.

"I studied interior design," she says with a smile that tells me people rarely guess this fact about her.

"That's quite a switch from working at FLU," Mrs. Blakenship says.

"I did work as a designer for a few years, but the market was competitive, and I found I didn't enjoy creating spaces as much when I wasn't the one picking out all the items or enjoying them."

"I like rearranging my bedroom," I say and then suddenly regret it. I know it isn't the same thing, but it's as close to interior design as I've ever (or will likely ever) come.

"Your bedroom is cool," Rowan says. Then he must realize that he's just admitted he's been in my room because he falls quiet and I blush hard, and everyone goes quiet at the table.

His knee finds mine under the table again, a silent sort of apology. If his parents didn't think we were dating before, they definitely do now.

"So, Rowan, you were asking Kristy about tips for your application." His dad saves us all with a quick topic change.

Kristy sets her fork down. "Most of my advice you've probably heard before."

"We'll take any guidance you have," I tell her honestly. At least I will.

"A good letter is probably the most important thing. What it says precisely is less important than it giving us a good idea of who you are and what you want or hope to get out of FLU."

"What if we don't know what we want yet?" Rowan asks, pushing a forkful of green beans around his plate.

"Then say that," she says with a smile. "Lots of people come in as a freshman without a set direction or plan. The first two semesters are mostly general requirements so you can explore different options while adjusting to college life."

"Who reads the letters?" I ask.

"At FLU, we have a committee that decides on all our applicants. Each goes through several rounds made up of admissions officers, faculty, and even students."

I don't know if it's reassuring that it's a committee instead of a single person or not. Not, probably. More people mean more opportunities for someone to say no.

"I'm sure you will have no problem getting into a good college," Rowan's father adds, looking at me. "FLU or any other school would be lucky to have you."

"Thank you."

No one seems to know what to say to that, so we eat quietly for a couple of minutes before Kristy compliments the food, and then Mrs. Blakenship tells her the potato casserole is a family recipe. After that, I'm lost in thought. About college and Rowan. His knee still presses against mine. He's different with his family, less talkative and not as playful. They adore him, that's easy to see, but I'm not sure they have any idea who he is or what he wants to do after high school. Though to be fair, Rowan's admitted he doesn't know either.

After dinner, we move back into the kitchen. Mr. Blakenship loads the dishwasher as Rowan's mom places leftovers in containers and sets them in the fridge. Rowan, Kristy, and I are talking about the next recruitment event.

"Oh, and we've added another to the calendar in late October if either of you are interested," she says with a smile.

"Definitely," I say, then add, "as long as I don't have a conflict with work or soccer."

"Where do you work, dear?" Mrs. Blakenship asks.

"At the country club," I say and pray they don't recognize me. "Mostly during the summer at the pool concession stand."

"Work, school, and soccer—that must be hard to juggle," Kristy says.

"I'm saving for college," I admit and will myself not to be embarrassed that my parents can't afford to just pay for it like the Blakenships can.

"It's impressive and says a lot about your work ethic." Kristy offers me another smile and then sighs. "I should probably be going. Thank you again for such a lovely dinner."

"Oh, thank you for coming. It's always so good to see you. Are you golfing next weekend with the women's group?"

While they talk golf and upcoming country club events, Rowan hooks one finger around mine. I look to him.

"Did you get all your questions answered?" he mouths.

"I think so," I whisper back.

"Rowan, Summer," Kristy says, facing us. "I'll see you soon."

"Let me walk you out," Mr. Blakenship says.

"No bother. I know the way," she says to him, and he gives her an appreciative nod.

"We're going to watch a movie or something," Rowan says to his parents as Kristy heads for the door.

"Okay." His mom waves and smiles at me. "Nice to meet you. Come back any time."

"Thank you," I tell her.

Mr. Blakenship gives me the same charming smile his

son does so often, then says, "Rowan, give me a hand with something in the den before you go."

Rowan arches a brow in question, but his dad walks off, motioning his head for Rowan to follow him.

"I'll be right back," he says to me.

"Sure." I watch him step toward his father, then peer down the front hall in the direction Kristy went. She's still putting on her coat in the entryway.

I go after her before I can talk myself out of it.

She smiles at me as I approach.

"Leaving too?"

"No, I just wanted to apologize."

"For what?" she asks, sweeping her hair out from the collar of her coat.

"I'm sorry if tonight was weird. I wanted to email and ask you about my application, but Rowan thought this was better." I shrug sheepishly.

She laughs. "Don't worry. Most of my dinner invitations are from well-meaning parents hoping to help their kids the same way Rowan's want to help him. And you."

"That feels…bad."

Another short laugh slips from her lips. "Not at all. I love my job. If I could sit down with every single person and help them with their application, I would. I know how hard it is to stand out among thousands of others and how much it means to get that letter of acceptance."

"You do?"

"I applied to twelve different colleges and got accepted to one. My last choice. Luckily for me it worked out, but I was devastated. I thought my life was over."

"That's how I would feel about not getting in at FLU."

She studies me for a beat. "And Rowan?"

I glance back toward the kitchen, but he's not back yet. It doesn't matter. I don't need to see him to know there's tension whenever someone asks about his plans.

"I'm not sure."

She smiles as if that were a test to see if I'd pretend he wanted to go there as badly as I do.

"I'll tell you what—send me your letter before you submit your application, and I'll read it personally and see if I have any suggestions."

"Really?" My chest lifts and expands as a weight lifts off. Her advice is everything. She's seen hundreds of thousands. If she thinks it's good, then I know I'll have a shot.

"Yes, but I need you to remember that I'm only one opinion. I don't make the final decisions alone. Ultimately it will be up to a committee vote."

"I know, and I understand. I promise I won't hold it against you if I don't get in." Though I might die a little inside.

She nods and turns to the door. With a glance over her shoulder, she steps out onto the front porch. "The same goes for Rowan. If he wants my help, have him email me at least a week before the deadline."

"I'll tell him. Thank you again."

—

When Rowan is done helping his father, he leads me upstairs to his room. I try really hard not to compare mine to his, but it's hard not to notice it's twice the size.

"Your bed is huge," I blurt out.

His lips pull up into a smirk that makes my stomach flip. He takes my hand and tugs me toward it, then flops down on top of it, taking me with him.

I squeal and giggle as I fall half on top of him.

"Your parents are going to think we're up here hooking up."

"Definitely," he says. "My dad just had a very uncomfortable 'don't forget to be responsible' talk with me."

"No." The blood drains from my face.

"Oh yeah. My dad thinks we are banging for sure."

I groan and roll over onto my side, covering my eyes with both hands.

Rowan pries them away. He's so close I can make out the small scar on the side of his face.

"What's this from?" I reach out and touch it. His skin is warm and smooth.

"Skateboarding. I tried to do a trick, fell down some concrete stairs."

"Ouch."

My heart pounds quickly as the air between us feels thick and heavy. I don't move, but I lift my left wrist to show him my own battle wound. "Silas threw a rock at me."

"A rock?"

"We were three and four, and I think I threw the first one."

"Antagonizing people from an early age," he says with a small smile. Then he captures my wrist between his thumb and middle finger and brings it to his lips. He places a soft kiss on the spot, his stare not leaving mine.

I pull my arm back slowly and clutch it against my chest. My breaths come too fast, and my head is light.

"Thank you for tonight."

"You're welcome."

"I should get home."

His mouth lifts higher on one side like he knows I'm

trying to run away. I don't know what's happening but putting distance between us feels like the most logical solution.

I don't move.

Rowan reaches out and fingers a strand of my hair. He pulls gently and watches the curl bounce back in place. Then he frees my hair and glides his hand up and rests it against the side of my neck. I wonder if he can feel my pulse racing.

No one is here to see us. No one to convince we're a couple. And still he's touching me.

"This is a bad idea," I say.

He nods, leaning closer. "Probably, but I can't stop thinking about you."

His admission sends goose bumps racing up and down my arms, and my stomach flips around like I'm on a roller coaster.

I think of a dozen more protests, but I don't say any of them as he guides his mouth down on top of mine. It's a gentle crush of his lips to mine, then he lingers there, almost as if he's waiting to see if I'm going to push him away. I don't have that kind of willpower.

Whatever this is. Whatever we're doing. It doesn't matter. I can't stop thinking about him either. I move only an inch, leaning toward him and pressing into the kiss. He lets out a small groan and then the hand at my neck pulls me harder against him and his mouth slants, more insistent this time.

Blood pounds in my ears and every nerve ending on my body comes alive. His tongue sweeps in and he groans again. The sound has heat pooling low in my stomach. Every second, the kiss gets less tentative and more demanding until somehow our bodies are pressed flush against each other. My hands press against his chest, lightly gripping the cotton material. He's warm and hard under my touch.

"Summer." My name is a tortured whisper as he pulls back and then dives right back in.

We kiss until my body is on fire and my lips feel swollen. His phone vibrates in his pocket. Once, then twice, then a third time. He doesn't make any move to check it, but the reminder of the outside world breaks us apart.

A million thoughts race through my mind as we lie there, unmoving, eyes closed, hearts racing.

Rowan is the first to move.

"Well, shit." He breathes out the words and rolls over onto his back, staring at the ceiling.

My thoughts exactly.

CHAPTER NINETEEN

Rowan

Summer aims a shy smile at me the next morning when I show up at her locker before first period.

"Hey." She clutches her notebook against her chest.

"Hey," I reply, my gaze inadvertently dropping to her mouth. I replayed that kiss for hours last night. And this morning. I was almost late to school because of that kiss.

Her face flushes. Yep, I'd say I'm not the only one thinking about it.

"I brought you something," I say, digging in my front pocket.

Her brows arch as she waits for me to pull out my hand. I reach out and open my palm to reveal the blue and pink flower ring.

She giggles, and the tension around us dissipates.

"Is that a paper ring?" she asks.

"Mm-hmm." I pluck it between my thumb and pointer finger and then take her hand, fitting it onto her middle finger.

"This is so cute," she says, admiring it. "Did you make it?"

"Of course. Finally got to use my origami skills for something other than fortune catchers." It took a few tries to remember how to do it, and then I had to rummage around to find supplies. I cut and folded a bunch of tiny strips of paper, then connected them.

The final result is a zigzag pattern with pink on top and blue on the bottom. Then I made a tiny pink rose and attached it to the ring. My fingers hurt from folding so many pieces of paper, but it was worth it to see the smile on her face now.

"Thank you." She holds her hand up in the air, admiring my craftiness.

"Perfect." I wink and then take her hand to lead her to class.

Mr. Hayes puts on a movie in first period. I don't see any of it. Summer takes notes, and I watch her. I push my desk up so that the front of mine touches the back of hers and I play with her hair. She keeps looking over her shoulder as I do my best to distract her.

Then at lunch she's working on her FLU admissions letter. I pull her right leg on top of mine under the cafeteria table.

"You should work on your letter too," she says with a grin.

"I'm composing it in my head," I say, then drop my mouth to her shoulder.

I kind of can't get enough of her. I don't think I've ever felt this way.

"Kristy can't review it for you if you don't write it," she reminds me.

It was nice of Kristy to agree to do that, but it only matters that she does it for Summer. She deserves the best chance at getting into her top choice school.

"I'm not even sure I want to go," I say.

"I know, but it gives you options while you figure it out."

I bob my head. She isn't wrong.

"Have you considered telling your parents?"

I answer her question with my own. "That I don't know what I want to do with my life?"

"Yeah."

"I tried a couple times, but they have it set in their minds. They've been talking about me going to FLU and taking over the business for as long as I can remember."

"Your mom said you wanted to work there when you were younger."

"Yeah, when I was like five. I just wanted to be wherever my parents were, and they were always at work, you know? I thought if I worked there, then I could spend time with them. But I grew out of that." The three of us being a family and doing stuff together like my friends did with their families. Now I realize they want me to take over so they can do other things—retire, travel, whatever.

And that's okay. I've made my peace with it, but I'm not going to work a job I don't want because I think it will change anything. It won't.

"I'm sorry." Her hand drops to the top of my thigh.

"It's okay."

She hums like maybe she disagrees, then her stare drops to my mouth. My lips twitch with amusement as heat pumps through me.

"Thinking about kissing me right now, aren't you, Lindsey?"

"Definitely not." Her tongue darts out to wet her lips.

"You're going to get me detention," I say as I consider

kissing her right here. I'm sure some teacher is watching us right now, just waiting for us to cross the line so they can send us to the principal's office.

The bell rings. Everyone moves around us like they're eager to get to their next period. Not me. The only reason I'm not blowing off the rest of the day and spending it kissing her is because Summer would probably regret it if I got her in trouble. So I stand and pull her to her feet.

"Saved by the bell."

"Yo!" Austin waves a hand in front of my face.

"Sorry." I blink and then pull my gaze away from the back field where the girls' team is practicing.

"Vaughn is going to blow a gasket if you don't lock in."

"I'm locked."

He cocks one brow.

"We were all worried about you partying away the year, but instead you're in a new relationship haze. I did not see this coming."

"I am not in…whatever this is," I say so I don't have repeat the phrase. "And I'm here. I'm good."

He looks like there's more on his mind, so I keep staring until he blows out a breath.

"This is a big deal. Senior year. One last chance. Redemption. Champions. Any of this ringing a bell?"

"Yeah, of course." I want all those things too. I just don't spend as much time as him or Vaughn stressing about it.

Still, he looks skeptical.

"Am I not here every day, putting in the work like everyone else?"

"Yeah," he says in a way that implies there's a *but* coming.

Irritating thoughts run through me like needles poking my skin. "Say what you need to say, Disco."

"It's important to me. To Vaughn. To a lot of us. And I get that soccer isn't in your future plans, but we need you. We want to do this with you. One last ride to state championships, then we'll relax. I promise."

I hear him. I don't agree with everything he's said, but he's telling me to step it up and I respect the nudge. "One last ride. Let's do this thing."

I hold out my hand. He takes it and pulls me against his chest, slapping me on the back in the process.

"Thank you," he says as he steps back. The relief on his face is another indication of just how much he's been stressing about me. Fuck, it's like they all expect the worst. I put my everything into our games, same as them.

"Yeah."

"Do you want to come over tonight?" Austin asks. "Vaughn and the twins are stopping by to watch the Brayson game from last week."

"I can't. Summer is taking me to the best pizza place in all of Oakley." There's no way it's better than Freddie's.

That look of doubt is back on his face.

"Send it to me," I say. "I'll watch it later tonight."

"Well?" Summer asks. She's sitting across from me in a booth at Momma Vi's, watching me chew.

I swallow the bite and nod. "Good."

A pleased smile curves her lips. "Better than Freddie's?"

"It's a tie."

"There are no ties!" The look of outrage on her face over pizza is cute.

"Sure there are." I go in for another big bite. It's really good. Possibly even better than Freddie's, but there's something nostalgic about that place that will always make it my favorite.

"I think your taste buds are broken." She grabs her own slice and digs in. A little moan slips from her lips as she chews.

I still haven't stopped thinking about kissing her, and that noise is not helping.

"How was practice today?" she asks, apparently not having the same loss of control over her thoughts as me.

"Good. Fine." My brows tug together as I think back to the end. "Okay."

She picks up on my uncertainty. "What happened?"

"Nothing. It's just something Austin said."

Silently, she continues to stare at me, waiting for me to continue.

"Basically, he told me that I wasn't taking things seriously and wanted to make sure I was going to step it up."

Her brows lift.

"He didn't say it exactly like that, but it was implied."

"Are you sure?"

"Yeah. And I think he was upset that I wasn't going to his house tonight to watch game clips because I had plans with you."

"You could have gone," she says like she thinks I wanted to do that instead of being here.

"No, I want to be here. I guess that's his point. I'm not built like him or Vaughn. I don't obsess for days on end leading up to a game."

"And you think because that's how he wants you to show up that your way is wrong?"

"Maybe," I admit. "It's more that he thinks I don't care about the outcome. I don't need to be planning a future around soccer to want to win this season."

I've been playing for a long-ass time, many of those years with these same guys. Of course I want to go out on top. I want it as much as any of them. Maybe more. This is my last season. I'm not moving on to another team. This is it for me.

"Did you tell him that?"

I shrug one shoulder. "More or less."

She lets out a small laugh that loosens the tightness in my shoulders. I don't want the guys worrying about me, and I definitely don't like the idea of them thinking I'm not locked in.

"You're a fantastic soccer player. If Austin's worried, it's probably more about him than you."

"Meaning?"

"We project our worries onto other people. Especially in a sport like soccer where we have to rely on our teammates so heavily."

"I'm not sure I follow."

"He wants to know that you're going to have his back in case he screws up."

"Austin is having an amazing season and he's already talking to several colleges. He'll have his pick."

"Which probably only puts more pressure on him this season."

"Yeah, I guess."

She rests both elbows on the table and stares at me like I'm interesting or complicated or...fuck, I don't know, but I like it.

"You're fun and easygoing, and you're always joking around." Something about the way she says all of it tells me this isn't a positive thing, but these are the attributes people love about me.

"Yeah."

"Because you're rarely serious, you're not always easy to read. Sometimes you come across so nonchalant, like nothing bothers you and whatever happens, you'll be fine. And that makes it hard for people like Austin or Vaughn or me when we wear our feelings so openly for everyone to see."

"Really?"

She nods.

"Huh." I consider that. I guess what she says is true. "You're not that easy to read either, not outside of soccer."

"No?"

I shake my head.

"What do you want to know?"

My mouth hitches up on one side. "Have you thought about kissing me all day?"

Her face flushes. Maybe she is easy to read.

"Not *all* day."

"Let's get out of here." I tip my head toward the door.

"We haven't finished the pizza."

I lift one brow. Like I care about food right now.

"Okay." She laughs.

I stand and then take her hand. I use it to tug her against me.

"In case I'm not easy to read right now, I'm planning to kiss you senseless as soon as we get in my truck."

CHAPTER TWENTY

Summer

"KEEP IT MOVING," VAUGHN YELLS TO THE GROUP OF SOPHOMORES walking in front of the bleachers. They're standing between us and the football field. But more importantly, they're blocking his view of the cheerleaders. Lacey, in particular.

Rowan's deep chuckle vibrates against my back. He's sitting in the row behind me, but he's leaning forward with both arms draped over my shoulders.

The whistle blows, signaling the end of the first quarter.

While the guys jog off the field to their benches, the cheerleaders turn around and start yelling, trying to get the crowd into it. I'm not sure what's wrong with everyone tonight, but the response is lackluster. That is until Vaughn stands up and puts both hands around his mouth, yelling, "Go, Frost Lake!"

Rowan doesn't stand, but he chuckles again and then lets out a whoop. Soon, the rest of the student section is yelling and cheering.

"Never thought I'd see the day," Rowan says, voice close to my ear.

I've only ever known Vaughn with Lacey, but the stories I've heard indicate that he wanted very little to do with school or football games or anything fun before they started dating.

"I think they're cute," I say.

"Not as cute as us." He winks, then nuzzles into my neck. "I really want to kiss you right now."

"We said no kissing while we're faking it," I remind him.

"I think we've already broken that rule, Lindsey." He's right, of course, but it's different when other people are watching. We weren't performing at his house or in his truck or in the parking lot after practice. Not like we are now.

We sit that way, chatting with his friends and watching the game, until halftime. Claire stands. "I need snacks. I'm starving."

"I'll go with you," Austin volunteers immediately.

"And you were giving me shit about Lacey," Vaughn says. "You two are attached at the hip."

"We are not. We don't have second, fifth, or sixth period together. Plus we're apart for two hours every day during practice, eight for sleeping..." Austin's voice trails off as we all fight back laughter. "Fine. I'll stay here. She's good. Right, babe?"

"I'll go with you," I offer Claire.

She smiles. "Thanks. My boyfriend just abandoned me for his pride."

"Gee, thanks. I'd rather Disco have gone," Rowan says, looking all sad and pathetic but still adorable. "Way to ruin it for all of us."

Austin nudges Rowan. "We'll stay here and do guy things."

"Yeah, and definitely not talk about you two." Rowan's eyes sparkle with mischief as he sits back.

"Do you want anything?" I ask him.

"No, but if you get M&M's, I'll help you eat them."

"How chivalrous," Claire notes with a laugh.

We leave the guys on the bleachers and walk side by side around the field to the concession stand.

"You two are really sweet together," Claire says once we get in the back of the line.

"Thanks."

"What's he like?" she asks, crossing her arms over her chest. There's a hint of chill in the air tonight that has me already missing summer.

"Rowan?" I ask, though I know that's who. It's more that I don't understand why she would ask me that question. "You've known him a lot longer than I have."

"Yeah, but not like this." She waves a hand back toward the bleachers where we were just sitting. "Not the boyfriend version."

"He dated Amanda."

"He was never like that with her." Claire shakes her head, making the blond strands fall over one shoulder. She has that perfect, straight hair. If I had to switch with someone, it would be her. I bet it takes her a lot less effort to brush her hair.

And yes, I am avoiding thinking too carefully about her words because I don't know what to make of them. I don't know why he's different with me, but the most logical reason is we're putting on a show. Sure, we've kissed a few times without an audience, but we've fallen into a rhythm of doing all these things so people believe we're together. I can't tell what's real and what's not at this point.

We step forward with the line. Claire continues. "He's different with you. He's still Rowan, all goofy and funny, but then he looks at you and..."

She pauses as if she's considering her words carefully.

"What?" I ask, my heartbeat picking up speed. I'm so desperate for someone else's take on us, even if it's clouded with what we've chosen to show them.

"You subdue him, but not in a bad way. It's like he seems more content. He's always been the guy who notices when someone is having a rough time and then tries to make them smile, but with you, he's just existing. I'm probably not explaining it well, but trust me, it's a good thing."

I'm not sure what to make of that assessment or if it's even true. Maybe he's comfortable with me because he doesn't feel the same way he would if he were really dating someone. His heart isn't on the line.

"What was he like with Amanda?" I ask. Part of me wishes I had seen them together and the other is glad I didn't so I can't torture myself with the memories.

"I don't really know." She shrugs one shoulder. "I only saw them together a couple of times. I don't think she liked hanging around with our group much. He usually hung out with her friends. The way she ditched him at homecoming was shitty though."

"Is that when she got together with Ronnie?"

"Yeah." Claire lowers her voice. "She could have at least waited until the next day. Instead, she abandoned him halfway through the night."

Amanda and Sophie are standing next to the line now, which explains why Claire stops talking. I mull over her words as we wait. Amanda and I are different, so it makes sense that Rowan is different with me. That's all Claire is seeing. Plus, it's not that much of a stretch for Claire to like me better than Amanda, because she cheated on Rowan.

"I'm going to pee before we head back. Will you hold my stuff?" Claire asks after we have our food.

"Yeah." I take her drink and popcorn, then move out of the way of the crowd.

I try to shuffle everything to one hand so I can get my phone out of my pocket but nearly drop everything and give up.

A soft chuckle makes me look up.

"Need some help?" Sophie asks. She and Amanda are standing in front of me. The latter looks... Well, she looks like shit. Her hair is up in a ponytail and her mascara is smudged. But it's more than that. She looks...sad.

"No. I've got it." I readjust. "Thanks."

"Ooh. The bathroom line is finally short." Sophie steps away. "Be right back," she says to Amanda.

"Hi," I say to Amanda when it's just the two of us.

"Hey." Her voice is quiet, and she glances down at the ground like she is in no mood to make small talk. I don't know Amanda super well, but something is obviously wrong.

I go back and forth on whether to ask or leave it, but Claire's still gone, and standing here awkwardly is painful.

"Is everything okay?" I ask.

Amanda looks up.

"Sorry," I add when she doesn't respond. "It's none of my business, but you seem upset."

"Ronnie and I broke up." Her eyes are glassy, and she crosses her arms tightly against her waist.

"I'm so sorry." My stomach bottoms out and a rush of panic washes over me. "When?"

"Tonight. Just before the game. His dad found out we were together."

I'm speechless and processing, but I seem to have given her permission to unload on me, because Amanda keeps talking.

"He isn't allowed to date during the season. His dad is all 'You need to concentrate on your future. Girls are a distraction.' And Ronnie refuses to stand up to him."

"That really sucks," I say.

She blinks and steels herself like she's forcing away the hurt feelings. "Whatever. I don't know why I'm so upset. This is dumb. There are so many other guys out there, right?"

"Right."

There *are* other guys out there. And she won't have any trouble landing one. Probably any she chooses.

But it's my guy I'm worried about. Particularly what will happen when he finds out his ex-girlfriend is single again.

CHAPTER TWENTY-ONE

Rowan

"You were incredible." Austin holds his fist up for me.

"Thanks," I say as a rush of pride fills my chest. We're walking off the field with the biggest win of the season. And better yet, it felt amazing out there today. I was locked in. Two goals and an assist. We beat Brayson.

This past week, I questioned if I was contributing to the team. Maybe Austin's worries were legit, and I was slacking off.

So I tried something different. I studied the game video on my own, I focused on every single practice (no matter how tempted I was to let a certain redhead distract me), and last night after the football game, instead of going out like I might have in the past, I went home and got to bed early.

Maybe none of it made the difference. Maybe all of it did.

After we shake hands with the other team, I turn my attention to the stands. The girls' team traveled with us today. They played just before our game. We're leaving here with two wins for Frost Lake. It was a damn good day.

And because I'm still me, I'm excited to celebrate tonight.

After Coach gives us a rousing pep talk that goes something like 'Good job, but don't get too comfortable because we have a long season ahead of us still,' we all pile back onto the bus.

On the way here, we were instructed that the boys had to sit in the front and girls in the back because apparently we can't be trusted to intermingle. Which means Summer is five rows back. So close and yet so fucking far away.

"Coach C," I say and lean forward over the seat.

"Yes?" he asks, not taking his eyes off his phone. I really wish he were playing Candy Crush or something. Instead, he's checking sports scores. Predictable.

"I have a big test coming up next week."

"Then I suggest you study," he says.

"I'd love to, but you see, my study partner is in the back of the bus."

He's quiet, but his mouth pulls up into a skeptical, slightly annoyed line.

"He wants to sit with his girlfriend," Vaughn calls from the seat across from me.

I shoot him a "What the hell?" glare and then focus back on his dad. "Yes. In this instance my study partner is also—"

"Fine."

I open my mouth, ready to give him more compelling reasons. "Wait. Really?"

"Yes. You all may sit where you like." He finally looks over his shoulder at me. "Don't make me regret it or we'll run all week."

"Yes, sir." I'm out of my seat and heading back to her before he can change his mind. As soon as the guys realize what Coach has allowed, they're moving around too.

It's a big game of musical chairs as we all rearrange for the drive back to Frost Lake.

"Do I want to know how you pulled that off?" Summer asks.

"I have no idea," I tell her truthfully. "He's in a good mood. I'm not questioning it."

I scoot closer to her. She has her AirPods in each ear.

"What are you listening to?"

She takes one out and offers it to me. When I put it in, my grin widens.

"Okay, Lindsey. Taking it old school, huh?" I bop my head to the nineties pop song.

"It's my victory playlist."

"What else you got on there?" I scooch down in the seat and lean over as she places her phone out for me to see. She scrolls slowly, letting me see all the songs on her playlist.

"Very important question," I say after she's shown me all thirty-five songs.

"What?" Her stare drops briefly to my mouth, and she flushes. We haven't kissed all day, though I've thought about it often enough. I'm glad to see she's as obsessed with doing it as I am. I don't think I've ever wanted to make out with someone so much. Don't get me wrong, making out is always fun. But with Summer I can't get enough.

"Do you also have a playlist for when you lose?"

"Of course."

"I figured as much."

"It's called Sad Girl Songs."

"Let's hear them."

She switches to that playlist. Most of the songs are more angry than sad, but it gives me a great visual of her sitting on the bus or at home listening to music and seething about the loss.

By the second song, we've stopped listening. The playlist is still going but the volume is down and we're talking about the game instead.

"MJ had a great game," I say after Summer brags on a particularly crucial save she made today. The girls' goalie stopped everything that came her way.

"She did," Summer says with a smile, and then her expression shifts to something a little less happy. "She's signing a letter of intent with Northern next week."

"No way. That's awesome."

"It is." She tries to fake another big smile, but she isn't nailing it.

"Your time is coming," I assure her.

She shoots me a sheepish smile like she's embarrassed I figured her out so easily. "I know. Or I hope so."

"It is."

"Hopefully I was more convincing when I told her I was happy for her."

"You can be pumped for her and still worried it won't all work out for you." I bump my shoulder against hers. "But it will. You were fantastic today. A total badass. Coach had to tell me to sit down and rest because I was jumping around and yelling so much that he was worried I was going to wear myself out before the game."

She giggles and rolls her eyes like she thinks I'm kidding.

"I'm not joking. You were carrying the offense. Amanda and Sophie both seemed off."

"Amanda wasn't feeling well," she says, glancing away.

"I could tell."

"Have you talked to her?" Summer asks.

"No." I shake my head. Not in days actually. Huh. I smile at Summer. "I've been preoccupied."

"With soccer?" She bats her lashes playfully.

"And kissing my hot girlfriend." I press my mouth to hers. I'm likely going to be the reason that Coach makes us run all week, but I can't help it.

I pull back a lot sooner than I want for the sake of my teammates.

Summer's cheeks are pink. "I don't know what's happening anymore."

"What do you mean?" I take her hand and interlace our fingers.

"This." She uses our joined hands to point between us. "We're kissing and hanging out and..."

"And?"

"Are we still faking it or is this... Are we a thing?"

"I haven't wrapped my brain around the exact label, but I'm not thinking about kissing you because I'm hoping to prove to anyone that you're my girlfriend."

"You're not?"

"Fuck no. I like kissing you. And I think you like kissing me?"

She nods and she stares at my mouth some more.

"Then we'll figure out the rest as we go." A chuckle slips from my lips. "Preferably with your mouth attached to mine."

She glances around. "Everyone can see us."

"True." I hum my disapproval. "What a waste of a bus ride."

Her laughter fills my chest with warmth. We slouch back in the seat together and use my phone to watch a movie. About halfway back to Frost Lake, the bus has gone quiet. There's a group of people playing cards in the back, but mostly people have on headphones and are watching shit on their phones like us.

I sit up to take off my warm-up jacket.

"Can I use that?" Summer asks.

"You're cold?" I ask in disbelief. I'm roasting in here, but then again, I've been pressed against Summer for an hour straight, and my blood is pumping hard as a million fantasies of kissing her and pulling her into my lap fill my head.

She nods.

"Yeah. Knock yourself out." I hand it to her.

Instead of putting it on, she drapes it over the front of her like a blanket, then rests her head against my shoulder. It's nice. All of it. Sitting here with her, watching a movie, holding hands. There aren't a lot of things I don't enjoy doing with her.

She pulls my hand farther into her lap. My pinky finger accidentally brushes against her inner thigh and she jolts at the unexpected contact.

"Sorry." I huff a small, tight laugh as my stomach tightens. Well, fuck, this ride just got a little more torturous.

I manage to concentrate (sort of) on the movie again and not think about where my hand is, but after another few minutes pass, Summer drags my fingers higher.

I still. Every nerve is coiled tight. It's dark on the bus but I can just make out a shy smile.

"Really?" I ask because this would be a bad time to misunderstand her intent.

She nods and my brain explodes. I did not see this coming. At least not today. Not here. Maybe I should have. Our kisses have become more insistent, and last night when

I took her home, we made out in my truck for almost an hour.

The pads of my fingers drag along her center over the slick material of her pants. My movements are slow and deliberate. When her breathing is shallow, I drop her hand but only to slide mine under the waistband of her pants. She sucks in a breath as I push my fingers down until I'm doing the same thing only with nothing between us.

"Rowan," she whispers.

"Do you want me to stop?"

"No. Just...I like you."

I chuckle. "That's good. Otherwise I probably shouldn't have my hand down your pants."

She shushes me with a playful smack and a giggle, but when I start to move my fingers against her again, she quiets.

My heart is hammering in my chest. Summer clings to my side as I make her feel good. Hopefully half as good as she makes me feel every single day.

CHAPTER TWENTY-TWO

Summer

"I might need to transfer to Frost Lake," Charlotte says as we walk into the party.

"Same." Jill nods her head. "It's a hot-guy-palooza in here."

Rowan's laugh is close to my ear. He's walking behind me, arms wrapped around my middle. The position makes us slow as we shuffle together, not breaking apart, but it's so packed in Boone's living room that it doesn't matter.

"Let me introduce you to some of them then," Rowan shouts over the music. "My friends are likely outside."

The four of us make our way through the house and out back. The soccer guys are here, exactly like Rowan predicted. They're off to the side, standing in a circle.

"Oh my gosh." Jill stops walking and turns to face me. "Your teammates are here."

"Yeah?" Surely she realized that was a possibility, given we're at a Frost Lake house party.

"Are they going to kick our asses?" She gives Charlotte a side-eye.

"No. Why would they do that?" I ask.

"We're the enemy, invading their territory hours before we face off tomorrow." Each word is a little more frantic than the last.

I fight a laugh because she sounds a whole lot like me a month ago. "Relax. I told them you were coming and they're cool."

"But maybe don't talk about how you're hoping to kick their asses or anything," Rowan suggests.

"Whose side are you on?" I tip my head back to glare at him.

His response is to brush his lips over mine. I guess that answers that.

On cue, MJ runs up to greet us.

"Finally. We've been waiting for you to get here," she says to me. "These must be the besties."

"Charlotte." I tip my head to one side, then the other. "And Jill."

"I know who you are," she says to them. "I'm MJ."

"We know who you are too," Charlotte says. "Every day at practice I picture your face inside the net, trying to stop me."

Rowan's deep chuckle vibrates through me.

MJ's brows rise. Jill starts coughing. Charlotte's expression turns to one of horror. "I don't mean like I'm trying to kick the ball in your face. I meant you're the goalie I am always trying to beat."

MJ's the first to bust up laughing. The rest of us join her. Everyone except poor Charlotte. She looks horrified.

"It's cool. I get that a lot," MJ says. "Nice to officially meet both of you. Do either of you like to play cornhole?"

"Yeah," Jill says. Then Charlotte adds, "Definitely."

"Awesome."

"I'm going to introduce them to the guys first," Rowan says.

"Okay. Catch you in a bit," she says, and then we're heading toward the circle of Rowan's friends.

They open up to let us join them. Rowan does the introductions. Vaughn, Lacey, Austin, Claire, Hunter, Eddie, and Eli. The last two stare unabashedly at my friends.

"Can I get you something to drink?" Eddie asks.

Eli rolls his eyes at his twin. "They have a game tomorrow."

"There's water and soda and stuff," Eddie insists.

"I'd love a Dr Pepper," Charlotte says.

"My fav," he says, stepping forward and tipping his head to the middle of the yard. "Cooler is this way."

Eli moves toward Jill. "You want something?"

"Yeah, that'd be great."

The four of them take off. Rowan is still wrapped around me. He rests his chin on my shoulder. "Well, that took no time at all. Now I have you all to myself."

"Ditching my friends was the plan?" I ask, twisting in his arms to face him.

"You make it sound so bad when really the plan was just having you all to myself." He smiles. "I like your friends."

"They like you too."

After I picked them up, we went to Rowan's house to get him and ended up hanging out for a bit. Charlotte was in awe of his house and demanded a full tour. I think Rowan was a little embarrassed, but he was a good sport.

"I think Charlotte is planning to move into your theater room," I tell him.

He chuckles. "For sure. Those recliners are comfy."

When the twins reappear with Charlotte and Jill, we're immediately pulled into a game of cornhole. MJ and Charlotte take on me and Jill. Then some of the other guys, including the twins, join in and me and Charlotte team up against Eddie and Rowan while MJ pulls Jill into a circle with some of our other teammates. Eli is stuck to her side.

"I think the twins are in love," I say.

"I'm just glad they stopped ogling you."

"Me?"

"Oh yeah. They were into you big time."

"No they weren't." I shake my head as I think back to my first interactions with them. I don't remember either of them doing anything that would have given me that idea.

"Oh yes. You're the first girl I've ever seen them both interested in."

"Is that supposed to be a compliment?" I ask with a chuckle.

"Hell yes. You're universally hot, Lindsey."

My face heats. "You're not so bad yourself."

His lips quirk up on one side as he brings his mouth to mine. My pulse quickens and my body lights up. I'm a little bit addicted to his kisses. To his touches. To him.

"Your turn," Charlotte yells from the opposite side.

As I pull back, my gaze snags on Amanda. She's standing with Sophie on the outskirts of the circle with MJ and Jill.

I saw Ronnie on our way into the party with some of the football guys. I guess they're really truly broken up. I thought, and maybe hoped, that their breakup last weekend was a temporary thing, but as the days have become a full week, I have to admit that maybe the reason I've not wanted to think about it is because I'm not sure what it means for me and Rowan.

As far as I know, he hasn't heard about the breakup. At least, we haven't talked about it. I know I should have told him as soon as I found out, but I don't want to deal with whatever it means. I like kissing him and hanging out and whatever it is we're doing. It's selfish but true.

I take my turn, spinning all this information through my mind again. Then Rowan takes his turn. After, he nudges me, bringing my attention back to the present. "You said earlier you had something to tell me."

"Oh right." I shake my head. "I got an email back from Kristy."

"She read your college application letter?" Rowan's eyes light up like he's as thrilled by the prospect as me.

"She did and she loved it."

"Of course she did. I knew it."

I roll my eyes. "You could not have known that."

"I did," he insists. "You worked so hard on it. There was no doubt in my mind you weren't going to ace that letter."

His confidence in me is completely unwarranted but sweet anyway.

I lift onto my toes. Charlotte is yelling at me that it's my turn again.

"One second," I call back without tearing my gaze away from Rowan.

He's smirking hard at me as I bring my lips to his. We linger that way, mouths fused together, but neither of us deepening the kiss. He slides his hand to my waist and threads his finger through my belt loop. Goose bumps dot my skin as his thumb glides against my bare skin above the waistband.

"Come home with me tonight."

I pull back far enough to study his expression. "What?"

"My parents are gone, and I keep thinking about the first time we kissed in my bed. Every night it replays over and over in my head. Tonight we could recreate it."

"I'm supposed to be sleeping over at Charlotte's house."

"So sleep over at my place instead."

I consider it for less than a second before I find myself nodding.

"Really?" His grin is big and happy.

"Yes. But I can't stay up all night." The game isn't until noon, but I still need sleep. Going up against all my old teammates is going to be brutal enough without feeling like crap. Still, the idea of being with him, just the two of us all night, is too good to pass up.

"I promise to let you sleep…a little bit." He winks and then bounces in place. "Fuck. Now I just want to drag you out of here. This is going to be so fun."

While he's celebrating, a nagging feeling eats away at my excitement.

"Wait. Before we go though, I need to tell you something."

He's still beaming but he waits for me to continue.

"Amanda and Ronnie broke up."

His smile falters.

"I found out last week at the football game. I should have told you, but…" I summon up whatever courage I can find. "I was afraid you'd want to end things so you could be with her."

"Seriously?" His brows lift.

I nod.

"I don't know how you could think that."

"It was the whole point of us getting together. Make

Amanda jealous so you can win her back and you'd help me fit in and introduce me to Kristy."

"And look at you now. You and your Oakley friends fit right in, and Kristy is helping you with your application." He's right. It did work out well. Better than I could have imagined. At least for me.

"Do you still want to be with her?" I ask.

"No." He says the word slowly like it's a realization he's just now piecing together. His expression smooths out and he smiles at me. "And I already knew about Amanda and Ronnie."

"You did?"

"Yeah, I overheard some people talking about it at school this week."

"When?"

"Does it matter?"

It shouldn't, but yes. If he's known since Monday and he's still hanging out with me, that has to mean something. But if he just found out today, then maybe he hasn't had time to process it.

"Wednesday, I think. Though I should have realized it sooner with how she was playing last weekend."

"And you aren't even a little bit curious to find out if she might want to rekindle things again?"

"This might have started out as a ploy to get Amanda back, but it stopped being about that the second I kissed you. Before that, even."

"I would understand if you were confused or wanted to cool things down until you were sure about us."

"I'm not confused. I appreciate you looking out for me, but I'm good." He gives me that smirk again. "Let's get out of here."

"Now?"

"Yes. Now. I just want to hang out with you."

"What about Charlotte and Jill?"

Shit. Charlotte. I look over to the other side of the game, but she and Eddie have abandoned us. I don't blame them. They're now over with Eli and Jill. The four of them are dancing, along with MJ and a couple of juniors.

"Okay."

"Yeah?" His grin widens.

"Yeah. I don't really feel like being out tonight either." Not when the alternative is kissing him. "Let me talk to Charlotte and Jill."

I weave through the party. As I approach, Charlotte spots me. She throws her arms up and runs to me, hugging me around the neck.

"Sum!" she yells as she rocks us side to side.

"Having fun?" I ask with a laugh.

"So much. You might have to drag me out of here tonight."

"I hope not, but if I do, then it might need to be sooner rather than later."

She tilts her head to study me.

"Will you be terribly disappointed if I ditch our sleepover?"

Now her gaze moves from me to Rowan, or where I presume he's still standing, waiting for me. Slowly, the surprise and excitement registers on her face with a huge smile and wide eyes.

"You're going home with him?"

I bite the corner of my lip to contain my grin.

"Does that mean you two talked?"

"We did."

"And you're a real couple??!!"

I nod and then think back to exactly what we decided. We aren't faking it anymore and we're still hanging out and he invited me over… I think that makes us official.

"Aww. I'm so happy for you. He's hot and sweet and really funny." She laughs like she's remembering something he did earlier, which is likely since he had her and Jill both in stitches.

"Thank you." I motion with my head over her shoulder. "And will you be hooking up with one of the twins tonight?"

"No. Not tonight, but I did give the one in blue my number."

"That's Eddie."

"Right."

Another soft laugh leaves my lips. "Might want to figure out how to tell them apart if you're going to date one of them."

"Wise advice from Miss Relationship."

My stomach swoops and flips. "I love you. Thank you for braving enemy territory to come tonight."

"For you? Anything."

I hug her again.

She pulls back first. "Now go home with your man and text me in the morning or I'll be forced to try to get it out of you on the field tomorrow."

The image makes me laugh. It's going to be bizarre enough tomorrow playing against her, but I can almost picture her trailing me all around the field and peppering me with questions about Rowan.

"Take my car." I give her the key. "Rowan and I are going to catch a ride and then he'll take me to your place in the morning."

She's grinning like a fool at me.

"Are you sure this is okay?" I ask again.

"Positive. Go." She shoos me. "I'm so happy for you."

"Thanks." I'm happy for me too.

Anticipation builds on the Uber ride to Rowan's house. We've been alone before, but tonight feels different.

He knows that Amanda is single, and he still wants to be here with me. I feel light and airy, like I'm floating.

When we pull up outside his house, Rowan thanks the driver, then pulls me out after him. We stand there, watching the taillights disappear down his driveway. My stomach flutters and my pulse races.

Rowan turns to face me. He's still holding one of my hands in his much-larger one. His smile is cocky but sweet.

"I can't believe you're here."

"What, like you don't have girls sleep over all the time," I joke.

"Never," he says, causing another intense fluttering sensation to zip through me.

"Not even Amanda?"

"Nope."

It feels impossible that they could have been together for so long and not had this opportunity. But I'm secretly thrilled to be experiencing things with him that no one else has.

"Well, I've had boy sleepovers plenty of times."

His brows lift. "Yeah?"

I stifle a laugh. "Silas's friends would sometimes stay over. That counts, right?"

His eyes narrow and his glare is playfully annoyed. "Brat. Here I was all jealous."

I don't know how he could be jealous of anyone. Not when the way I feel about him is so far beyond anything I've felt before. It's incomparable in every way.

He tugs me against him. His heat envelops me as his arms circle my waist, and I nuzzle into his chest. His heart beats rapidly in sync with mine.

"Wanna watch a movie?" he asks, still hugging me.

I gasp, smiling even though he can't see my face. "In the big, comfy chairs?"

"Yep. You can even pick what we watch."

Fifteen minutes later, I think Rowan is seriously regretting his last decision. His family owns an impressive number of movies, everything from romantic comedies to horror. I picked *She's the Man*, which was basically an excuse to stare at young Channing Tatum for two hours.

Rowan sits in a lounge chair next to me. Our feet tangle together on my recliner.

"How can you like this movie?" He groans at a particularly cringe scene where Viola, the main character, is pretending to be her brother—fake sideburns, wig, and all.

"It's one of the few movies about soccer and..." I wave my hand toward the screen to Channing.

"The dude is like fifty now." His tone is glum and, dare I say, jealous.

My laughter tinkles out. The giddy sensation that fills my chest is so all-consuming I wonder how I'm going to sleep tonight.

Channing takes his shirt off in the next scene and Rowan groans again, muttering something about old dudes. Giggling, I climb over the arm of our chairs into his lap.

He's still pretending to be grumpy, but the slight incline of his lips gives him away.

"Your abs are better." I slide my hands under his T-shirt and revel in the ridges of muscles.

"You don't have to gas me up. I saw your eyes light up when he came on-screen." He glances down at my mood ring. "And you're purple."

"That's because the movie is about soccer." And because I'm with him.

"You and your love of soccer." His hands find my waist.

I'm straddling him now, knees on either side of his hips.

He pulls me closer, and I fall into his chest. His mouth meets mine. Warmth pools low in my stomach and pleasure hums across my skin.

The anticipation and small touches all night have led to this, and there's no warm-up before we're making out like there's a timer and we're racing to the finish line. His tongue sweeps into my mouth, and one of his hands comes to my neck.

My core tightens as he shifts underneath me. The movement drags my center over his hard length, and I suck in a breath.

"Do you want to go upstairs?" he asks, the invitation clear. Down here we can pretend to watch a movie and make out until we're both flustered and breathless. Upstairs there's only one outcome. And it isn't sleep. At least not yet. I'm too keyed up. I don't want to pretend anymore with Rowan. I want it all.

"I don't have any condoms down here," he adds, solidifying his intentions. "Your call. We can keep watching your old-man boyfriend if you want. I'm happy just having you here."

"Upstairs," I whisper against his lips.

He stands, holding me to him. I wrap my legs around his waist and my arms around his neck, and he carries me out of the theater room, not bothering to turn off the movie. The house is dark, but he makes his way effortlessly back into the main part of the house and then up the stairs to his bedroom.

He drops me on top of his bed, then hovers over me. In the quiet of his room, all I can hear is our breathing and my own heartbeat. I'm not nervous. Not like I was my first time.

"I can't believe you're here," he says, studying my face like he wants to remember it. "Silas Lindsey's sister is in my bed."

I groan. "Please don't mention my brother right now."

He lets out a rough chuckle. "Sorry."

I sit up. He moves back to let me. I pull my shirt over my head and toss it to one side of the bed. His stare drops straight to my boobs.

"Still thinking about Silas?"

"Who?" he asks without lifting his gaze.

I let out a small laugh, but it dies off when his hands come up and cover me. His thumbs glide across my sensitive nipples over the material of my bra. My stomach tightens and a shiver rolls down my spine.

My hands shake a little as I reach behind me to unhook the clasp. The material falls slowly and then my back is against the comforter again and he's kissing me. Our tongues and teeth clash as we press into each other, trying to get impossibly closer.

His shirt comes off next. I toss it toward mine, then drag my hands over his stomach and chest and back down. He groans when my fingers brush against the front of his jeans, so I do it again, this time intentionally.

"Can I?" I ask as I hook one finger in the waistband above the button.

"Yeah." He makes another deep low sound as I undo his jeans and then slip my hand inside and touch him. "Oh, fuck."

His eyes flutter closed, and he tips his head back. His throat works with a swallow as I pump my hand slowly. His jeans are in the way, so I retreat but only so I can push both his jeans and boxers down. He rolls off me to help. We get his clothes off, then the rest of mine.

When we're both naked, we roll onto our sides, facing each other. He grins as he looks at me unabashedly.

"You're stunning."

"So are you."

That smile tilts, and he leans in to press a soft kiss to my lips. "Obviously."

I'm laughing again when he pushes me back, and then he's on top of me. He kisses me while he gets a condom from the nightstand. Then he covers himself and checks in with me again.

"Still okay?"

"Better than okay."

"Yeah. Same."

His touches are sweet and tender. His fingers dip between my legs, stroking me gently before he lines himself up at my entrance.

When he pushes inside, my breath hitches.

"You feel so good." His voice is tight and strained.

My heart is a wild beast trying to escape my chest. He moves slowly, each thrust making my body climb higher to the top of some invisible mountain.

"Rowan," I gasp as a million sensations explode all

at once. I grip onto his shoulder tightly as stars light up behind my eyelids.

"Summer." His reply is followed by a deep guttural sound. His body slumps on mine and then rolls. I place my head against his chest, letting the heavy pound lull me into a sleepy, contentment.

He kisses me again, then gets up to get rid of the condom. He pulls a T-shirt and sweats from his dresser, pulling on the latter and then tossing me the shirt.

It smells like him. Or maybe that's me.

"I'm never giving this back," I tell him as I pull it on.

"As long as you wear it in my bed, it's all yours, Lindsey."

CHAPTER TWENTY-THREE

Rowan

"MORNING," I SAY AS SUMMER'S EYES FLUTTER OPEN. SHE aims a sleepy smile at me.

"What time is it?"

"Seven."

She closes her eyes again and stretches out. "I need to go to Charlotte's house and get all my stuff for the game."

"No. Don't go." I roll on top of her, trapping her in my bed.

She's soft and small underneath me, so I hold some of my bodyweight up. "Okay. Tell Coach I can't make it for me."

I laugh. The idea of Summer missing anything soccer-related is hilarious.

"Great," I say, playing along. "Should we go downstairs and finish the movie?"

"Mmmm. Channing Tatum." Her eyes open and sparkle with trouble.

I nuzzle into the side of her neck with a growl. Her giggles egg me on. I nip at the delicate column of her neck, then lick, then suck. It'd be real easy to get carried away and make her late, but instead I force myself to roll off her.

"Fine. Fine. I suppose I can sacrifice for the good of the team. They need their star player."

She lets her head fall to the side so she can look at me. "I've never been more tempted to be late to a game ever."

I take that for the compliment that it is.

"Give me five minutes, and I'll drive you to Charlotte's house." I get up and pull on clean clothes while Summer puts on hers from last night. Except she keeps my T-shirt on.

I arch a brow. It's hard to look angry when she's so damn sexy.

"I'll give it back," she says, a smile spreading across her face. "Eventually."

"Keep it. Looks better on you." I walk back over to her and pull her into a hug. "Any chance you were also planning to sleep over at Charlotte's house again tonight?"

I could get used to having her here.

She chuckles softly against my chest. "I think eventually my parents would get suspicious."

"Right. One of the cons of having present parents, I suppose." I mean it as a joke, but when I pull back she's looking at me with pity.

"Have you ever told them how much you hate it that they're gone all the time?" she asks.

"I don't hate it," I say immediately, then backtrack. "They have demanding jobs that require a lot of travel. My complaining about it wouldn't change that."

"You don't know if you don't try."

"It's fine. I was only kidding. I mean, you couldn't have stayed over so easily last night if they were here. There are some definite perks."

"You should tell them. Or at least ask them to come to one of your games."

That one does hurt. I won't lie. But less so now that Summer's there cheering me on.

I open my mouth to make another excuse for them when noise outside catches my attention. I glance out the window and then blink several times to make sure I'm not seeing things.

"What are they doing home?" I ask as the shiny red truck comes to a stop in front of the house. My dad must like this vehicle because he's been driving it for more than a month. He usually swaps out as he gets bored.

"Is that your parents?" she asks, voice wavering.

"Yep. Looks like we summoned them."

"Oh my gosh!" Her eyes go big and round and she ducks down out of view.

I fight back laughter, slamming my mouth into a tight line as I stare down at her squatting in front of me.

"This isn't funny," she screeches but her own lips curve into a small smile. "I thought they were gone."

"They were."

"And you didn't know they were coming back this morning?"

"I think we've established that they don't exactly send me an itinerary."

Her expression softens momentarily, but when the front door opens downstairs she goes back into panic mode.

"How am I going to get out of here?" She looks all around the room like she expects a secret passageway to appear. Not going to lie, I've always wanted one of those. Sadly for Summer, the only way out involves heading downstairs.

I consider kissing the anxiety right off her face, but I need to focus.

"Stay here. I'll go down first and text you when it's clear."

"Okay." She nods. "Good idea."

Now I do drop my mouth to hers, lingering for just a moment. "Last night was…"

"Yeah," she says when I can't seem to find the right word. "It was."

My chest is light and every muscle in my body is loose. I like this girl. Really like her. I didn't see this coming, but it's better than I ever pictured.

Summer and I pull apart, and I walk backward to the door. "Avoid the third step. It squeaks."

Then I slip out of my bedroom, shutting the door behind me. As I pad down the stairs, my parents' voices filter out from the kitchen. I totally could have snuck Summer out without them seeing, but now that they hear me coming, it's too late.

"Rowan?" my mom calls. "Is that you?"

I step into the kitchen. Dad is making coffee and Mom is going through the stack of mail on the countertop.

"Who else did you expect?" I ask.

"No one at this hour," my dad quips. "Why are you awake this early?"

"Uhhh…" My tired, Summer-obsessed brain takes a second to come up with a good reason because he's right, normally I wouldn't be. "There's a girls' soccer game at the school in a bit."

"That's nice." My mom smiles. "Are you going to watch Summer?"

"Yeah." I nod. Normally I'd ask about their trip, but I can practically feel the stress rolling off my girl upstairs.

My girl. Whoa. I don't think I've ever thought of anyone like that before, but I don't hate it.

"Anyway. I better get going. I'll see you guys later. Welcome home." I'm one step closer to the door and pulling out my phone to text Summer when my dad calls after me.

"Wait. Before you go, I wanted to talk to you about something."

"Sure." I tap out a message to Summer, telling her to head out to my truck, as I walk back into the kitchen.

When I glance up, both my parents are looking at me.

Unease pricks along my skin before my dad continues.

"I've set up an internship for you at the dealership for after soccer season is over."

"You did what?" I ask, confusion and surprise making my words come out a little harsher than intended.

He gives me that signature dad grin, a little playful and a little patronizing. "It's only a few hours each day after school, so you'll still have plenty of time to hang out with your friends and all that."

"That isn't..." My voice trails off.

"It'll give you some experience to help you better decide which aspect you want to focus on and maybe give you a clearer direction for a major."

There are so many things wrong with this situation that I don't even know where to begin.

"I'm not worried about the hours. I want to work. I was thinking about applying at some places around town after the season ended."

"Great. Then it's settled."

I don't move, but I can't seem to find the words either. Then I hear the third stair creak.

"Can we talk about this later?" I ask.

"Sure, honey." My mom smiles at me. "Wish Summer a good game."

"Yeah, I will." I hurry from the kitchen to the front entryway. Summer is standing about three-quarters of the way down the stairs, frozen in place.

I glance back, but there's no sign of my parents. I grin at her as I open the door, then she sprints past me. Only when we're in the truck does she let out a giant sigh and speak. "Oh my gosh. I thought for sure they were going to catch me."

"I told you about that third stair."

"I forgot." She gives me an adorable pouty face, then covers it with both hands.

I pry them away with my fingers and then lean in and kiss her. She melts into me slightly, but I can tell she's still panicking, so I pull back and start the engine.

"How pissed would you be right now if my truck didn't start?"

Her eyes widen, but as the engine rolls over, she smiles. "So not funny."

I drop her off at Charlotte's house, and then I head to the soccer field. It's early, and we don't have practice today, but I'm not surprised at all when I spot Vaughn out there kicking a ball around.

"What are you doing here?" he asks when I walk out to join him.

"It's a long story."

Historically the girls' games aren't as well attended as the boys' games. We've gone to state several years running, plus we have Coach Collins. All of it has contributed to a loyal fan base that shows up at home games to cheer us on.

But today, Frost Lake has shown up for the girls' game against Oakley. Vaughn went home to shower, but I stick around as the teams are warming up and people are filling the bleachers.

Summer glances around like she's making sure no one is watching and then jogs over to me.

"Guess what?" she asks in an excited whisper.

"What?"

"Coach Endrews, the coach from FLU, is here today."

"Really?" I whip my head around in the direction she now stares. I spot the woman in blue, a tablet in her lap.

"That's awesome." Pride fills my chest. "You're going to be great."

"I hope so. This may be my only shot to show her what I can do."

"You've got this," I assure her.

"Thanks." Her smile widens and a little of her usual confidence resurfaces. "Okay, I better get back out there."

"Wait." I grab her hand before she can run off, then I tug her to me. She falls into me, standing between my legs and resting her hands on my shoulders. "Is it wild that we've only been apart for like four hours and I miss you?"

Her grin is sexy and playful one second, and then she looks past me and sucks in a deep breath, all other emotions replaced with surprise.

"What the fuck, Sum?" a deep voice asks from over my left shoulder.

I don't like the tone or the question. I whip around with a scowl and come face-to-face with the last person I expected.

"Silas?" Summer's voice is tight and questioning.

Her brother sneers, looking from her to me and back.

"What is going on? Why are you all couple-y with this asshole?"

He gives me another side-eye.

"Silas, you know Rowan."

"That doesn't answer my question." His jaw tightens.

She shakes her head. "I'll explain later."

"Explain now," he demands.

"I told you about this weeks ago." She keeps her voice low and quiet.

"Yeah, but you said you were faking it. That you didn't really like him."

I get to my feet and stand beside her. "Let's just all chill for a second. Maybe we should have this conversation after the game."

"Don't tell me what to do. I'm talking to my sister. Not you."

Well, fuck.

"Silas," Summer hisses. She looks around. Then I do the same. We're attracting some attention, and this is so not the time. It's the only reason I don't get in his face. That and he's Summer's brother.

"You said it yourself. This guy is an asshole." He meets my gaze again, sizing me up like he thinks I'm scum. "A world-class prick. A joke." He flicks his attention back to Summer. "He broke my foot for fuck's sake and busted Micky's face."

"I didn't—"

"I'm not fucking talking to you." His voice is louder this time. "I should hit you for dragging my sister into your fake-dating bullshit. All so you can get with some other girl. Who fucking does that? Meanwhile you're messing around with Summer like she's a fucking toy."

“Silas. That’s enough.” Summer shouts over him, then flushes as more people look our way.

I take a step back before I do something I can’t take back, like punch him.

“Lindsey!” Coach Bradley yells. “This isn’t personal time.”

Embarrassment creeps onto her features as she backs onto the field. She nods at her coach and then jogs back to join her teammates.

I look over at her brother in time to watch him step into my space. He’s only a half inch, tops, taller than me but he looms over me with a glare. “Stay the fuck away from my sister, Blakenship.”

He’s gone before I can respond.

CHAPTER TWENTY-FOUR

Summer

SILAS LEFT. MY TEAMMATES ARE LOOKING AT ME THE SAME way they did months ago, like they can't trust me. There's ten minutes left and we're down by one. It's a miracle it isn't more. And it's all my fault. I've made more errors than I have in the rest of the season combined. Not to mention the stunt before the game seems to have shaken everyone. I don't know how much they heard, but the way Amanda won't look at me says they heard the important things.

I dribble into the defense, trying to draw the defenders to me with the intent to pass to Sophie on the right, but I'm picked off by a sophomore from Oakley who is frankly not good enough to be giving me trouble. I growl in frustration. I'm saved only by the girl losing control and kicking a long pass wide and out of bounds.

Coach calls a time-out, and I walk to the sideline filled with embarrassment and shame.

"Rina, sub in for Summer," Coach says, not meeting my gaze.

I open my mouth to protest but think better of it. The

team is probably better off without me today. Even the Oakley girls are giving me pitying looks.

I make the tragic mistake of glancing up at Coach Endrews. She has an unimpressed scowl on her face as she stands and walks down the bleachers. I continue watching her even as she turns and heads for the parking lot, taking my dreams of playing for FLU along with her.

I can't believe it. Everything I want is right here and slipping through my fingers. All because of stupid Silas.

Rowan's still here, but he's not his usual self, cheering loudly and smiling. I'm not sure if he's upset or if I'm just not giving him anything to cheer about. Honestly, probably both.

On the very next possession, Amanda kicks in a rebound to tie up the game. My teammates cheer on the field, hugging one another, then refocusing on defense.

The momentum shifts without me out there screwing things up. Within another minute, we've scored again. Oakley is struggling now that we're playing like we can. Not *we*. *They*. I sit out for the rest of the game.

We shake hands with Oakley. Charlotte and Jill both spend a few seconds longer with me, hugging me and assuring me everything is going to be fine. Then I follow my teammates off the field. Rowan's nowhere to be seen. That might sting worse than anything else that's happened today.

The mood in the locker room is celebratory, but when Amanda is done congratulating everyone else, she walks over to me.

"Is it true?" she asks.

"Amanda, I—"

"It's a simple question. Were you and Rowan faking it to make me jealous or not?"

The conversations die off, and I can feel all eyes on us.

I swallow around the lump in my throat. "Yes."

Immediately there's a quiet, shocked murmur, and I know that whatever trust I'd gained is now lost.

"He wanted you back, and I wanted to fit in with the team."

She scoffs, then laughs and shakes her head. "You will never fit in on this team. No matter what desperate attempts you make. You proved where your loyalty lies today. And it's not with us."

Silas is sitting in the living room watching TV with Dad when I get home.

Dad grabs his cane and gets to his feet. "I think I'll see if your mother needs any help with the laundry."

"Real subtle, Dad," Silas mutters.

Dad squeezes my shoulder as he passes by me.

"I'm so mad at you," I say as I stand in the doorway.

"You're mad at me?" He sits tall. "That's rich, considering you lied to me."

"Oh, get over yourself. I did not."

"You said you were only faking it."

"We were." I throw my hands up in the air in exasperation.

"That didn't look like faking to me. Come on, Sum. I'm not stupid."

"Things changed. Just because you're not around anymore and don't bother to call to check in doesn't make me a liar."

"Uh-uh. You didn't tell me because you knew I'd be pissed."

That's maybe true, but him causing a scene today only proves I was right not to say anything.

"So what? I don't have to run my decision by you."

"Come on, Sum. Rowan Blakenship?" The way he says Rowan's name is full of disdain.

"You don't even know him."

"Sure I do. And even if I didn't, the shit he pulled, using you to win back his ex, is enough to tell me all I need to know."

"He was helping me too! You're twisting it to make him the bad guy because you don't like him. God. Do you have any idea what you did today? You ruined everything."

"I'm sorry, but what did you expect me to do when I show up to surprise my little sister and she's getting handsy with Rowan fucking Blakenship?"

"Did you know that the FLU women's soccer coach was there today?"

I can tell by his expression that he didn't.

"Yeah. Goodbye, dream college. And thanks to you, my teammates hate me again, so it's unlikely that any other college coach is going to bother coming to see me."

"You lied to me," he says in response but with a little less anger in his tone.

"No, I didn't." I take a seat in the chair across from him. "We *were* faking it. We just aren't anymore."

Silas arches a dark brow.

"Don't give me that look. He's different than you think."

"Unlikely," he mutters.

"I don't care what you think," I say, which isn't exactly true. But I'm so mad at him. "Why are you even here? I thought you weren't coming home until the end of the semester."

"Excuse me for visiting." He stands. "Jesus. That asshole is already rubbing off on you. I told you if things went bad, you'd be the one to pay the cost. He fucked you over just like I predicted."

Silas leaves me fuming in the living room. Hot tears sting the back of my eyelids.

Everything is so fucked.

CHAPTER TWENTY-FIVE

Rowan

"I SHOULD TEXT HER AGAIN," I SAY, EYES ONLY HALF-OPEN. I pat my pockets and search the couch around me, but my phone is nowhere to be found.

"Disco, have you seen my phone?" I ask, forcing my eyes open wider. He's blurry, but he's there, shaking his head.

"Vaughn took it."

"What the hell?" I whip my head around to my other side. The motion is too fast for my current state, and my head spins. "Whoa. There are two of you," I say to Vaughn and his scowly twin.

"You're drunk as fuck," he says. "You can have your phone back when you've sobered up."

"I'm not that drunk," I say, tipping back the bottle of Jack. Only I miss my mouth and whiskey trickles down the front of my shirt.

"Give me that." Lacey reaches over from the other side of the Vaughns and takes my alcohol.

"Not cool," I say to her but then rest my head back against the leather.

"Here's water." That's Claire's voice now. Did I know she was here too?

"Thanks," Austin says to her, then he nudges me. "Drink this."

"My mouth doesn't work right now."

"Seems to be working fine," Vaughn replies.

I flip him off as I pry open my eyes again. The room spins. I concede that I may have drinken too much. Drunken. Dranken. Whatever. Too much Jack. Too little time.

"I think it's time to get you home," Vaughn says, using his authoritative captain voice.

"No. My bed smells like her." I went home after the game, stepped inside my room, and walked right back out. I texted her a few drinks in, finally brave enough to hear what she might have to say. She hasn't responded. Or at least she hadn't when the guys took my phone away.

"I'm staying."

"Then you can come to my house," Austin offers. I do like his house. His mom makes the best pancakes.

"Tempting, but I'm not moving until I talk to Summer." I can still see the look on her face when Coach Bradley pulled her from the game. She worked so hard. I know how much soccer and proving herself to that FLU coach meant to her. And I fucked it all up. Bile burns in my stomach.

"She's not here, man. And I don't think she's coming."

"That's why you should let me text her again," I grumble. My head is clearing a little, and through the haze my anger and frustration are back. Not at them. I know my friends are trying to help, but I just need to talk to Summer.

"I will text her," Claire says. "From my phone."

I give her what I hope is a grateful smile and then watch as she taps around on her phone.

"What'd you say?" I ask. "Is she typing back?"

"She literally just hit Send," Austin says.

"Same questions."

"Hey." The soft, feminine voice comes from my right side.

Hope blooms in my chest, and when I look up and find Summer standing in front of me, I have to blink a few times to make sure she's real.

"You came." I aim a dopey smile at her. "I didn't think you would."

She's in jeans and a sweatshirt and her hair is pulled back in a low ponytail.

"You're beautiful."

Vaughn clears his throat beside me. "He's not in the best shape to talk."

"I can see that," she says, walking forward.

I fight to keep my eyes open so I can keep staring at her.

"Let's go...do something else for a minute," Lacey says, standing and then pulling Vaughn to his feet. Claire and Austin follow.

"Maybe don't give him any more alcohol," Claire says over her shoulder.

"Some friend you are," I call after her, mostly teasing.

Summer takes a seat a few feet away on the couch.

"How drunk are you?" she asks, sniffing me and then grimacing.

I let out a small laugh. "Not drunk enough." If I were, I wouldn't still feel so awful.

"Why?"

"I didn't know what else to do, and I couldn't do nothing," I admit. "I'm sorry about the game and your brother."

"You didn't stick around after the game."

"I wasn't sure if you wanted to see me."

Her brows pinch together. "Whatever it is you think I'm feeling, you're wrong. I don't blame you for any of it. Silas is the one who showed up unannounced, made a scene, and said all those awful things."

Her voice quiets. "And I'm the one who made the choices that put me in a position to have my teammates hate me again."

"I'm going to fix it. I'll fix everything. I never should have dragged you into my shit with Amanda."

She lets out a soft chuckle. "I don't think you're doing any of that tonight."

She stands. "Come on. Let me take you home."

I try to get up, but the couch seems to have attached to me. Summer laughs and pulls harder. She manages to get me upright, but then standing is a challenge.

Vaughn appears out of thin air and gets on my other side.

"Where'd you come from?" I ask him.

"Just standing by in case you tried to do something dumb like walk."

"Some Houdini shit there, Cap."

As we're walking out of the party, someone yells, "Go back to Oakley!"

It's followed by snickers.

Summer's face flushes before I've fully processed what's happening.

"Shut the fuck up," Vaughn shoots back at them.

"Want me to kick their asses?" I offer Summer.

"Maybe tomorrow," Vaughn suggests. "I'll make a list for you."

"Good man."

—

When I open my eyes, Summer is lying next to me on my bed.

"Are you really here?" I ask, almost afraid to reach out and realize I'm dreaming.

"Hey." Her voice is soft and husky.

My head is pounding, but I'm pretty sure she's real.

"How did you get here?"

"I brought you home," she says. "You don't remember?"

Do I? I think back, running a hand over my hair. "Fuck."

I glance around my room. I'm fully dressed, but my shoes are off.

"You texted me from Boone's, and when I got there you were pretty gone."

"What time is it?" It's dark out my bedroom window, but I don't know if it's late at night or early in the morning. Or even which day it is. Fuck, I haven't drunk like that in a long time.

"Around two. You've only been asleep a couple hours." Her grin lifts higher on one side. "It was not easy to get you upstairs."

"Damn. I'm sorry."

"Your parents saw you though."

Well, that's going to be an unpleasant conversation tomorrow.

"Are you going to get in trouble for being here?"

"Silas is covering for me."

My brows shoot up in surprise. "Does that mean you two made up?"

I've never had a sibling, so I don't know how that all works, but it seems like a quick turnaround. Especially considering what a dick he was to her.

"No, but I have enough dirt on him that he won't tell Mom and Dad."

"Just show up here and take out my kneecaps?" I joke, but actually...I wouldn't put it past him.

She gives me a sympathetic smile. "I'm sorry about him. And about what I said. It was before I really knew you."

She means the thing she apparently said to Silas at some point—that I was an asshole or a prick, maybe both. And that I'm a joke. It stings she ever thought it, let alone commiserated with her brother about me, but I don't hold it against her. Things have changed since we started this. A lot of things.

"What a fucking day." I run both hands down my face. "My parents show up during our sleepover, then your brother surprises you at your game."

"At least your parents didn't yell at me," she says.

"No, they just tossed an internship in my lap without asking." I grit my teeth at the reminder.

"They did what?" Summer asks.

"They want me to work at the dealership after the soccer season so I can better decide what I want to major in at college." I flash her a "Can you believe them?" look, or I try. My head is still killing me.

"Did you tell them you don't want to work there?"

I shake my head. "You were waiting for me in the truck, but we're going to talk about it later. Not that they'll listen to me."

"You have to try."

My skin pricks with unease at the slightly annoyed tone in her voice.

"I know."

"Do you?"

"Yeah, of course."

"Your parents just want what's best for you, but they can't read your mind."

"Why do you sound pissed right now?" I ask, genuine confusion marring my brow.

"I'm not pissed," she says but she still sounds annoyed, at the very least. "You never say what you want."

"Sure I do."

"No, you don't," she's adamant. "How do you think we got into this mess? You couldn't tell Amanda that you wanted her back, and so we faked an entire relationship. And now your parents are planning out your future, and you can't just speak up and say you don't want it."

I'm stunned speechless. I'll take the blame for Amanda and the fallout there, but she doesn't get what it's like with my parents.

When she speaks again, her voice is softer. "I don't want to be another thing that you fall into because you can't ask for what you really want."

"Where would you get that idea?"

She shrugs. "Would you have ever gone out with me if it weren't for Amanda?"

"That isn't fair. You thought I was an asshole. A joke."

"You're right. Maybe we jumped into this without really getting to know each other."

"That isn't what I said."

"I know." She sighs. "It's late, and it's been a long day."

I nod, thinking we'll sleep and talk later, but Summer stands.

"You're leaving?"

"I need to get home."

"Okay. Can we hang out tomorrow?"

"I have practice, and then my parents want to have dinner before Silas goes back on Sunday."

"Maybe after dinner?"

She frowns, and I can feel her pulling away emotionally from me. "Amanda is single. She knows how you feel. It's what you wanted."

"Wanted. Past tense," I clarify.

She shrugs. "Are you sure you're really over her?"

"Yes," I say immediately. Then it occurs to me that maybe the reason she's so hell-bent on me wanting Amanda has more to do with her feelings and less about mine. "Is this your way of saying you don't want to keep doing this?"

I guess I can't blame her after everything that went down today.

"Do *you*?" she asks.

My mind is spinning, and there's a throb behind my eyes. "You're talking in circles."

"And you can't even answer the question." She throws one hand up and walks toward the door.

I manage to get to my feet, albeit wobbly. "Wait. Fuck. Don't go."

She lets out a long breath and looks at me, some unnamed expression on her face that makes panic course through me.

"We jumped into things so fast," she says. "One second, we were faking it and the next we weren't. I wouldn't blame you if you were confused or if you still wanted to try to fix things with Amanda. I want you to be sure."

I pinch the bridge of my nose. "You want *me* to be sure or *you're* not sure?"

"Both, I guess."

She speaks quietly, but her words hit me like a truck. This day just officially became the worst of my life.

"Then I suppose that's that." My stomach churns with a mixture of anger and hurt. I did not see this coming. Not from Summer.

She hesitates like maybe she's torn about going. "Rowan, I…" Her voice breaks.

"It's fine. No big deal. It isn't like we were a real couple or anything." Every word feels like chewing glass.

"Right." Her hand rests on the doorknob. "I left some Advil and water on the nightstand."

"Thanks." My voice sounds cold and bitter even to my own ears.

"I'll see you around," she says, and then she's gone.

CHAPTER TWENTY-SIX

Summer

Dad looks up from the kitchen table as I enter the room. He eyes my outfit and bag. He's probably also noting the dark circles under my eyes and red, puffy skin from crying.

"Practice?" he asks.

"Yeah. I figure I should show up even if they don't want me on the team anymore." I glance at the biscuits on the table. They look and smell delicious, but my stomach is too upset to consider food.

"Pretty rough day yesterday," he comments.

I snort. "That's putting it mildly."

I don't know how much Silas has told him or what he and Mom have pieced together. Everyone gave me a wide berth after the conversation with Silas, and then I left to find Rowan.

Another wave of nausea hits me as I picture Rowan's face last night. He looked as upset as I feel, but I don't know if that was about me or if he just realized he wants Amanda back and didn't want to hurt me.

I think back to all the times I thought he was telling me he cared about me, but he never actually said that. He never said much of anything, and his actions can't exactly be trusted, considering we were putting on a show for everyone else a good portion of the time. It would have been so easy to sweep everything under the rug and fall back into the ease of whatever it is we were doing. I like him. I like him so much, and being with him is fun and feels right. But I don't want to be another person in his life dragging him along into something that he doesn't want to do. I want him to choose me on his own.

"They think I threw the game on purpose for my friends at Oakley," I tell my dad, focusing on soccer and not the destruction of my fake relationship.

"Did you?"

I shoot him a look of surprise. "Of course not."

He shrugs. "I didn't think so."

My temper levels out as I realize he's not accusing me, just trying to understand what happened. "I would never do that. Even if the FLU coach hadn't been there. I wanted to win as badly as they did."

I hate that I let it all get to me. That I cracked under the pressure. I want to blame Silas for all of it, but he isn't the one who couldn't keep it together on the field.

"Keep your chin up. They'll get over it," he assures me.

"I don't know if they will."

"And if they don't, then what?"

I consider that. "I'm still going to do everything I can to play my best, and if I don't get a college scholarship, I'll try to walk onto the team at whatever school I end up."

I can work to pay for school and take out loans. None of its ideal, but I can do it.

"That's what you'll do then," he says as if it were just that simple. Maybe it is. "Sometimes it takes a rough patch to figure out what it is you really want. If there were only easy days, we'd all be a lot less grateful and a lot more prone to living in the moment."

God, all this feeling sorry for myself and I know he's had to deal with so much more. I walk over to him and wrap my arms around his shoulders. He chuckles at my unexpected display of affection.

"I'm sorry."

"For what?"

"Being so selfish when your problems are a lot bigger than mine."

"You're seventeen. Your problems are supposed to be small but feel big." He rests his hand on top of mine and pats me gently. "Besides, I've been feeling pretty good for an old man."

"You aren't old, but I'm glad." I breathe in the smell of him. His cologne and the hint of flour from baking this morning. "I love you."

"I love you too, shortcake," he says as I pull back. He looks me in the eye, smiling but serious. "Now go show those girls you aren't going to run away just because things are tough."

When I walk out onto the field for practice, everyone stops talking and glares at me. No one says anything to me, but I feel their stares. Suddenly it's the first day all over again, and I'm the enemy. Except back then all I wanted was to be at Oakley with my friends and my teammates. I could never have imagined wanting to be here as much as I do now.

I swallow back my nerves and start warming up like it's any other day. I stretch, then grab a ball and dribble down the field. I take a shot from the right wing, pouring all my frustration into the kick. The ball slams into the back of the goal with a whoosh of the net.

"Surprised you showed your face after that stunt yesterday." Amanda stops next to me.

"I didn't pull a stunt. I had a shitty day and a bad game."

"Convenient," she says under her breath.

"Seriously? You think I would throw away my chance at playing at FLU so my old teammates could win? Do you even hear yourself?"

The irritation on her face flickers but she squares her jaw and lifts her chin.

"I want to be here, and I want to win just as badly as you do. We can either spend the rest of the season fighting about it or we can play together. But I'm not going anywhere." My voice is more confident than I feel.

"Play together?" She scoffs. "After you tricked me into thinking you and Rowan were a couple and tried to manipulate my feelings?"

"That isn't... I didn't..." Maybe it wasn't my intent, but I did lie to her and everyone else. "I'm sorry about Rowan. He wanted you back, and I wanted you to accept me. It wasn't supposed to turn out like it did." I swallow the lump in my throat. "This is my senior year. You think I wanted to switch schools and come to Frost Lake when you made it so abundantly clear you didn't want me here? You didn't leave me a lot of options."

"It still doesn't make what you did right."

"No, it doesn't. I can't take that back." Would I if I could? The thought of not having spent those nights with

Rowan, fake or not, is hard to imagine. I'd feel a lot less heartbroken right now, that's for sure.

"I should have known Rowan would never be into you," she says, teeth gritted.

The insult slices like a knife, exactly like she intended.

"All right, ladies. Time to warm up," Coach Bradley calls from the sideline. "Five laps around the field."

There's a collective groan. Amanda and I continue to face off even as the rest of our teammates start running.

"You're right. He only wanted you back. He still does," I say to her, throat thick with emotion.

Her gaze narrows like she's trying to decide what else to yell at me.

"Lindsey! Jones!" Coach calls us out. "You too."

Amanda takes off first, jogging to the back of the group. I leave several feet between us as I start, but she's on a mission today and quickly gets to the front. I don't have it in me to race her or anyone else today.

My legs feel like lead, and my chest is tight. I have spent a lot of hours on the soccer field. It's seen me through fights with friends, bad grades, tough games, and other heartbreaks. I've always been able to shake it away when I was out here. But none of them felt quite like this.

MJ falls back on the final lap. "You look like crap."

A surprised chuckle slips from my lips. She cocks a smile at me.

"Oh, it feels good to laugh," I say, surprised at the warmth that fights to spread through me. I keep thinking of my dad and how he always pushes through. I want to be as brave as him.

MJ and I continue jogging, side by side, around the field. As we pass two freshmen, they glower at me.

"Are you sure you should be seen with me?" I ask MJ. The last thing I want is for her to get iced out.

"Don't mind the rest of the team. They'll get over it."

"Does that mean you already have?"

"You had a shitty game, and you did a shitty thing." She shrugs one shoulder. "We all have."

"Even you?"

"Are you kidding? Every single time a team beats us, it's my fault. That kind of pressure can eat away at you if you let it."

Which is exactly what I let happen yesterday. The idea of going through that with every loss makes my entire body ache. "Oh god. Being a goalie must suck."

She laughs. "Nah, I love it. And you do too. Don't let one bad game get you down. We're having a great season, in large part thanks to you. Brush it off. We've got this."

She holds out her fist to me and I bump mine against it.

"We've got this," I say, and I hope by the end of the day I feel the words more than I do now.

CHAPTER TWENTY-SEVEN

Rowan

SUNDAY AFTERNOON, I FIND MYSELF OUTSIDE SUMMER'S house. I sit in my truck one house down, staring at the tree I once climbed to get to her.

I woke up with the world's worst hangover, but I don't think that's why I feel so awful. With one last deep breath, I get out of my vehicle. The sun is bright and mocking, and halfway to the front steps I have serious regrets about what I'm doing here.

I raise my hand to the door, hesitate, then knock. While I wait, I step back. Maybe no one is home, and I can turn right back around and go home.

The door swings open. *Well, fuck.*

"What are you doing here?" Silas asks, staring at me like he hopes lasers shoot out of his eyeballs. "Summer isn't here. Not that she'd want to see you."

"I'm not here to talk to her."

His brows lift. "I don't have anything to say to you either."

"I didn't expect you to, but regardless I wanted to say

I'm sorry." My palms sweat and I think I'm oozing Jack Daniel's out of my pores.

"You're sorry?" He repeats the words with enough skepticism to have me doubting myself for thinking this was a good idea.

"Two years ago. I wasn't trying to hurt you, but you broke your foot and that sucked. I'm sorry."

"I don't need or want your apology so if that's all..." He crosses his arms over his chest. He's broader than he was last season, and if he throws a punch I'm probably going to have to let him hit me. The only way I can think to make this situation worse is by hitting Summer's brother. She might be pissed at him in the current moment and want nothing to do with me, but I know how much he means to her.

"The shit talking on the field was mutual. You gave as good as you got. I think we're even."

"Yeah, except the part where you fucked around with my sister." He steps forward.

"I never meant to hurt her."

"Lot of good that does. Do you have any idea how hard she's worked to play college ball? And then you come in and get her involved in your bullshit and ruin everything."

"You are not putting yesterday on me. You're the one who made a scene."

"How the fuck did you expect me to react when I show up and you're all over my sister?"

"To be honest, I didn't care."

His gaze narrows on me, and he clamps his mouth shut. A muscle in his cheek flutters like he's grinding down on his molars.

"I didn't come here to pick a fight with you," I redirect before I cause more harm than good. "I care about Summer.

I'm sorry that pisses you off, and I'm sorry that it played any role at all in her missing an opportunity to show the coach at FLU what she's capable of. That's the last thing I wanted."

"I told her to stay away from you." He shakes his head. "She should have listened."

"Yeah, well, we ended things, so you don't need to worry about that anymore."

"Then why are you here?" He quirks one brow.

"To tell you that she didn't lie to you. We *were* faking it, and then...things changed. She never meant to hurt you. She looks up to you. Fuck knows why." I mutter the last part.

He works that tight jaw back and forth.

"Be mad at me. Hate me. But don't hold it against Summer. You two were tight before I came into the picture. Whatever happened shouldn't come between you."

I told her once that when things were over, she and Silas could sit around and commiserate about how much they hated me. Maybe I wasn't so far off from reality.

"That it?" he asks.

"Yeah."

"Wish I could say it was nice chatting with you." Silas unfolds his arms and steps back. "See you never, Blakenship."

The second Summer walks into the lunchroom on Monday, I can feel it. My gut twists, and I bounce my leg under the table.

Austin must feel the tension radiating off me. He glances at me, then follows my line of sight. "Have you talked to her since Saturday night?"

"No." I shake my head, not taking my eyes off her. She

looks good today. Jeans, white T-shirt, hair down. She tucks a strand behind one ear, and I catch the glint of her mood ring under the lights. I wonder what color it is today.

I was late this morning and missed first period. I sat in the parking lot for an hour, picturing her face when I walked in. Best-case scenario, it was going to be awkward as fuck. Worst case was a toss-up between her giving me the cold shoulder or avoiding me all together.

"You were pretty fucked up," he says.

"I wish I still was." I look down at my tray and push it away. I'm not hungry.

"You should try to talk to her again," Claire suggests. "Now that you're sober and things have had time to settle."

"There isn't anything to talk about. She doesn't want to be with me."

"Are you sure?" Lacey asks from across the table.

I dip my head in a small nod.

"Have you tried groveling?" This from Vaughn. "I hear a protein bar is the way to a girl's heart."

"It worked for me." Lacey beams.

I smile, but I don't have it in me to laugh. Last year when Vaughn was trying to win over Lacey, I suggested he get her a gift. I did not mean a protein bar, but it worked out, so what the hell do I know?

"I don't think that's going to do the trick in my situation," I say. "Besides, we're both better off. Relationships are dumb. They're messy and complicated. It's way easier to just hang out and keep things casual."

The table is silent and all four of them are staring at me. Claire, Austin, Vaughn, Lacey.

"Ahem." Lacey's brows rise.

"What, like you don't know it?"

None of them looks like they're going to admit all the trouble it caused them, so I shake my head.

"When Disco first moved to Frost Lake and fell for Claire, Vaughn literally punched him." Vaughn and Claire had been a thing before that, and it caused a whole lot of drama. Then I look at Lacey. "And you and Vaughn spent months trying to decide if you hated each other or wanted to rip your clothes off."

"That is not how that went down," Vaughn says.

"Close enough. My point is, think of all the pain you caused each other. And for what? High school relationships are fucked. What are the odds that either of you will make it after graduation?"

"Rowan." The way Claire says my name, voice full of hurt and shock, gives me pause but they know I'm right.

"He's upset. He doesn't mean it," Austin assures her.

"No, I do. Enjoy it while things are good, boys, but don't be too surprised when it blows up in your face." I stand and grab my tray.

"Don't be an asshole. Sit down," Vaughn says.

"No. I..." I squeeze my eyes shut. I'm being a dick, and I know it, but I can't sit here another second. "I'll see you guys later."

I dump my trash and put my tray away. As I'm leaving the lunchroom, my gaze snags on Summer. She's sitting at the end of the soccer table. MJ is across from her, but everyone else is putting a good four feet of distance between them. My gut twists.

Some junior football player walks over. He glances over his shoulder at his buddies before asking, loud enough that the whole lunchroom can hear, "Yo, Summer. Wanna fake date me?"

I head toward her before I've decided to intervene.

She's responding, but I can't hear her, and there's a red haze blurring the edges of my vision. I still see it when the guy looks up and sees me coming though. His eyes widen.

"Fuck off," I say to him.

He chuckles. "You can't blame me for trying."

Someone else yells out, "I'll fake fuck you."

I want to find the jerk and smash his face in with a lunch tray. Instead, I focus on the kid in front of me.

"I can and I do." I motion with my head for him to get lost. His smirk stays in place, but he goes.

I finally turn to Summer. "Are you okay?"

"I'm fine." She stands with her tray. "You didn't need to do that."

"It's my fault they're giving you shit."

"I can handle myself," she says, then brushes past me.

CHAPTER TWENTY-EIGHT

Summer

On Friday, the team travels to Pacific. MJ is still the only one talking to me. It's been a long week, but Coach has me back in the starting lineup today, and I'm determined to push everything else aside and play well.

As we pull up to Pacific High School, Coach stands at the front of the bus.

"We're a few minutes behind schedule so change quickly and get out on the field for warm-ups. Pacific is big and aggressive. I expect them to come out hard on defense from the start. They'll want to rattle you and see if they can't take advantage of the fact we lost the last game. Do not let them break your focus or shake your confidence. We're still the team to beat this season."

The bus comes to a stop. The mood has shifted. A few of the girls are bobbing their heads along, others are standing eagerly. I feel the same anticipation, but I linger and wait for everyone else to get off the bus first before I move.

"Are you ready?" Coach asks me as I pass by.

I let out a long breath. "Definitely."

"Good. We're going to need you."

I don't think the team would agree with her, but I nod anyway.

In the locker room, I change and then walk over to Amanda.

She glances up as she zips her warm-up jacket over her jersey. When she sees me approaching, she lifts both brows in challenge.

"I'm sorry." I doubt she's going to let me say much, so I don't wait for acknowledgment before I continue. "I shouldn't have gotten involved in your relationship with Rowan. It was none of my business."

There's a flash of something in her expression—surprise maybe.

"I love soccer and being a part of this team. I may not have chosen it, but the longer I've been here, the more it's felt right. Like maybe there's a reason all this happened to bring us together for one magical season. We're good. Really good. I wouldn't have thrown that away for anything. Not even my friends back in Oakley. In fact, they'd be just as pissed at me if I pulled something like that. I let the team down last weekend. I know that. I have to live with it. But I didn't do it on purpose. I *want* to win, and I want to win with this team."

I force myself to stop talking and wait for a response that doesn't come. Amanda's face softens, then hardens again before she brushes past me.

As Coach predicted, Pacific pressures us from the jump. They have mostly seniors, and what they lack in talent, they make up for in hustle. They've been close to the playoffs the past two years, and they're desperate to make it this season.

I'm locked in. Focused. Ready.

Two defenders run at Amanda, trying to trap her on the sideline. I yell to let her know I'm open, but she attempts a pass to Sophie on the other side instead. It's picked off and I bolt down the field to get back on defense.

It goes that way for most of the first half. With only a few seconds left, Pacific scores. MJ's expression is pure fire.

"Fuck," she mutters under her breath as I jog up to her.

"You got this. Embrace the pressure, right?"

Her mouth pulls into a tight line. "Right."

I offer her my fist, and she bumps hers hard against mine. I laugh off the bite of pain from her knuckles and we head off the field for halftime.

Coach's pep talk sounds a whole lot like the one before the game. Keep our heads up, take our time, don't let them take us out of our game.

I'm winded and my legs are tired. For as little as I touched the ball in the first half, I feel like I ran a marathon. Judging by the look on my teammates' faces and the slow way we walk onto the field to start the second half, we're all feeling it.

Our only saving grace is that the other team is tired too.

There's a lot of back-and-forth as we find our rhythm. I'm trying to stay patient, but the only time I touch the ball is when I strip it from the other team. I'm hesitant to pass even when I see Amanda ahead of me. I take a chance, pass, then cut. I'm wide open and I know she sees me, but she dribbles farther into the defenders and eventually loses it.

"I was open!" I yell at her, running behind her back to the other side of the field.

"I didn't see you."

My anger gets the best of me. "Bullshit."

MJ makes a save and I sigh with relief. Still, I glare at Amanda. The only way we're going to win today is playing together as a team. She knows it too. She's just too stubborn to admit it.

On the next play, Sophie gets off a long shot that goes high, just out of reach of Pacific's goalie. Amanda and the rest of the team crowd around and congratulate her. I hang back slightly.

"Nice shot," I say to her.

"Thanks." She looks toward me but not directly at me.

For the next thirty-five minutes, neither team scores. Coach subs us in and out to keep everyone fresh, but it's only sort of working. We're tired, and Pacific is doing just enough to stop us from scoring again.

Amanda dribbles down the field, passes to Sophie, then the ball moves to Rina. Rina looks to me, hesitates, then passes. That second of indecision costs her, and the Pacific defender intercepts. I'm already anticipating it and manage to clip a tiny piece of the ball. It's just enough to get it away from her. I head toward the goal. All the defenders have shifted toward me, so I send it back to Amanda. She's open and has a clean look. She takes the shot. It goes just wide. Frustration bleeds out of her. I turn to head back, but as I do, movement catches my eye and I look just in time to see one of the girls on the other team elbow Amanda in the face. It's deliberate and has my teammate keeling over immediately. The Pacific defender sprints down the field like nothing happened.

The referees are watching the action at the other end and don't see it. I race toward Amanda. Her hands are up covering her mouth, and her eyes are wide with panic.

"Are you okay?" I ask.

She lets her hands drop just enough that I can see the blood pouring down her chin.

"Oh my god." I look over at Coach and wave to her.

By this time, other people have noticed, including the referees. Amanda heads slowly to the sideline, dripping red as she goes. I stay by her until Coach jogs over. Then I look for the girl who elbowed her. She's standing at the centerline, hands on her hips.

I walk straight for her. There's a hint of a smirk on her face until I get close.

"You did that on purpose." I shout.

"It was an accident," the girl claims.

I'm seething. I start to take another step forward, but Sophie appears in front of me.

"Don't do it. It isn't worth it," she says, putting her tall, lanky body between me and the other team. She walks forward, forcing me back.

I know she's right, but I still think shoving that Pacific girl will make me feel better.

Time-out is called, and Sophie and I head to our bench to check on Amanda. She has a rag to her mouth, but it's already soaked through.

"I'm fine," she says as we all look in on her.

"She needs a stitch, but she'll be okay," Coach Bradley says.

The referees confer, and whether they actually saw it or not, they seem to decide it was intentional. The Pacific crowd is pissed, but it feels like a small vindication for Amanda.

"Okay. We still have a game to win," Coach Bradley says. "Who's going to take the penalty kick for Amanda?"

There are murmurs and everyone looks to one another.

"Summer should do it," Amanda says. The words come out a bit jumbled from her injured mouth, and I stare at her like maybe I didn't hear her correctly.

Then everyone looks to me.

"You want it?" Coach asks.

I'm nodding even before she finishes asking the question.

"She favors her left side," MJ tells me as she lowers her forehead to mine.

"Got it," I say.

My heart is hammering in my chest but as I walk out onto the field, a calm resolve spreads through me. I get in position and wait for the referee. He blows the whistle and hand signals for me to take my shot.

My stare flicks up to the Pacific goalie. She shifts her weight from side to side as she watches me. Inhaling, I run forward and kick the ball hard to the right of the goalie and pray MJ is right.

Everything slows down as the ball soars toward the net. The goalie lunges, hands outstretched, but she's a second too late. The ball flies past her. I stare, a little stunned, until the cheers of my teammates break through my haze.

"You did it!" Rina is the first one to hug me. Others pile on until I can't tell who is who. We move in a big huddle toward the sideline.

Coach wears a pleased smile as my teammates scatter around me. "Nice job, Summer."

"Thanks, Coach."

As soon as the game is over, Amanda's parents take her to get stitched up. The bus ride back to Frost Lake is loud and happy. MJ and Rina ask me to play cards, but I just want to sit back and soak it all in. I don't know if the camaraderie will continue, but for tonight, I feel like part of the team.

When we arrive back at school, I help the managers take the gear to the locker room. The rest of the team is already gone by the time we're done.

Coach's office door is open and the light is on. She looks up as I appear in the doorway.

"You're still here," she notes.

"Heading out now." I point to the locker room doors.

"Do you have a minute?"

"Sure." I step fully into her office. She sits behind her desk and motions for me to take the chair in front.

"I know I lost my temper out there today. I shouldn't have confronted the Pacific player."

"No, probably not. If the referees had seen you, it would have cost us the penalty kick."

I swallow down my shame at the thought.

"But that isn't what I wanted to talk to you about." She smiles, a small curl of her lips. "Coach Endrews from FLU called this week."

My stomach flips and twists. "I can't imagine she had a lot of good things to say after the game last weekend."

"It wasn't a good showcase of your talent, but luckily for you, she understands that young players like you are still working things out. She wanted me to pass on her contact information."

"Seriously?" My entire body lights up, and I sit forward.

Her smile curves higher. "Mm-hmm."

"I don't know what to say. Thank you."

"Don't thank me. You did it. You're a great player, Summer. One of the best I've had the pleasure of coaching."

"I..." I can't even think straight. "Thank you."

"You're welcome." She stands. "Now get out of here and enjoy what's left of your weekend."

"I will. You too, Coach."

As I stumble back into the locker room, I'm in a haze. Coach Endrews wants to talk to me. It's so surreal.

The slam of a metal locker makes me look up. Amanda turns, bag on her shoulder, then slows when she sees me.

"You're back already," I say, focusing on her mouth. Her jaw and bottom lip are swollen, but otherwise she looks okay. She has an ice pack in one hand.

"Two stitches. We were in and out." She grimaces and puts the ice to her face. "Why are you still here?"

"I was helping with the equipment." I hitch my thumb over my shoulder. Then we stand there awkwardly. I don't feel any animosity from her, but we aren't friends, so neither of us seems to know what to say.

"You looked like you were going to punch that Pacific girl," she says finally.

"I might have if it weren't for Sophie." Tonight could have ended a lot differently if she hadn't intervened, but I'm not sure I would have been sorry.

Amanda drops the ice to her side again. "Thank you."

"I didn't do anything," I say, confused.

"You had my back even though I haven't had yours."

"Oh." That. "Believe it or not, I haven't been secretly wishing you'd get knocked in the face."

She laughs, then winces.

"Sorry." I eye her swollen lower lip. "Does it hurt?"

"Like a bitch." She lets out another small chuckle, then we fall quiet.

I'm about to make my excuse to leave when she surprises me by saying, "I was jealous."

I open my mouth to speak, but only a small squeak comes out.

"Of you and Rowan," she clarifies. "He was different with you. The guy I always wanted him to be, you know?"

I don't but nod slowly.

"But also, I was jealous of you."

"Me?"

"Yeah." The look on her face tells me she hates admitting it. "This was finally my year to lead the team. Then you showed up, and everyone was looking at you that first day with so much awe like you were the answer to us finally having a winning season. I didn't want to hold it against you, but I think I did."

I'm dumbstruck.

"And they were right," she says. "I'm sorry that I let it get in the way of the team."

"I don't know what to say."

"You don't have to say anything. We don't have to be, like, besties or anything; I just wanted you to know we're good."

The idea of me and Amanda being best friends is almost weirder than this conversation.

"Are you going to Boone's house tonight?" she asks, shifting toward the door.

"Oh, uh…"

"The whole team will be there. You should come. We wouldn't have won without you."

"I might need you to repeat that about a dozen times," I joke. I can't quite believe she's being so nice to me.

"You've got it. So I'll see you there?" She takes another step toward the door.

"No. I…" My words trail off.

Amanda nods her head like she understands. I'm sure she knows exactly why I'm resisting. The team might have stopped hating me for the moment, but the rest of the school hasn't forgotten yet. I can't take another night of guys teasing me or watching Rowan have fun and party with his friends like nothing happened.

Even thinking about him has my chest squeezing. School was torture this week. I don't know how to be his friend or exist in a world where we aren't a couple—even a fake one.

"If you change your mind, I owe you a drink." She smiles and then heads out of the locker room.

CHAPTER TWENTY-NINE

Rowan

"HEADING OUT?" MY DAD ASKS AS I COME DOWNSTAIRS.

"Yeah." I'm surprised to see him. "I thought you and Mom were heading to..." I let my voice trail off. They told me where they were going, but I've already forgotten. Somewhere else for some important business something or other.

"Green Bay. And the meeting got pushed a week." He's kicked back on the couch in the living room with his bare feet on the ottoman in front of him. It's such a rare sight to see him relaxed and chilling that I almost sit down and abandon my plans for the night.

"Cool. Well, I guess I'll see you tomorrow then."

"Yeah." He has his laptop resting across his thighs and the remote poised in one hand. "Since I'll be in town this week, why don't you come by the dealership one night after school, and I can show you around and introduce you to some people. It's been awhile since you've been there."

That isn't an accident. I used to love going there, true,

but not in a long time. The thing I used to enjoy about it—being near my parents—became just one more place where they ignored me for work.

"Uh, yeah, sure thing."

His smile lifts higher. "You're going to love it."

Every muscle in my body tenses as I turn to leave. How is it possible he knows so little about me that he can truly believe that? I know how. Because I'm a fucking coward.

I pause at the edge of the living room, squeeze my eyes shut, and then spin around.

"Actually, Dad. No."

I open my eyes in time to see his forehead crease as his brows lift.

Before he can ask, I say, "I don't want to work at the dealership."

His smile returns, and he nods his understanding. "It's only a few hours a week. You have to start somewhere. Graduation is just around the corner."

"It isn't about the work. I'd be happy to get a job after the season is over, but I don't want to work at the dealership."

He mutes the TV like the quiet will help him better make sense of what I'm saying. "I don't understand. You've been talking about working there since you were a kid."

"No, *you've* been talking about it. I gave up that dream a long, long time ago. About the time I realized that it was pathetic to want to work with your parents just so they might want to see you."

I hate that I've admitted it as soon as the words are out, but it's too late to take them back. My body is coiled tight with frustration of holding things in for too long. "You and

Mom built this empire, so I get why you want it to stay in the family, but it isn't what I want."

"But..." He seems to grapple with my words, brows furrowing and mouth pulling into a tight line.

"The only reason I ever wanted to work there was so I could spend time with you. I don't have any interest in business or finance."

"You're young. You might change your mind."

"You aren't listening to me." I pull at my hair with both hands. "You never listen. I'm telling you how I feel, and you aren't listening. I don't want to go to FLU. I don't want to study business, and I'm *never* going to work at the dealership. Ever. I might not have it all figured out, but I know what I don't want."

His voice softens. "I had no idea you felt this way."

"How could you? You're never here. And when you are, you're working. You have no idea who I am or how I feel because you don't know me at all."

"That's not true."

"What position do I play?"

He stares at me.

"In soccer. What position? Fuck, what jersey number do I wear?"

I huff a laugh when he can't answer either. Hurt and confusion are splashed across his features, but I'm too pissed to care. I leave him gawking at me as I storm out of the house.

I don't take a full breath until I'm in my truck. I let my head fall back, and I grip the steering wheel hard with both hands.

Well, shit.

I go to the party anyway. I wasn't really feeling it before the blowup with my dad, and now I'm really not, but I don't want to sit at my house either.

It isn't a big crowd tonight. The football team had an away game and the hockey team is on some weekend bonding retreat. The girls' soccer team played in Pacific earlier too.

I try not to look around for a familiar head of red, curly hair, but I scan the party anyway. Disappointment sits heavy on my chest when I don't spot any of the girls from the team. Or more specifically, Summer. I highly doubt she'll come tonight, and I'm not sure what difference it would make anyway.

Staring at her across the party is probably not healthy. Fuck, I miss her though.

I make a circle around, saying *hey* to some of my teammates before finding a quiet spot inside on the couch. It's me and a couple cuddled up on a love seat across the room. They probably want to be alone. But so do I, so I guess we're both not getting what we want.

Leaning to one side, I pull my flask out of my front pocket. I unscrew the top and take a drink.

"Hey." Vaughn takes a seat next to me.

I stare at him a moment, sure I've hallucinated him.

"Where's Lacey?"

"She and Claire were going to the movies tonight. Thought I'd stop by and hang for a bit."

"I'm fine. You don't need to babysit me." It's the only explanation for his presence here without Lacey. Vaughn hates parties.

"Good, because I wasn't planning on it." He nods his head toward the flask in my hand. "Can I have a drink?"

I arch a brow in question but offer it to him.

He brings it to his lips and takes a sip, hesitates, then drinks a little more. "Is that root beer?"

"Alcohol didn't help last weekend, so I'm trying something new." I take my flask back and chug more of the soda. It isn't helping either, but at least I won't wake up feeling any worse than I do now.

Vaughn's quiet chuckle cuts through the faint music from outside.

"Look, I know you're hurting, and I'm sorry if I haven't been there for you this week," he says.

He has a look of genuine regret on his face that only makes me feel worse.

"No, I'm sorry. I was a dick to you." And many others. I see an apology tour in my future.

"You don't need to apologize. I get it." He settles back into his chair beside me and kicks one leg out. "When Lacey and I were figuring things out, I was a mess."

"It isn't just this thing with Summer." Though that is the worst of it. "Everything is fucked. I don't know who the hell I am or what the fuck I'm doing anymore."

"What do you mean?"

"All of it. College. Career. Life. You have the next five years all planned out. Soccer. Lacey. Dreams and goals." As I speak, irritation at my own indecisiveness makes me fidgety. "And same with Austin. You guys know what you want. And I can't even picture next week, let alone an entire future."

"You aren't like us," Vaughn starts.

"Yeah, no shit." A gruff, deep-sounding laugh works its way from my chest to my lips.

"It isn't a bad thing."

"No? Because you two have both been side-eyeing me all season like you think my lack of concentration is going to cost us the playoffs."

"Fuck the playoffs."

Those are three words I never thought I'd hear come out of Vaughn's mouth.

"Yes, we want to win state, but the reason we give you so much shit is because we see how talented you are."

"I'm nowhere as good as you and Austin."

"That's where you're wrong. The only difference between us is we know what we want and we channel all our focus to it."

"I doubt that very much."

"Seriously. Do you know how hard we work?"

I do actually. Really fucking hard. And to me it never seemed worth it. It was like my parents, channeling everything into work and neglecting other areas. I always chose balance over perfection.

"You don't, and you still outperform us some days. It's fucking annoying." His lips pull up on one side.

Not often, but I think I get his point.

"You want to nomad around the country? Take over your parents' businesses? Be the best soccer player ever? Whatever you decide, you will succeed. I believe that. So does Austin. So why don't you?"

I shift in my chair. Now I really wish I had booze. I didn't know this conversation was going to turn into a therapy session.

"Because there were no expectations for me. Ever. I see how your dad pushes you, but my parents never cared about school or soccer or anything else I did." I shrug. "So why do it?"

"Because *you* want it. Whatever it is." He pauses, runs his palms down his thighs. "As long as I have known you, you've been the guy who lives in the moment. Things happen and you adapt and acclimate immediately."

"Yeah, I know. I can't live in the moment forever. Graduation is coming and then what?"

"No, that's not…" He shakes his head. "You think it's a bad thing, but it isn't. You're looking at the situation from the wrong angle."

"How do you mean?"

"The way you see the world is a skill, not a detriment. On the field when everything we've practiced goes to shit and everyone else is stressing about how to adjust, seeing you there acting calm and steady is what we all need. You don't know how rare that is. The only time I've ever seen you rattled is when you're protecting guys. I can't tell you how many times I wished I could adapt as easily as you do. Austin too. We'll never have that because we work too hard to perfect the things we can control. It's a trade-off. And *that's* why we give you so much shit. We're jealous, man. Nothing can take you out of your game when you're in it. You don't let anything get you down, and there's no way to rattle you. At least until Summer."

I bite down on my back molars, suddenly wishing I had gone ahead with Jack instead of root beer.

"Hey, I'm here." Austin's breathless as he comes to a stop in front of us. "Who's ready to party?"

I do the only thing I can think of and laugh. They really are the best friends a guy could ask for even if they are terrible at subtlety. "You two are so obvious."

Austin looks from me to Vaughn. I lean forward and hold out my flask to him. "Chug the rest of this."

He takes it from me and shakes it a little as if weighing how much liquor is in it.

He hesitates, because yeah…that would be a lot of booze to chug.

"You said you want to party," I remind him.

He pales but then brings the flask to his mouth. Slowly he tips it back and drinks and drinks and then…lets it drop and looks at me, confusion etched into his features.

"What the fuck is this?" he asks.

Vaughn and I share a laugh.

"You're good friends," I tell them. "Thanks for showing up."

Austin takes a seat on the other side of me. "Fuck. I thought I was getting carried out of here tonight."

He lets out another sigh of relief.

"Are Claire and Lacey really at the movies?" I ask.

"Yes, but we were tracking you down tonight either way," Austin says.

"We figured a week of sulking and drinking yourself stupid was long enough," Vaughn adds.

"I'm sorry," I say to Austin, since I already apologized to Vaughn. "I said a lot of shit I didn't mean."

Austin holds up both hands. "We're good, man. I get it. It's been a tough week."

"I don't think high school relationships are bullshit. Or at least not yours." I look from him to Vaughn. "Now…can we talk about something else?"

"Sure," Vaughn says.

Austin nods.

We sit in silence for several long seconds. Time ticks by and no one says anything.

"Okay, but can I just ask one thing about Summer?" Austin asks.

I groan.

Vaughn shoots him a wide-eyed "We had a plan" sort of glare.

"One thing."

"Were you really with her just to make Amanda jealous?"

"Of course he wasn't," Vaughn answers for me. "You saw them together."

"My sister says I have a tendency to ignore everything else when Claire is around, so it's possible I wasn't paying close enough attention," Austin says, giving me a sheepish look.

"Your sister is correct, but in this case, I don't think we can blame Claire or the love bubble the two of you live in."

"Love bubble." Vaughn snorts.

"Oh, please, don't get me started on you and Lacey." I shake my head. It feels good to joke around and give them shit.

They laugh softly and then let me take my time, figuring out how to answer Austin's question. But before I do, Amanda steps into the living room.

My heart leaps, and I look behind her for a flash of red, curly hair. Stupid. I don't know why she'd be with Amanda anyway, but if Amanda's here, then that means the girls' soccer team has made it back from their game.

Amanda approaches slowly, like she expects I might yell or tell her to fuck off.

"Can I talk to you for a minute?" she asks.

"Sure." I dip my chin, feeling Vaughn and Austin staring at me.

The two of them get to their feet.

"We'll be outside," Vaughn says before they leave me with Amanda and the couple who is now making out. Ah, making out. I've missed that this week too. Kissing Summer was fun. I can almost feel her giggling as she lay next to me or smell her shampoo.

Amanda takes a seat next to me, and I blink to stop the barrage of memories.

"How are you?" she asks. Now that she's closer, I can see that something is off with her. Her jaw is swollen and she's holding her mouth funny.

"I'm fine. What happened to you?"

"Your girlfriend let me have it."

"She did what?" My brows shoot up.

Amanda laughs quietly, still holding her mouth awkwardly so the sound comes out stilted. "I'm kidding. Some chick on the other team elbowed me during the game. You should have seen your face though."

"Fuck." I chuckle softly but the more I think about Summer, the harder it is to breathe.

"We're good, actually. Me and Summer. Or..." She glances up at the ceiling as she considers her words. "We will be, I think. She won the game for us today."

A shot of pride zips through me, followed by sadness that I'm not hearing it from her.

"I'm glad you two worked things out. If you're going to be pissed at someone, then I'm your guy. I shouldn't have dragged her into my bullshit." Summer didn't deserve any of this. None of it was her fault. Not being forced to switch schools or fake dating me.

"I'm not mad."

I bob my head.

"Confused, but not mad."

"That makes two of us." I chuckle softly.

"So... you're *fine*?" she asks in a way that suggests otherwise. "Really?"

"I've had better weeks."

Her lips pull into a knowing smile that morphs into one of understanding.

"I should have already said it, but I'm sorry. It was a dumb plan, and I shouldn't have tried to manipulate your feelings like that."

"Thanks for saying that."

One more apology down.

"I was jealous and hurt. Not that it's an excuse. We've always fallen back to each other. I think I started to expect it'd always be that way. When it seemed like that wasn't going to happen, I felt like it had to be my fault. And I think I wanted to prove that I could be the guy good enough to be in a relationship and not whatever casual bullshit we had going on."

"Me too. I think everyone thought that. All summer, every time I wasn't with Ronnie, people would ask me where you were." Her smile is a little wider now, like she's adjusted to the injury and it doesn't hurt as much. "I should probably apologize too."

"For what?"

There's a moment of hesitation before she says, "I knew you were jealous. I liked it even."

That is not what I expected. I wonder if it changes anything, then decide it doesn't. Everything is still fucked.

"She thinks you still want me back."

I know exactly who she means even though she doesn't say Summer's name.

"Yeah. She told me."

"Do you?" Amanda asks.

I don't want to hurt her more than I have, but I shake my head. "No. I don't think so."

All week I could have talked to Amanda if I wanted or made some sort of plan to get her back now that she and Ronnie are over, but the truth is that I barely thought about her.

"Good."

"I guess that tells me how you feel." A short puff of laughter leaves my lips.

"Do you remember what we were like together?" Amanda asks, brows arching together.

"Vaguely." I think back. We weren't the perfect couple, but we had some good times together.

"When we were hanging out, you were always so chill about things. I knew you liked me, but I never felt like you really wanted to be with me. I can't explain it. It was like I wasn't quite good enough to be more than a hookup. It almost felt like I was convenient."

My stomach drops. That's an awful way to make someone feel. "I am so sorry. I wish you had said something. I did like you. A lot."

Though admittedly maybe not as much as I thought I did. I liked her more than I'd ever liked anyone before, but that isn't true anymore.

She shakes her head. "I didn't say anything because I was afraid. You seemed to like that I wasn't into having a serious, traditional relationship like everyone else, and I didn't want to lose you. So instead, I hit on other guys and did things to try to make you jealous." Her face flushes with embarrassment.

"Fuck, that's..." I rub the back of my neck, wishing I could go back in time and kick my own ass. "I'm really sorry."

"I think deep down I knew you didn't feel the same way about me as I did about you, so I sabotaged things and secretly hoped it would force you to see how great I am." She lifts one shoulder and plays it off like it's no big deal, but I can see the hurt on her face. "Then I met Ronnie. At first, I thought he was going to be another detour before you and I got back together and then...I really started to fall for him."

"For the record, you are great."

"I know." She gives me a coy smile. "You are too, just maybe not great at seeing when a girl is super into you but too nervous to speak up."

"I guess not."

I'm going to have to filter through everything that's ever happened between us with this new information, but I can already see it's true. The flirting with other guys in front of me. Her and Ronnie. All of it.

"What are you going to do about Summer?" Amanda asks while I'm still reeling.

"Nothing. She doesn't want anything to do with me."

"Are you sure about that?"

I open my mouth to say yes, then reconsider. Maybe I don't know shit about anything.

"I don't know how you really feel about her, but I know that if I had spoken up a year ago, things might have been very different."

"In other words?" I need her to spell it out for me because I don't trust my own judgment anymore.

"If you want to be with Summer, and I think you do,

try telling her that." She laughs like it's so obvious it's silly. Maybe it is, but there's one problem.

"I already did."

"No."

"What do you mean, *no*? I was there. You weren't." I think back to last weekend in my bedroom.

"I don't need to have been there to know you left some room for doubt, because if you hadn't, then she wouldn't believe you still want me back."

After Amanda leaves me, I stumble outside to find Austin and Vaughn.

"Hey. Everything okay?" Austin asks.

"Yeah," I say slowly.

Vaughn's brows lift.

"Sorry. The world just tilted on its axis. Everything I thought I knew was wrong."

"Are you sure that's root beer?" Austin asks, staring at me like he thinks I took a dozen shots in the past fifteen minutes.

"He's not drunk," Vaughn says, eyeing me carefully.

"He isn't making any sense either," Austin grumbles. "This isn't the 'I'm getting back with Amanda' face, is it?"

"No, we're done."

"Thank fuck," Vaughn says. "Nothing against Amanda, but you two were a disaster."

"Yeah, so I've heard." I shake my head and then a laugh bubbles up in my chest.

My friends look rightly confused at my sudden change in emotion.

"I need your help," I say.

“Anything,” Vaughn says and Austin nods.

“Sleepover at the Kellers’ house?” I ask hopefully. “Pancakes for breakfast?”

“Sure.”

“Great. And between now and then, you two can tell me all about your relationships.”

That gets an eyebrow lift from Vaughn.

“I figure I should learn from the best,” I say, grinning. “Then you can help me figure out how to tell Summer I want her back.”

CHAPTER THIRTY

Summer

"WHAT DID SHE SAY?" MJ ASKS, EYES WIDE AS SHE LEANS across the lunch table.

"Don't leave anything out. I want to memorize her exact words so I can manifest her recruiting me next year," Rina says with the same eager expression from beside her.

I let out a small laugh before repeating my call with Coach Endrews yesterday as closely as I can remember. "She said that she was impressed with my quick transitions and the improvements I've made on offense this year. And then she asked if I'd be interested in visiting FLU this fall."

After that I think she went into details about touring the facilities, all the things I'd see and people I could meet, but I sort of blacked out from excitement.

"I'm so excited for you. And for us." Rina grins, looking at Amanda and Sophie. They're sitting on her other side. The four of them crowded around me as soon as I sat down. Apparently the news traveled fast after I told MJ this morning.

"Us?" Sophie asks.

"Summer can put in a good word for her old teammates," Rina clarifies for her.

The girls at the table laugh. Everyone except Amanda, who is still nursing a swollen lip. It looks better, but she has to miss practice until Wednesday.

"It's really cool," she says. "And you'll be close. We can come watch."

"And you can introduce us to college guys," Sophie adds.

They all nod at that. A giddy, hopeful feeling has taken root in my stomach, but when I look up and see Rowan entering the cafeteria, it's overtaken by the crushing sadness I can't seem to shake.

It's been more than a week. I should be over him. Things with the team are better. Coach Endrews wants me to visit FLU. Silas even started sending me funny videos again, which I'm pretty sure means he forgives me.

Everything is right in the world except one tiny thing. My heart is still broken.

He walks into the cafeteria with his friends. He glances over at our table, but as soon as he catches me staring at him, I look away. I've mostly managed to avoid him. In first period, I switched seats to be in the front, and in our academic prep hour I have been laser-focused on homework and appearing busy so he hopefully won't notice how I flinch every time he talks. I miss him. I miss him so freaking much. I have no idea how he worked his way under my skin so deep in such a short time.

I know I need to move on, but it's hard when everything reminds me of him. Even my bedroom at home. I keep staring at the window, thinking he might appear on the other side to hang out. Last night, my parents suggested we go to Momma Vi's for pizza to celebrate the FLU interest, and I nearly burst into tears.

So yeah, everything is great except one thing that's making all the rest a little dimmer. That's the thing about Rowan. He makes everything better and brighter somehow.

The girls have moved on to talking about our next game. Thursday is our first conference playoff match. There's a lot of excitement about the possibility of making it to regionals for the first time.

I force myself to enjoy it and soak up these moments with my teammates. Regardless of the outcome of the season, it's almost over, and I'm going to miss playing with them.

"I hope we get another shot at Pacific," Sophie says.

"Me too." MJ nods her agreement. "I need redemption. I cannot believe I let that sophomore score on me."

"Hey." Rina elbows her.

"You've been playing varsity since freshman year, so you don't count," Sophie says to her.

Rina's smile stretched wide and proud.

I catch Rowan in my line of sight again. It's like I have freaking radar for the guy. Every time he moves, my body is intensely aware of it.

I try not to track him, but when he gets closer and it's apparent he's walking toward me, I finally glance up again.

He stops at the edge of the table behind my teammates. They must feel his presence or notice me gawking because the four of them turn.

"Hey, Rowan," MJ says. The other girls stare at him a little more warily.

"Hey," he says back to her, but he's looking at me.

My face warms, and I seem to have forgotten how to

breathe. I'm taking too long to respond, but the way he's staring at me has temporarily broken my brain. I wasn't sure if he'd ever speak to me again or look at me like he didn't hate me. Last week when he stopped that jerk from teasing me about fake dating, Rowan still looked so upset. But today he's more his usual self. It should hurt to see him happy again, but there's something irresistible about him like this. Cheery and playful and smiling. Specifically, smiling at me.

He finally looks away from me, takes a step toward the table beside ours. A couple of juniors are sitting on the far side.

"Do you mind if I…" His words trail off as he points to the table.

They shrug and move down, giving up their spot for him.

"Thanks."

I watch, confused. Even more so when he steps on top of it.

"What is he doing?" Rina asks in a voice that sounds concerned.

Everyone is looking at me like I have the answers. I look to Amanda.

"Beats me," she says, but there's a smile on her face that makes me feel like she knows more than she's saying.

"Excuse me, everyone," Rowan says, voice loud enough that it carries through the lunchroom.

The noise all around quiets and then stops.

"Sorry to interrupt, but I wanted to clear a few things up," he says.

My stomach dips and my pulse quickens in warning. I have a very bad feeling about this.

"As most of you heard, Summer Lindsey and I were fake dating."

There's a murmur of soft conversations, and now I'm the center of attention. I duck my head but only after shooting him a glare that I hope communicates exactly what I'm thinking: *What the hell are you doing?*

People were just starting to move on. No one has asked me to fake date or fake fuck in at least seventy-two hours.

"It's true," Rowan says. "It was my idea. Not hers."

"This isn't necessary," I hiss toward him. "Get down!"

For some reason that makes his smile lift higher.

"We had rules. No kissing. No falling for each other. She'd help me and I'd help her and then we'd go our separate ways. Unfortunately, I screwed it all up. I broke the rules. I fell for her."

All the air leaves my lungs in a *whoosh*.

"And then when I had the chance to make it right, I didn't say the things I should have to make sure she knew how I felt. So..." He turns to face me. He has that playful, cocky smirk on his face and his blue eyes are full of trouble. "Summer Lindsey, I like you. Getting you to fake date me was the smartest thing I've ever done. You have made my life so much better since you came into it. You're funny and talented, hardworking, smart, and so damn beautiful. I never a stood a chance of not falling for you."

My face is on fire but my heart...my heart is tripping over itself to get to him.

He jumps down off the table and stands next to me. "What do you say? Will you be my real girlfriend?"

He reaches into his pocket and pulls out an origami rose. As I get to my feet, the cafeteria explodes with cheers and catcalls. Someone yells out, "I'll date you if she won't," and I glare in that direction.

Rowan chuckles and closes the gap between us.

"No need to be jealous, Lindsey. I'm all yours. If you'll have me."

The only reason I hesitate is because it feels unreal. I must be dreaming. Then I decide if I am, I better enjoy it.

"Yes. I want that. I want you." I launch myself at him. He's ready for me. His arms circle my waist, and he picks me up and spins me around.

"Thank fuck," he says in a rush of air like maybe he was worried I'd say no. Silly boy.

"I was afraid it was all in my head," I admit. "That everything I thought you wanted was only me projecting my feelings."

When he sets me down, he holds on to me and stares down into my eyes.

"I'm sorry I didn't make it clear how much I like you. I stopped wanting anyone else a long time ago. I thought you knew. I thought…I thought there was no way you couldn't feel how absolutely obsessed I am with you."

Now I'm the one smirking. "Obsessed, huh?"

"It's kind of a problem. My friends are starting to get tired of listening to me yap about you."

I glance over at Vaughn and Austin. They're at their usual table with their girlfriends. All four of them are grinning so big like they knew exactly what he had planned.

He holds out the paper flower to me and I take it and hold it to my nose like it's real. The rest of the cafeteria has gone back to their lunch now that the show's over.

"Now what?" I ask him.

He moves to stand beside me and hooks his fingers through the belt loop on my jeans. "Now we get to be one of those really annoyingly happy, cute couples."

CHAPTER THIRTY-ONE

Rowan

"It's nice to meet you. I heard you got an offer from Northern with MJ." Coach Collins smiles at Summer.

She gapes back at him, pupils blown wide and completely speechless.

I bite back a laugh.

"She did, but she's holding out for FLU," I tell him, pulling Summer out of the doorway.

Vaughn and Lacey are in the living room. Austin and Claire too.

"Congratulations," Lacey says to Summer as we take a seat between the two couples.

"Thanks." She finally manages to speak, glancing over at Coach.

"I'm heading out for a bit." He grabs his keys off the kitchen counter.

"Hot date?" I ask.

Summer elbows me.

Coach gives me a dry, apathetic stare. "Dinner with the athletic director."

"No judgment, Coach. She doesn't look a day over sixty-five."

He shakes his head as he leaves for the garage. I can't help messing with him. Especially now that the season is coming to an end. I'm going to miss him next year.

"Oh my gosh. I can't believe I just met Jude Collins." Summer stares ahead, unblinking.

"Well, sort of. He met you, and you just gawked at him."

She elbows me and then laughs a little self-deprecatingly. "I couldn't help it. He's such a legend. Wow. I've seen him at school and on the field, but he actually talked to *me*." She fans herself. "This is the best day of my life."

Summer looks to Vaughn. "I'm so sorry if I'm being weird."

"Oh no, I'm used to it." He waves a hand.

"Ahem," I say and then actually clear my throat as I watch my girlfriend go completely mind-blown over my coach.

She aims a guilty smile at me. "It's only a soccer crush. Those are allowed, right?"

"Hell yeah. I have a soccer crush on him too."

"Me too," Austin says, grinning.

"Me too," Lacey adds.

Vaughn turns slowly, brows lifted, to stare at his girlfriend.

"What?" She shrugs. "It's like looking at future you. And I like you."

She leans forward and brushes her lips over Vaughn's, and all is forgiven.

The six of us order pizza and watch a movie. Regionals start this week. October is always a busy month, but this year I've been pulling double duty attending as many of Summer's games as I can manage with my own schedule.

The conversation turns to our first game against Brayson. We're ready and heading into the playoffs undefeated. It's been our mission this season to prove we're the best team in the state, and now it's time to prove it.

"Maybe we should rewatch their game against Springfield earlier this season," I say.

"Yeah." Austin nods.

Vaughn looks around the room.

"I'd love to watch," Summer says.

Claire and Lacey share a look, then shrug.

"Fine," Lacey says. "But I'm making popcorn."

She gets up and goes to the kitchen, opening cupboards with a comfort that shows how often she hangs out here.

"I'll grab my dad's laptop from his office," Vaughn says.

Austin juts his chin toward Summer. "You should see the office. It's like a museum."

Her eyes light up. "Seriously?"

"Oh yeah. Game balls, trophies, jerseys, everything you can imagine," Austin says.

Summer gasps. "Can I see it?"

"I've lost her," I say, fighting a grin.

Vaughn snorts. "Yeah, come on."

He leads a very excited Summer to his dad's office.

"What do you think the odds are that I can get her out of here later?" I ask Austin.

"Trust me, if it were an option to live in Coach's office, I would have already moved in."

When Summer finally returns, she's got a wide-eyed, dreamy look on her face.

"As good as you imagined?" I ask, draping an arm around her shoulders.

“Even better somehow.” She nuzzles into my side. “I’m going to have a room like that one day.”

“Hell yeah, you are.”

We make it through about half the Brayson/Springfield game before we lose focus.

“I should get home,” Summer says. “I have an anatomy quiz tomorrow.”

“Need a study partner?” I ask hopefully. I’m not ready to say good night to her yet.

“Yes, but you have to come through the front door. My mom threatened to put a lock on my window.”

I chuckle. Oops. I guess I wasn’t as sneaky last night as I thought.

I officially met the parents last week, and they don’t hate me. I’m not sure if they like me yet, either, but I’m sure I’ll win them over eventually. By not climbing through their daughter’s window, for starters.

“Let’s do it.” I stand and pull her to her feet. “Later, boys. Lacey. Claire.”

“Bye,” they say in unison.

At Summer’s house, I say hello to her dad, and then we head up to her room.

“Are your parents back in town?” she asks as she grabs her laptop and study notes.

“Not as of this morning.”

She gives me a sympathetic smile as she takes a seat next to me on the bed. Then she takes my hand and squeezes. “I’m sorry.”

“It’s fine.” We’ve barely talked since I told my dad I

wasn't going to work at the dealership. My mom cornered me one morning and had the same questions my dad did, but ultimately it ended the same way. With them frustrated and me angry.

"You did the right thing telling them the truth," Summer says. "Maybe they just need time to adjust their vision for your future."

"Or they've written me off because I'm not doing what they want."

Summer looks at me like she wants to fix all of it for me. I love her for that. I wish it were that easy. Regardless of how things have shifted, I'm glad I told them. I still don't know what's next for me, but for the first time ever, I feel like I have options.

Instead of dealing with any of that tonight, though, I want to enjoy this time with my supersmart and sexy girlfriend. It turns out, I'm a relationship guy. Who would have thought? Not me. But I think I might even be good at it. I'm enjoying it, that's for sure.

I pull out my phone and hold it in front of us. She laughs. I have so many pictures of us, I had to buy more storage.

I snap the pic, then look at it.

"Aww. We're cute."

"You always say that." She glances at it. "That is a good one. Send it to me. I want to post it."

My finger hovers over the share button.

She rolls her eyes, reading my hesitation. "Silas knows we're together."

"Yeah, but the less he sees my face, the less likely he is to think about punching me."

She presses her palms against my cheeks on either side,

framing my face. "I promise I won't let him get your face. It's too pretty."

I huff a laugh, then lean forward and lick her nose. She giggles and I dive in closer, burying my face in the crook of her neck.

"I need to study," she says as we fall into a heap, limbs intertwined and me partially on top of her.

"Five minutes," I murmur, placing a chaste kiss on her collarbone and then working my way up her neck.

She sighs.

"Ten tops," I amend, and she laughs.

CHAPTER THIRTY-TWO

Rowan

When the final seconds tick off the clock, the crowd erupts. I run to the centerline, colliding with my teammates in a giant huddle. Sweat-soaked, dirty, exhausted, and so happy it can't be contained.

We jump up and down, yelling and cheering.

"We did it! We're state champs!" Austin shouts. His expression is pure awe, like he can't believe it even as he says it.

"Hell yeah, we did it!" Vaughn pumps both fists into the air.

I sling my arms over their shoulders, and we let out another round of whoops into the night.

After we shake hands with the opposing team, we head to the sideline where we douse Coach C with the leftover water and ice from the cooler. He's a good sport about it. And it's too late for him to make us run.

Fans are making their way onto the field. I stand on my toes, looking for Summer. She's here somewhere, wearing my name on her back and my number painted on her face.

I could hear her yelling for me too. I might miss that more than anything else about soccer. I hope I do a lot of things in the future that make her proud.

I accept congratulations and pats on the back from familiar faces as I weave around families and groups looking for my girl.

I come up short when I spot two people I did not expect. My parents.

"What are you doing here?" I gawk at them. They're really here. Correction: They're here and they have buttons with my face on them pinned to their jackets.

"We came to watch you play," my mom says, like *Duh, why else would be here?* except I can't remember the last time that was true. To be honest, I wasn't even sure if they knew I was playing tonight. Things have been awkward and tense.

"I thought you were in Phoenix." At least that's what the latest note said: "Gone to Phoenix, back next week."

"We changed our plans to be here," Dad says. "I know it doesn't make up for all the ones we missed, but we didn't want to lose another opportunity to watch you play."

"We met your coach, too." Mom smiles.

"Coach C?" I whip my head around to the last place I saw him, but he's lost to the crowd.

"Before the game." She nods. "He told us how proud he was of you and what a pleasure it's been to be your coach."

"We're proud of you too," Dad adds. "I should have said it a long time ago."

"I don't know what to say."

My dad steps forward and hugs me. "You were incredible out there. I'm so sorry we didn't see you play sooner. I had no idea just how good you've become."

Mom is next. She's teary and doesn't get out any words, but I feel her pride and sorrow.

"Thanks." I'm still a little stunned that they're here. And while it doesn't make up for missing all the other games, it means something to me that they're here now.

Before I can fully let it all sink in, Summer runs up to me. She's a blur of blue as she jumps into my arms.

"Congratulations!" Her hair whips me in the face. "You won! You're the best team in the entire state!"

"I had to get a big trophy like my sexy girlfriend's."

She grins all big and happy like she's done all week anytime anyone's mentioned the girls' epic playoff run. They lost in the sectional finals, but it was a hell of a season. The best in Frost Lake girls' soccer history. Thanks in large part to Summer. Since then, she's had a bunch of colleges reach out, and she got her official early acceptance letter from FLU. She's still considering her options, but I have no doubt that's where she'll end up. Her future's looking bright, and for once I can see mine. Or at least a part of it. I'll be cheering her on from wherever I am.

When she pulls back, she finally glances at the other two people standing with me.

"Oh." She does a double take. "Mr. and Mrs. Blakenship. Hi!"

"Hi, Summer. Good to see you," my dad says to her. My mom waves, still looking as if she might cry.

"We're going to let you celebrate with your friends, but dinner tomorrow?" Dad asks.

"Yeah, I'd like that."

"I hope you'll join us," he says to Summer.

She nods and then hooks her arm through mine, and we watch as my parents disappear into the crowd.

"Did you know they were coming?" she asks.

"No. I had no idea." I shake my head. "Coach C called them."

"Wow."

"Yeah." I turn to face her, resting my hands on her hips. "Wow."

What a fucking night. Month. Year.

"Very important question," she says as she lifts her arms up and curls them around my neck. She has a sassy, seductive glint to her eye that I like. I like it very much. "How would you like to celebrate?"

"Easy. Me, you, Freddie's Pizza, and Channing Tatum."

Her body lifts and falls with her laughter. "Seriously?"

"I still haven't seen the end of the movie." I step closer and drop my mouth to hers. And something tells me I won't tonight either.

After most of the families and fans have left, Summer and I walk off the field hand in hand. I finally see Coach Collins by the bench, cleaning up trash from the celebration.

"Congrats, Coach," I say to him.

"You as well." He stares out at the field. "It was a good night."

"A very good night," I agree.

"Sure you want to give all this up?" he asks, glancing over at me with a sly smile. "A friend of mine at Valley University called me about you this week. I know you haven't made up your mind about next year, but it's worth considering. They're building a great program there."

"Seriously?"

"He thinks you'd be a great addition. Then again, he

doesn't know you like I do." The playful wink he gives me tells me he's kidding. "Think about it."

"Yeah, I will." To my surprise, I don't hate the idea. It'd be nice to get out of Michigan for a few years, and I can't imagine never playing soccer again. I might not be quite ready to say goodbye.

He nods and continues cleaning up.

When I glance at Summer, she's smiling so big at me.

"Rowan, that's amazing! Are you seriously considering it?"

"Maybe? It'd be a long way from you, but we could text and visit on weekends."

"It is pretty far, but there's a direct flight out of Green Bay, and sometimes it's pretty cheap."

It's like she's already figured it all out, and then it clicks. "Wait. Isn't that where your brother goes to school?"

Summer busts out laughing as she nods.

"Well, this should be interesting."

EPILOGUE

Rowan

"Finally." Summer plops down on my bed with a tired sigh. She stretches out her legs and arms like a starfish. "I'm never leaving."

"Oh, no. Don't get comfortable. I promised your brother I wouldn't keep you locked in my room all weekend."

"You did not run that plan by me." She sits up, grinning at me and somehow looking more beautiful than she did when I saw her a month ago. She glances toward the open door of my bedroom and then fights a smile. "Is that why the door is open?"

"Noooo," I say, not all that convincingly.

I live in an off-campus house with Silas and two other soccer players, Rodrigo, a sophomore striker who is obsessed with Dolly Parton (seriously, he blasts her music nonstop), and Dom, a junior defender who speaks four languages but rarely speaks at all. I'm pretty sure Silas only lets me live here to keep an eye on me—or he's planning to murder me in my sleep.

But despite the fear of my girlfriend's brother, I love this place. This house. This school. The Arizona sunshine. Every day I walk outside and look up at the clear, blue sky, barely a cloud in sight. It's gorgeous. Almost as gorgeous as the woman smiling at me.

"Don't tell me you're still scared of him," she says.

"I'm not *scared* of him. I have a healthy fear of my girlfriend's brother, who frequently threatens to kick my ass." I think he's kidding. I hope.

She lets out a soft chuckle. "What time does he get back from class?"

"He's done at three, so..." I check the time on my watch. "Soon."

Summer stands slowly. That curly red hair is down and falls over her shoulders as she walks toward me. It's been a long three weeks since she was here last. She came with my parents to drop me off at college but had to go right back to Frost Lake to get herself settled. Since then, we've both been busy with classes and soccer and getting used to campus life. We text and video chat constantly, but I've missed her so damn much.

When she reaches me, Summer places her arms over my shoulders and laces her fingers behind my neck. Goose bumps dance across my skin.

"Then you better hurry up and kiss me again."

My lips hitch up at the corners as I lean in. "Yes, ma'am."

I slant my mouth over hers and don't waste any time before deepening the kiss. Electricity hums under my skin and my stomach dips low. No matter how many times we do this, it never stops feeling this way—all-consuming, exciting, and somehow comforting too.

"I love you," I murmur, not wanting to break the kiss any longer than necessary to get out the words.

"I love you too," she says, breathless as she tightens her grip around my neck.

"I know. Your ring has been purple since you got here."

"Maybe I was thinking about soccer."

I lean down and scoop her legs up. She squeals as she wraps herself around me. I walk her back to my bed and then carefully drop her onto the comforter. I've barely let my weight drop on top of her when someone clears their throat loudly behind us.

I freeze, body clenching tight, and look down at Summer. "Oh shit," I whisper.

"Seriously, Blakenship?" Silas sighs heavily.

Summer peers around me. "Hey, Silas."

She reaches up to peck her lips against mine, then rolls from under me. I sit on the edge of the bed as she races across my room to hug her brother.

Silas glares at me over his sister's head as they embrace.

When Summer pulls back, she looks between us and laughs. "Is this what you two are like all the time?"

"No," I say at the same time Silas says, "yes."

With a shake of her head, my sexy girlfriend comes back and takes my hand, then pulls me toward Silas. "Well, not this weekend. I want to hang out with both of you."

There's a beat of silence.

"Of course," I say before Silas does.

"Whatever you want," he adds.

"Good." Summer steps away from both of us. "Can we grab food? I'm starving."

Silas studies me carefully.

"I liked it better when we hated each other," he says, but there's a hint of a smile on his face.

"Me too. I wasn't so jumpy when I didn't have to care what you thought."

"This is you caring what I think?" His brows lift.

"Well…more than I used to." I backhand him softly in the middle of the chest and then hurry after Summer.

After the three of us have an early dinner, then show Summer around the soccer field and some of campus, we head back to the house.

Dom and Rodrigo are back, and several of our other teammates are over. "9 to 5" is blasting on the speakers, and they're all sitting around our dining room table playing cards.

Most of them have met Summer before, but Silas introduces her to the few guys who haven't.

"Let's switch up and play Spades," Silas says as he takes a seat. He pulls out an empty chair next to him. "Sum, you can be on my team."

She looks to me and I nod. "Yeah, sounds good. Dom and I usually pair up, and I would hate to disappoint him."

Dom grunts.

I take the only available seat next to the quiet defenseman while silently glowering at Silas. He's grinning at me in a way that tells me what I already knew—he's fucking with me—but since I plan to spend all night with Summer, I guess I can share her for another hour or two.

Unfortunately for Dom I'm not very good at Spades… or concentrating when my sexy girlfriend is sitting across the table.

"Geez, Blakenship. You're killing me." He tosses the cards down on the table, then mutters something in French…I think. Maybe Spanish. He talks so fast I can't make any of it out.

"It isn't my fault." I wave my hand toward Summer.

"Aww, come on, Si, let the guy hang with his girl," our goalie, Sonny, says to Silas.

"His girl is my sister," Silas says as if everyone else doesn't already know.

"Let's play washers or something." Rodrigo pushes back from the table.

Everyone else slowly murmurs their agreement and heads outside to our small backyard. We have a nice setup with a stone patio, some mismatched furniture, and a firepit.

Summer and I go out with them, but instead of playing washers, I pull her over next to the firepit. She sits on my lap, earning a side-eye from Silas.

"Are you two going to be okay this semester?" Summer asks.

"Yeah, we'll be fine. I think he's starting to like me."

"Really?" She laughs.

"We're cool," I say more definitively. We like to give each other shit, and we'll probably never be as close as I am with my friends from high school or the couple of teammates here at Valley U that I've become tight with, but I understand him, and I'd do anything to make it work for Summer.

"I like it here." She glances around the yard.

"Thinking about transferring?"

She huffs another quiet laugh. I know she isn't. FLU was her dream, and I think it's been even better than she imagined.

"Do you like it?"

"Yeah, I really do. It doesn't quite feel like home yet, but it's good."

"Speaking of home, I texted with Claire yesterday. We're planning a get-together over the semester break."

"I heard," I say, then add, "Austin told me and Vaughn last night." The three of us play *Call of Duty* every Thursday night. Vaughn and Lacey ended up at Stanford together. They both got full rides, him for soccer and her for academics. Austin ended up at the University of Michigan and is loving the soccer team there and the proximity to Claire, who's about an hour away at Michigan State. I miss them and I'm excited to hang in a few months, but it's cool to see everyone doing big things.

"You're still planning to come home for break, right?" she asks.

"Yeah, I promised my parents."

That makes a grin break out on her face. "I'm glad."

"Yeah, me too. They're coming out for parents' weekend next month."

"That's great."

"It's still weird," I admit. They call every Sunday and we FaceTime. It's always a little awkward to start, but they're making an effort, so I'm not complaining.

"Oh, I almost forgot." I shift, curling one arm around her to hold her in place as I reach into my pocket to pull out the fortune catcher I made earlier.

When she sees it, a surprised puff of laugher escapes. "Seriously?"

"Pick a color, Lindsey."

She hesitates but I can see the excitement on her face. "Purple."

I spell it out, moving the paper around. She picks a number, then another. I peel the paper back, then turn it so she can read.

"'Someone sexy will be cheering you on at your next game,'" she says. One side of her mouth pulls higher. "I assume you mean you?"

"Duh."

She presses a kiss to my lips. "Thank you. I love picturing you cheering me on from here. Sometimes I swear I can hear you screaming and catcalling."

"I love cheering on my girl, but this time you won't have to picture it. I'm coming to Frost Lake."

"What?" she asks, then, "how?"

"We have two days off practice, so I bought a ticket and I'm going to come up."

Her mouth falls open and her eyes widen. "Really?"

"Yeah. I've been dying to see you in action. Frost Lake University's star midfielder."

"Well that might be stretching it, but oh my gosh, I'm so excited."

"Me too."

She kisses me again, and it isn't long before I've forgotten everything and everyone else. We're interrupted by someone tossing a ping-pong ball at us. My guess is Silas.

Summer takes the fortune catcher from me. "My turn. Let's find out your fortune."

Unfortunately for her, they all say the same thing. But it doesn't matter. I don't need a fortune catcher to tell me how lucky I am.

READING GROUP GUIDE

1. Summer is furious about switching schools her senior year. Why is the loss of her old team and identity so destabilizing for her? How does this upheaval shape the way she reacts to Rowan and the Frost Lake girls early in the story?

2. Rowan initially proposes fake dating to win back Amanda. Do you think he truly believes this plan will work, or is he already looking for an excuse to spend time with Summer? What might Rowan be avoiding by focusing on Amanda instead of acknowledging his own insecurities?

3. The Frost Lake girls are wary of Summer, especially Amanda. Why is it so difficult for the team to trust her at first? How do existing rivalries, assumptions, and team culture influence their reactions to her?

4. Rowan and Summer both struggle with pressure—Rowan from his parents' expectations, and Summer from her need for a scholarship. How do these pressures manifest differently in each character? Who copes in a healthier way at the beginning of the book, and how does that shift by the end?

5. Silas arrives unexpectedly during one of Summer's games and confronts Rowan. Why is this moment so emotionally explosive for Summer? Do you think Silas is protecting her, or projecting his own unresolved issues?

6. Rowan is known for being laid-back and rarely serious—traits others admire but also misinterpret. How does his emotional avoidance affect his relationships (with Amanda, his teammates, and Summer)? What changes once he starts making active, intentional choices?

7. The fake dating agreement includes rules—no kissing, no feelings. Which rule do you think they break first emotionally, even before physically? At what point does their relationship clearly shift from "fake" to real?

8. Soccer functions as more than a sport—it's a source of identity for both protagonists. How does the game reflect their inner struggles throughout the book? In what ways does their shared passion bring them closer together?

9. Rowan's public confession in the cafeteria is a major romantic gesture. Why is this moment so meaningful for Summer? How does it contrast with Rowan's earlier reluctance to open up?

10. By the end of the story, both characters have started envisioning their futures differently. How have Rowan's goals changed? How have Summer's? Do you think their relationship helps them grow independently as well as together?

ACKNOWLEDGMENTS

Thank you to everyone who read the Frost Lake High series and especially Summer and Rowan's story.

I should start by acknowledging that I took liberties with the Michigan high school soccer schedule. Admittedly I started plotting this book before I realized the girls typically play in the spring, but it didn't take long for me to go down a rabbit hole of the disadvantage for recruitment opportunities and school involvement (because they're often playing beyond the school year) that ended in me feeling like I wanted to stand by my original vision for this fictional world!

There are so many people to thank. My agent, Georgana, for helping me through this new journey into traditional publishing and the young adult genre.

My editors at Bloom: Christa and Kylie, thank you for all your insights and support. I loved working on this series with you!

My team: Jamie, Kayla, Sahara, and Tori. You're the best!

To my childhood besties: Becca, Emily, Jenn, Jess, Lydia, Shari, and Tasha. Thank you for the memories. You showed up in so many ways while I was writing this series and I know what I do about friendship because of you.

Dad and Natalie—Long John Silvers and Slice of Pie?!

Also to my book club girlies, love you!

Thank you to my daughter, who provided endless ideas, beta read, and cheered me on. Hopefully she forgives me for not writing a heroine who does color guard. They'd never compare to you <3.

And, last but not least, to my readers who took a chance on this new world with me. THANK YOU.

ABOUT THE AUTHOR

Rebecca Jenshak is a *USA Today* bestselling author of sports romance for teens and adults. When she isn't writing, you can find her cheering on local sports teams, hanging out with friends and family, or curled up with a good book.